CARAV[AN]

An Erotic Fantasy

by
Janey Jones

SILVER MOON BOOKS LTD LEEDS
PO Box CR25, Leeds LS7 3TN

New authors welcome

Sil er Moon Books of Leeds and Sil er Moon Books of London are in no way connected.

Also by JANEY JONES:
ISBN 1-897809-10-7 CIRCUS OF SLAVES
Introducing Mr Columbus and his fantastic speciality circus!
£4.99 from shops, £5.60 by post from Silver Moon

If you like one of our books you will probably like them all!

For free 20 page booklet of extracts from our first 16 books (and, if you wish to be on our confidential mailing list, from new monthly titles as they are published) please leave name and address on our 24-hour message/order line. Please speak slowly and clearly and repeat post code if known:

0113 287 6255

(also fax)

or write to:-

**Silver Moon Reader Services, PO Box CR 25
Leeds LS7 3TN**

Surely the most erotic freebie ever!!

[Sil er Moon Books of Leeds and Sil er Moon Books of London are in no way connected]

Caravan of Slaves copyright Janey Jones
First published 1995

Contents

A MONDAY MORNING IN MAY

1: At The Gipsy Training Camp 6
2: Cassie Cycles Into Adventure 12
3: Daisy Meets Her Destiny 17
4: Jo Explores The Wood 30
5: Daisy And CJ Meet 43
6: Chained In The Corral 48
7: Troy and The Hutch Bunny 52

THE MORNING AFTER

8: Maggie Suffers Further Humiliation 62
9: - And Meets Her Match In CJ 71
10: CJ Learns About Discipline 80
11: Gathering Fuel Leads Shorsa Into Trouble 89
12: Commotion In The Camp 99
13: A Surprise Find Beside The Lake 106
14: Jo Returns To Dropwell - Daisy Is Left In The Stables 114
15: Training In The Temple 122
16: Davy Goes looking For Damien And Finds Daisy 127
17: Snookered! 131

THE BIG DAY

18: CJ Receives A Proposition 140
19: Visitors approach 145
20: A Missed Opportunity For CJ 148
21: Success For Maggie: Abduction For CJ 153
22: Is This Folly? 157
23: An Unforgettable Evening 160
24: The Future 173

A MONDAY MORNING IN MAY

1: At The Gipsy Training Camp

Dark-haired and dusky-skinned, the naked, collared figure of the gipsy girl Maggie crouched all alone beside the swiftly flowing stream.

She picked up a well-soaped shirt from the pile of clothing dripping at her side and banged it hard on a wide flat stone. Shifting her weight on thighs that were sore and throbbing, she dipped her hand into the tumbling brook, and cupped water, fresh and cold, to splash onto bare haunches still glowing from a recent beating.

The shirt shone whitely in the sun, dazzling against her dark skin, and she nodded with satisfaction before plunging it into the clear fresh water, one well-scrubbed cuff held tightly in her right hand.

"I hope that pleases you now, Troy Dempsey," she said to herself. Her naked body, lithe and slender, glistened in the sunlight and Maggie, servant and bond-maid to Dapper Troy Dempsey, commander of this gipsy training camp, smiled, humming happily, and remembered her recent punishment almost with pleasure. The quiet humming turned into low song and she worked her way through the laundry with vigour and enthusiasm enhanced by the memory of her beating. A laugh, deep, and throaty burst from her and her supple body shook with elation.

Maggie was eighteen years old, although she would not have been able to put so precise a number on her years had she been asked. Born into a gipsy colony, and assigned to Troy at the appropriate time in a gipsy girl's life, she had grown from a wiry rapscallion of a child into a wilful, wide-eyed young woman.

Humming and singing her way through his washing, she remembered with pleasure the night Troy had taken her for the first time. Troy, wide-shouldered and sleepy-eyed, with long dark hair, brushed straight from a high forehead and caught in a thick tail that snaked down his back, Dapper Troy, so clean, so neat, his clothes always immaculate. Even on this warm and sunny morning, Maggie shivered at the memory of that night.

The flames from the campfire had illuminated and warmed the chill air of the September evening when, on the green-sward in front of his peers, Troy had initiated her into the adult gipsy world. She had been proud to become the woman of such a high ranking man. She was still proud, and continued gladly to submit to his will, by both day and by night.

Whipped, bound, loved, Maggie was a willing slave to Troy's demands. And Maggie was pleased with herself for she had learnt many new tricks and Troy could not leave her alone. Always free to take another woman, whenever and wherever he chose, it would need a determined opponent to disengage Maggie from Troy.

Leaning back on glowing haunches, she shook a lock of hair away from her face, hair that was thick and curled roughly over shoulders that were narrow and slight. It curled in heavy unkempt tresses and was the colour of wet pitch. Her eyes, velvety as bitter chocolate, gleamed bright and alert beneath fine black brows and her nose tilted skywards. Her mouth was generous, perhaps a little too large, richly red, the colour of ripe cherries, and she grinned widely as she continued with her wash. The grin revealed small teeth, sharp and white, and the tip of a pink tongue clasped in concentration between them. The lips glistened, the tongue curled, and the teeth, always willing to nip and nick at tender flesh, shone brightly.

With the sun beating on her back, Maggie worked hard. This was not the first time today she had tackled this particular heap of washing. Earlier that morning, when she had returned from the stream to the gaudily decorated caravan she shared with Troy, he had taken one look at the basket of laundry and roared his disapproval into her smiling face.

"And just what do you call this, you useless lazy baggage? Do you call this clean?" He had held up one of his shirts, the same shirt she was now admiring, and wound it tightly into a thick wet rope. The heavy basket was flung from her arms, the clothes scattering drunkenly about the field. Troy had torn her shift of fine muslin embroidered with flowers from her shoulders, revealing a bronzed body, completely naked, petite and perfect. With slender hips and parted thighs, bottom cheeks clenched, her small, full-nippled breasts had heaved as she caught her breath in surprise at the violence of his reaction.

"Troy! I've been up since six, working hard, washing all your lovely things. They're clean, or they were until you threw them into the dirt!" Maggie had stooped to gather the discarded items. Some had caught on twigs, others were strewn about the grass, and some unfortunate pieces had fallen in the cold dead ashes of last night's fire. Kneeling on one knee, picking up a pair of jeans coated with ash, she had tried to shake the dirt from the wet material.

The first blow sent her reeling. The shirt that was now a rope, cracked across her stooping back, threw her small body sideways, knocking the breath from her lungs. Maggie rolled over on the grass, curled up into a ball, hair flying, arms clasped around her gasping frame.

"You no-good little trollop. I'll give you working hard. Work - you don't know the meaning of the word." Troy leapt at her, grabbed hold of wrist and ankle, thrust her flat onto the damp dew-covered ground, spread-eagled and helpless. He swung the shirt above his head and Maggie could hear it whistling through the air. She lay quite still, trembling and impatient, waiting for the first thwack to home in soundly on her flawless apple-round rump.

"I'll teach you to give me lip, you hussy." He beat her until the smooth bronzed flesh of her bottom and thighs shone with a deep and glowing red. Maggie knew with a quivering certainty what the next move would be. That prick, always excited by the sight of whip-lashed buttocks, was now growing thick and hard between his thighs.

The pounding ceased. A strong arm scooped her body, shaking and sore from the ground. With crotch unzipped Troy plunged, urgent, hot and hard, inside her wet and willing slit. Maggie bounced, hair tumbling, breasts swaying, belly jerking at his long insistent thrusts. Hot spasms exploded into her and as his cock withdrew from the sweetness of her, Troy let her fall, discarded, onto the earth.

"Now, collect this lot of filth together. Then when you've done that, light the fire and get my breakfast."

"What about the clothes, Troy, when shall I get them clean?" Feeling elated after the quick fuck, Maggie knelt on all fours, head down, tousled hair falling forward over her face, a pretty face but covered in cinders now and grubby as the clothes she had been trying to retrieve. "Do you still want me to clean the clothes?" Her voice was pleading, low-toned, almost whispering, and she stayed where she was just in case Troy wanted to beat or fuck her again. With small breasts swaying and neat bottom exposed, she knelt very still, ready willing and waiting for any further attentions.

"Oh, forget it, forget it." Irritation made him spit the words in her direction. "I'll go over to Jem's van, I need to talk to him, I'll have breakfast there. I have arrangements to make with the boys if we're going to be ready in time for the arrival of the Big Man. Jem and the others will have to be getting out and about to do some recruiting now we're here." Troy swung a booted foot heavily against her waiting bottom and lazily brushed back a loose lock of long black hair from his eyes.

"We are staying here then, Troy?" Maggie glanced cautiously upwards at her man's glowering face. "You've come to a decision?" She saw his expression lighten, the thin lips curved and fine lines creased the corners of his deep-set eyes.

"Yes, yes, it's true. I have made - no, what I should say is the decision has been made for us. This field is ours for the summer. And not just this field. The woods beyond the stream," he waved a muscular arm, "and the parkland we passed through last night on our way here, though I don't suppose you saw any of that."

Maggie grinned, stood up, brushed the dirt from her knees and wiped her soot-smeared face with the back of her hand. She could see his mood had changed. He was pleased to be here. "No, I didn't see anything much at all on the way, did I?" With head to one side her big eyes looked at him mischievously. "I would have had difficulty in seeing anything the way you left me, now wouldn't I? Trussed up like a chicken all ready to go to market." She rubbed her wrists where the deep marks left by the ropes still glowed. Happy to see him pacified, she gathered together all her bits and pieces and placed them back in the basket. "So now I'll be off and get this washing done - again."

A grunt had been his only reply and Maggie had returned to the stream and here she was, happily completing the same wash for the second time in as many hours. As she knelt on the bank, she sang a song of love and loss in a lilting voice, and didn't hear the swish of bare feet moving quietly through the lush water-side grass. A lithe willowy figure was creeping slowly towards her.

A low lazy voice drawled, "Struth, Maggie, you look like an animal, crouched there, bare-titted and bare-arsed."

"Jeez, Shorsa, you frightened the life out of me, creeping up like that. I could have lost the clean washing all over again and then where would I have been?"

"Strung out on Troy's rack, if I know Dapper Troy Dempsey. And receiving plenty of lashes from his best cow-hide belt. Does the thought tempt you, Maggie? Shall I throw that shirt in the deeper water for you?" Grinning lazily, Shorsa Colquhoun flung herself down on the grass, selected a long juicy stalk from a clump beside the brook and began to suck the tender creamy coloured flesh.

Where Maggie was small and slender, Shorsa was taller, full-bosomed, narrow-waisted and wide-hipped. Like Maggie, her hair was dark, but fine and straight, parted in the centre. It framed her fine-boned face, two black silky curtains, translucent and shining in the sunlight.

"I've had one beating and fucking already this morning. Look," Maggie stuck her bottom out so Shorsa could get a better sighting of her glowing rump and dripping lips. "But, I'll tell you this, we're here for the summer. We're setting up the camp in this field until the Big Man arrives."

"Here? Are you sure of that, Mags? It's nice enough. Oh, but I would like to have been nearer the sea." Sighing heavily, Shorsa stretched herself on the ground, languid and lazily content, screwed up her eyes and stared into the heavens. Her long hair spread around her head on the grass like a fan. A skimpy shift of deep purple muslin hand-embroidered with leaves of gold and slashed open to the waist revealed her magnificent full-bosomed body right down to her navel. A stone in the dell of her stomach, an amethyst, bluey-purple, sparkled in the sunlight, and the contrast with the tautly drawn dusky skin of her flat stomach was startling.

"The boys'll be out recruiting then, eh?" Shorsa's eyes glittered. "We'll soon be having some fun with the local girls." Her face relaxed, as she considered this. "That's what I really enjoy about the summer months, Mags. Seeing all those naive bitches learning what life is really about." She burst into a fit of high-pitched giggling, rolling about on the ground and her voice contracted into a simpering whisper, *"oh no, please, please don't do that, Mummy wouldn't like it."*

Maggie smiled, but looked thoughtful. "That's all very well, Shorsa, but I've heard - you know - it means we have to share the men and - well - I -" Maggie began to blush furiously under Shorsa's hard gaze. "Don't look at me like that. Just because you don't give a damn who you go with - or where - Troy is special and I belong to him."

Shorsa stared at her friend. "Don't get too fond, Mags. I've heard there's something special happening this year. I don't know what yet, but it's all to do with the arrival of the Big Man. He's been here before. I've seen him."

"What's he like, Shorsa? I've only heard talk of him.

"Oh, believe me, he's big, enormous!" She rolled her eyes and puffed her cheeks. "Big face, big chest, big hands, big cock. But so far," she sighed, "no matter how hard I've tried, I haven't managed to get near him. It's a real shame. There's something about him. Something compelling and very sexy."

"Oh, you think anything in breeches is sexy, Shorsa. For me, there's only Troy." Maggie stopped her scrubbing and stared dreamily at the shirt grasped in her wet fist.

"Maggie," Shorsa pushed herself up onto her elbow and gazed at her friend. "You've joined us here in the training camp, and, well, life's different. You can never be sure quite what's going to happen next - or who you'll be with."

"But I was assigned to Troy, I'm his, he's mine!"

"Don't ever think that, Mags. No man is yours and you can be given to any man in the camp. Life is good, Maggie, and we should make sure we enjoy every opportunity to the full."

"Uh-huh, Shorsa, I do understand. But, you were saying about the Big Man."

"Yes. He's been here before. He comes to select certain girls. Usually the recruited ones, but sometimes he takes a fancy to a gipsy girl. He's of gipsy blood himself."

"What does he want the girls for, Shorsa? Just for his own amusement?"

"No. No, it's more complicated than that. He runs a circus, a Speciality Circus. This training camp provides some of the girls."

Maggie frowned. She didn't want to join any circus. She wanted to stay here, with Troy. She turned back to her laundry. "Ah well, I don't imagine he'll be interested in the likes of me, there's nothing special I can do, besides my dancing. Now, help me get this washing back in the basket and together we can carry it back up the slope and put it out to dry - at last."

Shorsa rolled over, kicked her legs high in the air, momentarily revealing pussy lips, soft moist and juicy, ripe for pleasure. "No. I think you're safe this year. This year he wants only fair-haired girls, blondes, red-heads, apparently he has something particular in mind."

Maggie stood up and looked down at her friend. "Troy's mighty fond of red-heads himself." She looked round anxiously, as if she expected to see red-headed girls popping up from behind every bush. "It looks like I'll have to keep my wits about me this summer, Shorsa."

Giggling, Shorsa sprang to her feet. "It's not your wits Troy's interested in. It's your tits," she squeezed, "your fanny," she stroked, "and your cunt." She pressed her warm soft body against Maggie and dug two fingers, long brown and tipped by nails painted a deep and glowing purple, inside the wet and accommodating cunt.

"Keep everything well-oiled and ship-shape, Mags, and you'll have no problems." She massaged Maggie's clit, still aroused form Troy's earlier attentions. Her long brown fingers rubbed, slowly at first, round and round, up and down. Probing and gentle, she caressed the responsive pussy until it creamed and moistened. Maggie moaned and wriggled her hips. "Let the red-heads and the blondes invade, Maggie. We're ready for them, all of them. We'll fight 'em on every front."

The two girls kissed, mouth to mouth, tongue to tongue. They squeezed one to the other in loving arms, warmly and tenderly. Then, dropping to their knees, they folded the clean clothing into the basket and slowly made their way back up the slope to the training camp on that fine and balmy Monday morning in May.

2: Cassie Cycles Into Adventure

The bicycle skidded on the loose gravel and Cassie, auburn curls flying, tumbled onto the scrubby verge and into this story.

"Damn and blast!"

She rubbed a bruised knee and clutched at a tender elbow. Rueful and exasperated, she examined the wayward bike. It looked odd, not right, no longer the shining and exciting vehicle that would take her over distant horizons. Only the second day of her holiday and it had to start like this.

The rucksack, which had helped unbalance and deposit her so regrettably, weighed heavy. Groaning at the unaccustomed ache in her shoulders, she let it fall to the ground with a thump. Perhaps this solo cycling holiday hadn't been such a good idea after all. She had planned it so carefully, gathered together every map, got all the right gear, bought the best second-hand bike she could afford. She had decided to book into B & B's as she went. Wander wherever the fancy took her. Become a gentleman - or rather, lady - of the road, a free spirit. Cassie had decided to take her whole month's holiday entitlement in one go. Get away completely. Leave behind everything - and everybody. Try to forget the stinking relationship she had just come out the back end of - though she realised it would take a lot for her ever to truly forget that man, her boss. He had loved her, she thought, used her she knew, then dumped her and gone back to his wife.

She had started this holiday with a heavy heart, but yesterday had managed to get forty miles under her saddle, travelling into unknown territory. Now her calf muscles ached, her bottom was sore, and the sun had caught her tip-tilted nose and it was a mass of freckles. She should have got a bigger sun hat. The wide-brimmed straw had flown from her head when she fell and the russet curls, bunched untidily underneath, now flopped in a golden tangle, dazzling in the sunlight.

Cassie drummed her heels on the ground and felt the damp morning dew seep through the seat of her satin shorts. Her emerald eyes prickled with tears, her throat felt tight, and she knew that, if she did not take a firm hold of herself, misery was not far away.

A girl friend had suggested they go on holiday together, but Cassie had wanted a complete break from the past. Now she wished she had accepted the offer. She realised she needed the company of friends. Someone to chat to, giggle and argue with whilst cycling along together. Perhaps it would be a good idea to give up the holiday now. Pack up and go home. But Cassie had her pride and, after the failure of her relationship, defeat in this venture was not something she wished to contemplate.

She had a tool kit, and whatever had caused the bike to tip her so ungracefully onto the verge could surely be tackled by someone as bright and intelligent as herself. She had learnt how to mend a puncture, and that must be the trouble. All she had to do was get on with it. 'Don't be such a wimp, CJ, pick yourself up, do your stuff, keep going. You never know what might be round the next corner.' Unpacking her tool-kit, she wiped her damp hands over the seat of her shorts and prepared to tackle this unwelcome task.

The sun was beating onto her back and she jammed the sun hat back on her head. One crop of freckles was enough. Even if there was nobody to see her, Cassie intended to try and stay looking presentable. She settled to the tyre, unsure and ignorant, but more than willing to give it a go.

"Do you need any help, sweetheart?"

Cassie started in alarm, the spanner slipped from her inexpert fingers and she squinted upwards, screwing startled eyes tight against the brightness of the morning light. Standing over her were two young men. Both were dark-haired, the one small and wiry, and the other much larger, this one appearing to Cassie to have something of the cart-horse about him, with his long mane and enormous feet.

She blushed, embarrassed when she realised the smaller of the two was staring with blatant interest down the front of her loose cotton top. When she leant over her damaged bike, the white T-shirt sagged away from her body, clearly revealing unfettered breasts swaying freely beneath the flimsy material.

Cassie was an independent girl and didn't want any help. She adopted a nonchalant air. "No, no thanks, boys. I'm fine." She turned away and looked at her useless wheel in despair. A furious blush flamed her pale skin.

"You quite sure about that, darling? From the look of you, I would say you could do with a bit of a hand." The one who had spoken, the smaller wiry one, crouched down beside her, a concerned smile puckering his handsome features. His companion guffawed loudly and shuffled his feet on the roadside gravel. "Be quiet, Damien. Can't you see you're embarrassing the young lady? Here, let me have that." He lifted the bike away from her grasp. "By the way, my name's Davy, what would they be calling you, my darling?"

Cassie's mouth dropped open in amazement at the utter cheek of him. Then she saw the twinkle in his eyes and knew he was trying to send her up. She relaxed and smiled. His bravado was rather attractive - and masterful. Cassie liked men who knew their own minds. She always tried to assert her own independence, but there was something about a powerful man, a man who took charge, a man in control.

"Have it your own way then - Davy. Here's the spanner, you're welcome to it. My name is Cassie, but my friends call me CJ.

"Right then CJ, let's see if we can get this little devil fixed for you. Give the lady your hand, Damien. We don't let young ladies sit about in the dirt, now do we?"

Damien guffawed again and, holding out a grubby hand, offered to pull Cassie to her feet.

"It's all right, thank you, Damien." Discomposure made her sound prim. "I'm quite capable of getting up on my own - thank you." But Cassie's muscles were stiff from yesterday's exertions and having swung herself onto her knees, could get no further. Humiliated, she was forced to accept Damien's proffered hand.

"Looks like this young lady could do with some refreshment, don't you think, Damien?" Davy's eyes, bright and alert, surveyed her from where he knelt next to her useless bicycle. "We could take her back to our place - that's if she'd like to come. Offer her a cup of coffee, be hospitable like."

There was no reply, just a snigger and more shuffling of feet in the gravel from Damien.

Detaching her hand from his grip with difficulty, Cassie shaded her eyes and gazed round at the undulating landscape. "Where do you come from, the pair of you? Did you walk here?"

"We come from just over there." Davy waved his hand vaguely in the direction of some woods on the other side of a small valley. "We're here for the summer, right Damien?" His silent side-kick merely nodded his head in agreement.

"Over where?" Standing on tip-toe, Cassie surveyed the countryside. "I don't see a house or anything. Are you camping? Are you? Is there a camp site?" She suddenly felt more amenable towards these two strangers. After all, if there was a camp site, perhaps she could stay there, then she would have some company. Cassie felt cheered at this thought.

"Right. We are camping, just the other side of those trees. You won't see it from here though. It's well hidden."

"Is it a nice site? Do think there would be room for me?" Cassie smiled encouragingly at the one who called himself Davy. "I could do with some company, are there any other girls there? Girls of about my own age?"

Davy looked at her, head on one side, and rubbed a thoughtful hand, the fingers oily from her bike, down the front of his shirt. "And what age would that be? Eighteen, nineteen perhaps?"

Cassie felt herself blushing again at his appreciative stare.

"Now that's a pretty sight, isn't it Damien? All flushed and eager, that's what we like to see. And yes, there are plenty of girls there already. And you," he looked her up and down appraisingly, "you would be very welcome to join us, very welcome indeed."

Cassie glanced from one man to the other. They looked harmless enough, even if the big one hadn't so much as uttered a word yet. And this was a lovely part of the country. The fields were lush, the trees handsome, and the stream she could see running at the bottom of the valley looked very inviting. Cassie felt a surge of excitement, her tummy flickered, and she decided to take a chance. After all, what was the point of not taking a few chances in life? She would only live to regret it if she allowed tempting opportunities to pass her by. Cassie did not want to end up old and resentful. She could hardly bear to contemplate such a fate.

"I'll come," she said, suddenly sure of herself. "I was going to ride another forty miles today, but by the look of my bike, I don't think I'd get very far. And my bottom's sore from all the cycling I did yesterday."

"Is it now?" Davy glanced at her neat little rump encased in shiny green shorts. "And this bike isn't going anywhere. You've buckled the front wheel badly."

His gaze travelled up her body. The T-shirt's fine white cotton clung to breasts that stood proud and firm beneath the thin material, nipples like two pearly shells clearly outlined. The sun hat dangling from strings over her shoulders framed her extravagant chestnut curls. Cassie knew she created a very attractive picture.

"So, would you be able to give me a hand?" She dimpled prettily at the pair of them. "I'll never be able to manage all this by myself." She indicated the rucksack still lying heavily on the grass. "I could only just manage it when my bike was in working order."

"Don't you worry your pretty little head about such things, sweetheart. Me and Damien, we'll be bringing all your gear along. You, you little darling, you just bring yourself." And so saying, Davy nodded at Damien who, with one huge fist, swung the bike across his shoulders, picked up Cassie's rucksack and strode down the lane, sliding effortlessly through a gap in the thick thorn hedge.

"He's strong, isn't he?" she said in amazement.

"Aye, Damien's a big lad. Lots of muscle, but not so much up here." Davy tapped his forehead. "You understand what I'm saying?"

Cassie looked at him, slowly reassessing. Perhaps he wasn't such a brash lout after all. He obviously cared about this other bloke. They must be old friends, or perhaps they were related.

"Are you close, you and Damien? Have you known each other long?"

"You could say that," said Davy, an impish grin lighting his face. "We're twins. Not identical, but born to the same mother within twenty minutes of each other - I'm the older. I look after him - and he looks after me, in his own way. I'm the brains and he's the brawn. We go everywhere together. Now let's be off. There's a lot of people I'd like you to meet, and you've such lovely red hair." He stroked her curls. "You wouldn't happen to have any beautiful blonde companions lurking about here anywhere, would you?"

CJ looked puzzled.

"No, I suppose not," sighed Davy. "But now, I reckon you could do with that cup of coffee."

Cassie beamed at her new-found friend, This holiday might just turn out to be fun after all.

3: Daisy Meets Her Destiny

"White heather, deary, buy some lucky white heather, only fifty pence."

The whining and insistent voice was impossible to ignore. Keeping her head down, Daisy averted her gaze, but by hesitating for those few vital seconds, lost the opportunity to dash past the old gipsy woman who was blocking her path. A hand, sharp as a cat's claw, clutched at her arm.

"I don't want your white heather - I'm in a hurry. Out of my way!"

Daisy felt herself blush scarlet with annoyance and embarrassment. Her reaction to the old woman had been abrupt and rude, a bad start to this all-important day. For Daisy really was in a hurry. She had to catch the bus. If she missed the bus she would be late for the interview. If she was late for the interview, she would leave a bad impression on the interviewing panel. If she left a bad impression, she would probably not get the job, and Daisy needed a job, this job, any job.

Daisy was broke and Daisy was late, and still the gypsy woman blocked her way. She lifted her head and tried to glare fiercely at the gipsy. But Daisy's eyes, big, round, innocent, softly grey speckled with blue, bright as freshly bloomed gentians, opened wide with wonder.

The old woman was not alone. Just behind the small figure, and slightly to one side, stood a young man, his shoulders hunched, hands thrust into the pockets of jeans that clung to narrow, bony hips. Black eyes, hooded and intense, stared directly at her.

The young man was studying her, and her blush deepened from scarlet to crimson. There was no way she could push past these two, not on her own, and, in this small market town at this hour of the day, there was no one to appeal to for assistance.

Normally, she would not have used this alley, but she had been late leaving her bleak bed-sit and it was such a handy cut-off to the market place. It was still early on this fine Monday morning in May. Not so early that commuters were dashing down the ginnel to get to work on time, but still too early for shoppers to be surging through on their way to the shops.

That whining and insistent voice drew closer and Daisy thrust herself back, her whole body quivering with alarm.

"You've a lucky face, deary, and pretty too, very pretty. If you cross my palm with silver I could tell you many things about yourself - and your future, I see that something special is about to happen to you."

Daisy danced from foot to foot, shifting her weight impatiently. She was dressed in her best and knew she looked attractive. A pale grey jacket, fastened with one large button, nipped her narrow waist and flared over hips that were full and rounded. Her silken shirt, ivory in colour, deep cuffs buttoning almost up to her elbows, clung softly over her generous breasts, the low front revealing a promise of dark and mysterious cleavage. Her skirt, the same dove-grey as the jacket, short, skimming dimpled knees, fitted close and displayed the line of plump thighs nestling beneath the fine material.

Nervously, with shaking hands, she smoothed the skirt, glanced up at the two gipsies and saw that the young man's gaze was fixed, with no hint of embarrassment, on her long legs, legs that shimmered in fully-fashioned stockings and were already aching slightly because the shoes, which matched her outfit, had pointed toes and too high heels and made her unsteady and in no position to run away, even had she wanted to.

Daisy patted her hair. It was because of her hair that she was late, had decided to use the ginnel instead of walking the long way round to the market place. She had spent a long time that morning dragging the heavy blonde tresses into place. She had gone to a lot of trouble, put much effort into pulling the heavy hanks of hair into a pony-tail on the crown of her head and then tying it into a tight knot. The remaining tendrils, the ones she could never tame and pin into place satisfactorily, framed her heart-shaped face with fly-away corkscrew curls. They tickled over her high forehead and dangled provocatively in front of her ears. Fine golden curls framed her face in a dazzling halo and this shone in the semi-darkness of the narrow alley-way.

Daisy fingered a fifty pence piece in her jacket pocket. Her bus fare was safely in her shoulder bag. This would only go towards a cup of coffee, and fifty pence was a very small sum to pay to have your future told.

"Go on, then. I'm sorry if I was rude just now, but really, I am in a hurry."

She slid the coin from her pocket and held it out towards the old gipsy woman. The gnarled fingers grasped the money, dropping it quickly into a leather pouch that hung over a long, gaudy skirt, that swirled with patterns of silver, black and scarlet. When the old head bent forward, large hoops of gold hung from each ear, and Daisy noticed white scalp clearly visible beneath the greying hair.

"Give me your palm, deary. Let me take a closer look." The old woman clasped Daisy's hand. "The future is always clear in the palm, especially in delicate young things like yourself."

Daisy, her large breasts swaying under the silky fabric of her blouse, shivered as her soft warm hand felt the touch of one that was wizened and old. The bones were sharp beneath the skin, their texture like the scraping of dry twigs, fragile and liable to snap if squeezed, but the voice resonated, calm and clear, very different from the original high-pitched wheedling tone.

Entranced, Daisy concentrated hard until a stifled snort of laughter made her look up in surprise. In her excitement, she had forgotten the gipsy woman's companion. The young man slouched against the brick wall of the narrow passage, his hooded gaze fixed on Daisy's breasts, his grimy thumbnail flicking the end of a spent match. There was an air of sneering menace about him and Daisy shivered.

Her attention was recalled with a jolt. A sharp intake of breath sucked between the old woman's discoloured teeth made her pulse quicken and her stomach flicker with excitement. Perhaps the gipsy really had seen something in her trembling palm, something unusual, something unexpected, something that might change her dull and boring life into one of thrills and adventure.

"Have you seen my future? Am I going to get this job?"

The old woman, her thin brown fingers clutching the palm that was plump and pale, looked up, her eyes glittering. "There is a future for you, my dear, and such a future. You are about to set out on an adventure that will change your life. Around a corner - and it could be the next one - your destiny is waiting to gather you up. You have been unhappy and lonely, but all that is about to change. I see colour and fire, two good omens. Flames of deepest red swirl in your palm. There is a heat, great heat - and passion - some darkness, but very little - the future is full of promise. But you must follow your heart. Follow your heart and you will enter a world previously undreamed of."

The gipsy's words pounded in Daisy's ears. Her destiny, the word was so thrilling - an adventure - round the next corner - follow her heart - Daisy trembled and a previous reluctance to be bold evaporated. A tingle of fear mixed with excitement trickled down her spine. It was all true. She had been unhappy and lonely and she had always tried to do the sensible thing and where had it got her? - nowhere: living in a bed-sit, on her own, no job and broke, when somewhere out there her destiny waited.

She stared down the alley-way, grey eyes darkly dilated, glazed with a delicious terror, and gazed into the unknown. Unseeing, she stared past the two dark figures blocking her path, stared past the shadows and out into the clear sunlit market place. She stared into her future, her mind full of vivid imaginings. Buses trundled past the passage entrance, blocking the sun and throwing the whole alley-way into even deeper shadow. One of those buses was the one she needed to catch. The one that if she missed would mean the end of her chances for that sensible job in the Town Hall. But Daisy, a secret smile playing about her lightly painted lips, had made a decision. This gipsy woman knew something, something special. She had seen the future in Daisy's palm and no way did it sound as if the Town Hall was going to play a significant part. Out there, beyond the market place, her destiny waited and it would be tremendous - and romantic. Of that, Daisy was convinced.

A sound, half-way between a snigger and a snort, brought her bumping back down to reality. The young man, his narrow hips thrusting towards her, grinned at the look of surprise, almost shock, on her scarlet face. His gaze was insolent and she squirmed under the intensity of his stare. His eyes, narrow under their heavy lids, glittered with amusement, and from the expression on his face, Daisy could almost believe she had left home naked that morning. He seemed to be appraising and assessing every curve and dimple of her young body and his thick mat of black curls swung loosely over his forehead, as he nodded in appreciation at what he saw.

When he spoke his voice was low and husky. Daisy's hand flew to her breast in an effort to cover what she felt was her nakedness. Her toes curled, uncomfortable and cramped, inside the narrowness of her pointed shoes.

"Tell her, Rosie, tell the girl her 'destiny'. We haven't got a lot of time. Get on with it, or I will, you silly old -"

"Quiet Jem, be quiet," the old woman growled in annoyance at the interruption. "I'll be the one to tell the girl what's to happen. You keep your own counsel and do as you've been instructed, d'ye hear me?"

"Yes, I hear you Rosie, but time's short, and I'll not let this one get away, not without a fight." As he spoke he glanced over his shoulder, but nobody was there. They were quite alone. Three figures, one, blonde hair glimmering, pale skin translucent, the other two, dark-haired, swarthy-skinned, almost shadows in the dim light. "This one suits me fine." He stared hard at Daisy. "And you'd like some new experiences, wouldn't you, girlie?"

The stare was penetrating, his expression moody, and Daisy quivered with what, she realised with surprise, was desire. He was attractive, very attractive in an animalistic sort of way. He was mysterious, and firm muscles slid effortlessly beneath his coarse skin. Although he still slouched lazily against the brickwork there was a dynamism about him which could spring into action at a touch - her touch! She giggled nervously and a silly grin spread over her pretty face. Moisture dampened the white cotton panties caught tightly between her cleft and, unconsciously, she wriggled her bottom in anticipation.

Perhaps her destiny would include lying in the arms of this man, and he looked like a real man. Her gaze dropped to his jeans. They clung to his hips and a wide belt of leather, deep brown, well-worn, fastened by a heavy clasp, stuck crudely out over a crotch that bulged enticingly. There was an odour about him, far from unpleasant, and Daisy felt the dampness between her thighs increase.

The clock in the market place chimed the half-hour. "I've missed my bus!" she wailed. "I'll never get that job now."

Iron-hard fingers dug into the soft flesh of her upper arm, and stayed her from flight. "That is fate." The voice of the man was soft in her ear, the breath hot and smelling of stale tobacco. "Destiny awaits you. A destiny that might free you forever from the shackles of normality. There's a lot more to be discovered in life if you give yourself the chance to find out."

Frozen in flight, Daisy stared into the darkly hooded eyes. The expression hidden behind those shining orbs burned deep into her soul. It was a determined look, a hungry look. His hooded eyes glittered with a menace that thrilled her to the core.

"I am that destiny - you know that, don't you?"

Daisy nodded. She was dumb. Her head was spinning with the sight, the sound, the smell of him. Musky, manly, an outdoor smell. Hard work had firmed those muscles to iron and she longed to reach out and touch.

His gaze smouldered, and made her shiver from head to toe as if a ghost had passed her by.

"We are going to the woods and fields. My home is in the natural world. The hedge rows around me, the trees above my head, the soil beneath my feet. That is where I belong, in the natural world. I belong to it and it belongs to me. It is my destiny."

The gipsy was standing next to her and she could feel the heat from his body. The ring in his ear tickled the knot of blonde hair and his breath rippled down the back of her bare neck. She winced at the tightness of the pointed toes as he took her arm and urged her forward.

Jem's stride was brisk and Daisy had to take two steps to every one of his. She tottered, her arm still firmly in his grasp. It was only a small market town and they soon left behind the bustle of the pavements, the fumes and throb of the traffic, and were walking down a tree-shaded lane that Daisy knew, but had hardly ever used. It led to Dropwell Park. Unless you were going to Dropwell there was no cause for any vehicle to drive along its narrow winding way.

"Are we going to Dropwell?" Daisy asked breathlessly. She was hot and sticky and would have liked to sit down, somewhere cool, under the trees.

"No, not quite. Not to the house." Jem's voice was abstracted. "I told you, I live in the natural world. The woods and fields are my home - and yours, if you desire it."

Daisy didn't reply. She needed every ounce of breath to keep up. He was very fit and wiry and his feet seemed to spring along the hard surface of the track, a surface that was becoming rougher, and more unkempt. Trees arched overhead. The lane became a tunnel. Steep banks loomed on either side; the roots of the trees, gnarled and twisted, snaked through the stony soil. A few late primroses nestled on the banks, and above the sun filtered through the tracery of dark branches fringed with the frothy green of new leaf.

Daisy struggled on. The lane rose steeply, the trees thinned, became occasional, and the hedgerows lining the narrow road were heavy with may blossom.

Without warning, Jem came to a halt. Daisy stumbled at the suddenness of it. Her right foot twisted and she heard a sickening snap. She knew the heel of her shoe, her best pair, had broken. "Oh sugar! Can we stop, please? I can't go on. Not with one heel."

There was no reply. He did not even look her in the face. Without releasing her arm, Jem sank to his knees, removed first the broken shoe, then the good, and tossed them both into the roadside ditch. Daisy stood in her stockinged feet, sharp shards of gravel cut her toes. Her jaw dropped in amazement.

"Where you're going," he said curtly, "you won't be needing them. Stop griping and come with me." He grasped her wrist and dragged her a few yards more along the lane. She tripped and staggered. Her feet, not used to such rough exercise, were soon grazed and bruised and she whimpered at this harsh treatment.

"Come on, we're here." Jem pushed aside a large branch of hawthorn, snowy with blossom, and stepped through the gap, dragging Daisy behind him. The branch swung back into place. The entrance from the lane was concealed entirely.

Relieved to be off the hard and punishing road, Daisy welcomed the comparative softness of the woodland floor. Twigs cracked, abrupt and sharp, but the earth, covered by centuries of leaf-mould, felt soft and luxurious to her tortured feet. A sweep of bluebells shimmered in the suffused light and the air was heavy with their perfume. Wave upon wave of iridescent blue flowed into the distance and Daisy looked at the sea of sapphire in delight. She began to relax. Here it was cool.

They were alone, she and Jem. Daisy's nipples stiffened and she glanced at him shyly. The thing with the shoes - he must have been annoyed at her clumsiness. Daisy smiled. It was obvious Jem had been as keen as herself to get somewhere private, somewhere like this, somewhere they would not be disturbed, somewhere they could indulge themselves without fear of interruption.

A low whinny made her look up in surprise. A horse, white with dabs of black, was cropping a patch of grass. It was tethered to a beech tree and at the sound of Jem's call looked up from its grazing, neighed softly in welcome, dark-eyed gaze fixed firmly on its master. Fascinated, Daisy stared at the horse, delighted to be involved in Jem's secret world so soon.

"Is he yours?" Her grey eyes were wide with wonder. "What's his name? He looks so sweet." She wanted to pat the sturdy flank and nuzzle the strong neck, and she struggled in Jem's grip, but he held her firm.

She looked at the horse, saw the reins, the bit, the bridle, the saddle. Surely the saddle was unusual? To Daisy, who knew little about such things, it looked odd, curving steeply, back and front, with high pommels - weren't they for fixing lassoes? And there, draped over the patient haunches, was the rope. Dark and sinuous, tough but smooth, long and sensuous, was coil upon coil of rope, fine but with a look of strength about it.

Surprised, Daisy struggled again. "Keep still!" A slap stung across first one cheek and then the other, making her cry out. Tears spilled from her eyes and ran in glittering droplets down cheeks flushed with the red hot marks of his palm. The shock of the blow made her bottom lip quiver and the knot of hair, always precarious, shook loose, and blonde curls tumbled about Daisy's shoulders. She wriggled in his clasp.

"I said, keep still."

He twisted her arms behind her back, threw her to the ground, dropped to his knees. Astride her prone body he lifted the cuff of his jeans and removed a knife, small and curved, from a sheath bound to his bulging calf muscle.

Daisy gasped at the sight of the weapon and tried to roll away. His strong thighs pressed against her hips and she was trapped on the woodland floor. His dark body loomed over her own that was pale and soft and shivering.

"You've nothing to be frightened of, girl." He ran a grubby thumb along the blade that shone in the dappled light. "This little beauty has the lightest of caresses." And with one swift movement he slit through Daisy's clothing. His words were truthful, the touch was precise.

The grey skirt fell away, taking with it the slashed remains of white panties and suspender belt. Her thighs quivered in the warm air but the knife left no mark on that translucent flesh. Her stockings, the finest of black nylon, torn and ragged now, still clung to the suspenders, the inky blackness of the stocking tops contrasting darkly with a curve of dimpled thigh. The plump flesh was ghostly white but coloured by a thin red line where the nylon had cut and marked the skin.

The point of the blade proceeded upwards. The sleek blouse, ivory silk, ripped with a sensuous sigh and Daisy's bra, skimpy and always bursting with the swell of her meloned breasts, sprang away, the heavy orbs spreading, soft and plump, a tracery of pale blue veins focusing on the rosy nub of her nipples. Her long hair, loose and unkempt, tumbled about her shoulders and a gentle breeze blew strands of gold across her heaving breast.

Jem stood, slid the blade back into its sheath. He looked her up and down. Daisy closed her eyes but could still sense his stare slithering, sliding, scrutinising, appreciating her naked and vulnerable body. The excitement of it made her forget about the total destruction of her one and only decent outfit. She longed for him to touch her, massage her aching tits, squeeze her throbbing nipples, cup her moist sex in those scaly hands and rub a horny finger over her quivering clit. She lay there, tense and ready to welcome his advance. The lightest fondle of any part of her would send shock waves coursing into every intimate fold.

Her lips curved into a smile and she opened her eyes in welcome.

He'd gone!

Frantic, she looked round the clearing. He was standing by the horse, one hand cupped under its muzzle, the other resting on its flank. She smiled. He cared about that horse. This thought endeared Jem to Daisy even more. He would be back soon. With a sigh, she closed her eyes and waited for his return.

A cut, sharp - but sweet - lashed across her legs. Daisy screamed in surprise, her head jerked from the ground. A circle of rope, dark and sinuous, entwined like a snake round her ankle. A snake that now lay coiled, snug and exquisite, tightening and terrifying. Her eyes widened and she stared at the sight, a sight that both fascinated and frightened her. She tried to push herself up but the ground was soft, the branches that lay around her were loose. There was nothing to hold on to. Her hands fluttered uselessly and her nails, the varnish so carefully applied that morning, scrabbled helplessly. Several tore in her haste. Her mind was in torment. Her eyes, filmed by tears, sparkled and glittered. The flecks of gentian blue shone deep within the two dark wells of self-doubt. She wept, piteous in her plight.

Now her hair hung in golden hanks. No semblance was left of the neat knot she had fixed so carefully that morning before leaving home. Her shoes were gone. Her clothes destroyed. She was half-naked and vulnerable, and standing over her, the other end of the rope wound up his forearm, swayed Jem.

His eyes were vulpine, his mouth sardonic, and his free hand stroked lazily at the front of his jeans as he watched her struggle. With legs straggled, he gained purchase on the soft soil, and pulled on the rope with the skill of someone well-used to handling such prey. He dragged her over the floor of the clearing, and Daisy, staring helplessly at his laughing face, opened her mouth in silent protest. Her bottom scraped painfully over the damp earth and he yanked her, arms flailing, torn garments trailing, towards his arrogant and thrusting body.

"I can see, from the look in those big grey eyes of yours that this," he unzipped and a cock, bulbous and stiff, sprang into the daylight, "this is what's playing on your mind. Am I right, sweetheart?"

Daisy lay directly below the swaying knob, and stared in dumb amazement. Without loosening his hold, Jem stepped backwards, slowly unwinding and paying out the rope, bit by bit, from his arm.

"What - what are you doing?" Her voice was quavering. She could not take her eyes off his prick. He had turned away from her and the sight of his backside, narrow and firm, the black jeans clinging, the magnificent prick swinging as he strode towards one of the tall beech trees, was riveting. There was no reply.

She was his prisoner now. She trembled at the thought and her nipples, already tingling, stood rigidly to attention. She was at Jem's mercy and she watched him eagerly. She saw him secure the other end of the rope to the trunk of a tree and her heart beat ferociously. She waited, desperate to know what his next move would be.

He span round and stared at her. Her one leg, the one with the rope cutting cruelly into the flesh of her ankle, was strung up into the air. The rest of her, clothes shredded, hair entangled, lay naked and exposed. Daisy could feel the soft breeze playing over the lips of her gaping pussy. She knew he was looking straight at those open lips. A shiver of desire made her moan and she pouted, wiggled her hips, arched her back and thrust her large white breasts in his direction. She longed to entice him back to her body. The buzzing in her head and the velvety contractions pulsing inside her told Daisy that a touch would send her bounding into the realms of ecstasy.

She moaned again. "Please, please..." With a hand that was grubby, stained from her previous struggles, she stroked her belly and touched the point of her pussy where her clit throbbed and yearned to be massaged. She jerked at her own touch. Sweat trickled between her breasts and she flung her head from side to side. Moaning and mewing, Daisy raised her bottom from the ground, right forefinger nestling deep in the mass of golden curls bushed between her thighs.

A slap echoed round the clearing and Daisy cried out, a long and piercing lament. Her eyes opened wide. Jem's belt dangled in front of her. The curve of her belly, previously unblemished, boasted a weal the width of that belt. It glowed, hot and scarlet.

"You have a lot to learn, my girl." Jem brought the belt down once more, hard and incisive. It slashed across her spreading breasts, across her thighs, it struck her again and again. "You take your interfering fingers away from your cunt, you slut." His voice was a hiss. "When you're in my presence you do not even think of pleasuring *yourself*."

Daisy quivered. She longed for relief. The touch of the belt, a new and thrilling experience, had aroused her to an aching desperation. To Daisy sexual satisfaction was the ultimate enjoyment, one of life's many pleasures. She whimpered in despair.

"What - what do you want?"

Her leg was stiff. The rope cut into her ankle. Neither of these pains diverted her from the longing for Jem's cock. Since her beating, the iron rod, full and rigid when originally released, had grown in stature. Daisy bit her lip. The sight alone of that prick was sending waves of longing, sizzling, uncontrollable, through her loins, down her legs, turning her breasts into lush pulsating mounds, her nipples into glowing buttons.

"You really are a hot little number, aren't you darling? Can't think we'll have much trouble getting you up to standard." And with these incomprehensible words resounding in Daisy's head, Jem sank to his knees between her thighs. With rough fingers he spread her lips, lips that were wet and soft with desire. Daisy urged him on. The tip of that cock nuzzled at her. She lifted her hips and his hands clasped her bottom. He pulled her, willing and shivering, over the dusky shaft and rammed the cock home sturdily. The thrusts were deep. Daisy shook and cried out with joy. Her face, naturally pale, turned a warm and rosy pink, she jumped and juddered and the gipsy grunted, and shot hot thick juice deep inside her thankful body.

She flopped back, relaxed and with eyes closed, stroked her belly in lazily gliding caresses. A smile of pleasure lit her face and with lips pursed in expectation of a kiss, held out her arms. No kiss came. But hands, coarse and insistent, pulled at her hair, bent her head forward, pushed her face down towards the dark warmth of her juicy cleft. Daisy opened her eyes. She could see the plump and creamy curve of her thigh, sticky with fluid, smell her own odour mixed with Jem's. The sight, the smell, brought a heat to her cheeks and desire began to build once more.

She struggled against his restraining hand, tried to look up - catch his eye - smile invitingly - but what happened next made her cry out. Darkness engulfed her. A blindfold pressed close and she could feel the loose ends tickling her neck, then entangling in her tousled hair. Jem grabbed the dangling ends and tied them with a deliberate and satisfying flourish behind her head. She waved her hands, tried to feel for him in the darkness.

"Jem, Jem, I can't see! I -"

She was cut off abruptly. Something soft and warm was stuffed into her mouth and, from the taste and perfume, she realised with surprise, these were her own torn and useless knickers. Daisy could neither see nor speak. She tried, but only muffled groans gurgled inside her throat. She tried to spit the knickers out, but more material, probably her bra, was bound round her lips. The stuffed knickers were firmly held in position.

"There, young lady, that's a pretty sight." Jem's voice was soft and lilting, his hands smoothed her hair and caressed the back of her neck. He patted the blindfold, then the gag, his fingers dancing over the bonds with light fluttering strokes, and then he left her.

Daisy heard him whistling softly, zipping his jeans, moving farther away, the rustle of dead leaves shuffling under his feet. What was he planning? From what she had heard him say, and the way he had said it, Daisy was convinced he had no intention of really harming her. Her body was tense with waiting. Her leg, still tied by the ankle to the trunk of a tree, ached. She wanted to move into a more comfortable position but could only manage the slightest of wriggles.

"I shall have to get moving. The horse wants to get back to his stall, don't you?" A low whinnying appeared to confirm that the horse was ready to go.

Daisy sat where he had left her. Dead twigs dug into her bottom. And then the rope was loose. Her leg fell to the earth with a bump. She bent her stiff knee, squirmed her toes, grateful for the return of movement. She wanted to thank Jem, throw her arms round his neck, fuck him again. But everything was silence. Had he gone? Had he got what he wanted and left? Swinging her head from side to side, listening hard, she tried to work out where he was standing. She could hear nothing.

Panic seized her. Had he left her, with no clothes to speak of, no shoes? Daisy was devastated. She scrambled to her feet, caught hold of the blindfold. Perhaps it was just a game. Really, he was only inches away staring at her, laughing at her helplessness.

Before her fingers had even touched the knot, they were grabbed. Jem's body pressed against her. She could feel the rigid rod between his legs thrusting against her thigh.

"Don't move," his voice hissed in her ear. "The blindfold stays exactly where it is, and so does the gag, but," he tore the remaining tatters of her best outfit from her shoulders, "these rags can go." They slid from her body and Daisy felt them slither into a sad pile at her feet. Her stockings drooped below her knees and Jem ripped them deftly away from her legs, leaving her totally naked. "These hands of yours could do with some restraining, don't you think, girl? Give me an answer. Nod your head, commit yourself or this belt will loosen and tickle your backside."

Daisy nodded, her mind confused but craving agreement. The rope that had earlier wrapped itself round her leg now secured her wrists. Swift and professional, Jem tied it round Daisy's forearms, pulled it tight, looped it again, slowly and determined, wrapped it around her arms until they were fastened into a single rigid formation behind her back.

A convulsive shiver of delicious wantonness embraced Daisy. She thrilled to the bite of the rope. She longed to thank Jem for her fucking, to show him how grateful she felt and to fuck him again. Her pussy was wet, her belly quivered. She tossed her head, opened her thighs, and thrust her cunt forward. She hoped that Jem would understand her mute message.

"You really are a willing little madam, aren't you?" Jem's hand delved between her legs and squeezed her sex. Two fingers jammed inside her. "There will be plenty of time for that later. Now," he said, "I have some more trussing up to do before I can deliver you to your new home."

Daisy waited patiently. Silently she urged him on, willing to submit to any demand if it meant she could have more of that cock. The rope cut into her arms and her shoulders hurt. As she attempted to ease them they were jerked by sudden jolting spasms. Jem, the remaining length of rope clasped in his hand, thrust it between her legs, moved round in front of her, drew it tight over her tummy. He bound it round her waist, once, twice, three times, knotted it firmly over her belly and marched her across the clearing.

Daisy stumbled, the rope scorched between her pussy lips, and she felt explosions of ecstasy shoot from her sensitive clit. Dizziness engulfed her, her legs wobbled, she staggered, clumsy and weak, only Jem's firm hold on the lead rope prevented her from falling to the ground. A pulsating, all-consuming spasm left her enraptured and shaking. Jem kept walking and she had no choice but to follow. Her knees felt ready to buckle when strong arms wrapped round her waist and he lifted her bodily from the ground.

The horse, stolid and strong, waited patiently for this charming burden to be slung into position on its back. Daisy's head flopped forward, her nostrils breathing in the sweet warm animal smell, and her naked stomach squashed onto the supple leather of the saddle. Her legs kicked, Jem grasped her ankles, secured plump knees with the remainder of the rope, fastened and strapped her legs tightly from knee to ankle. She sprawled on the horse's back, heart thumping, frightened of falling, and screamed a muffled scream.

Think you might fall, do you? No need to fear that."

Grabbing the loose end of rope that hung from her waist, Jem tied it, first to one, then to the other pommel that curved steeply upwards from the saddle.

"Gee up!" His belt swished through the air, landing on the horses flank. The horse walked forward, slowly at first, then hastening into a trot. Daisy, constrained and blindfolded, bound and gagged, bounced up and down on the broad warm back.

Jem's leather strap continued to thwack, sometimes to encourage the horse, but more frequently to land smartly on Daisy's big white bottom.

4: Jo Explores The Wood

With her long blonde hair shining in the sunlight, Jo flicked the yellow duster out of the attic window. Her eyes were glazed, unfocused, the normal blue of clear lavender clouded with frustration. She stared into the far distance. This summer job had turned out to be a non-starter. She'd only been a few days in this lovely old house, Dropwell Park, and already she had been given the sack. Not that it was her fault: her boss had lost his job too.

"It's like this, my dear," her boss had explained. "The new owner, a strange man, not that I've met him, just spoken on the phone ... He rang this morning ..." He paused, frowned, shook his head, then continued. "Yes. Well, I had great trouble understanding what he was saying. Something about the woods and the meadow, it didn't make sense to me. Then he said the house would be remaining vacant and any staff I had appointed, luckily that's just you, my dear, were to be given their cards, and I could push off as well. Quite rude, I thought. Most abrupt. Not my usual kind of gentleman."

Agitated, he polished the silver candlestick in his hand with unnecessary vigour.

The man looked so sad. Jo had felt quite sorry for him as he pursed his lips and shook his head, a expression of acute discomfort flitting across his normally placid features.

"I've had a such strange feeling about this job ever since that day - about ten days ago - when a very odd young man turned up. He said he was the owner's assistant. He locked himself in the billiard room for the day. And then for the rest of the day, there were some very strange noises - quite a racket. There was banging, clanking. the rattling of chains."

Jo's ears pricked.

"After he had gone, the key to that room had disappeared. I haven't been able to get in there since."

Jo smiled sympathetically.

"Anyway, the new owner won't be coming to live here after all." He sighed, smiled at Jo, put down the well-polished candle-stick and patted her bottom. He pressed a week's wages into her hand, and said: "So, that's the end of it for both of us, my dear. Not that you will have much trouble finding another position, not with your looks."

Jo dimpled prettily at the compliment, well aware though that compliments would not keep her fed and watered for the summer.

And now, hold-all packed, Jo had finished tidying her lovely little room. There was no excuse to linger. She kicked her toes, long brown and tipped with polish the colour of ripe damsons, against a battered skirting board. She had liked this bedroom the minute she had set eyes on it. She had looked forward to waking up here every morning for several weeks, and now her dreams of country living had come to an abrupt end. Hey ho, back to the stinking city. Back to bed-sit land and hamburgers.

Jo sighed, leaned her head against the cool glass of the dormer window and watched the duster flutter from her fingers, floating in slow yellow swirls, down, down, down into the cobbled yard below.

It was a beautiful morning in mid-May and blossom coated the gnarled apple trees in the orchard beyond the stable yard. The pink and white blooms cushioned the branches and a perfume, sweet and heady, wafted on warm currents of air to where Jo stood, moody and miserable, at the open window high in the creaking old house. Her lavender blue eyes, fringed by lashes that were thick and sooty, flashed with annoyance. A heavy fringe cut straight across her broad forehead, and curtains of hair framed a face that was square-jawed, high cheek-boned and very determined. Shaking the fringe out of her eyes, she pushed the heavy locks behind her ears.

The long tresses brushed over her bare shoulders, tickling her spine. Jo knew this mane of hair was one of her best features. It was not possible to put one single name to the colours that shimmered with the shine of youthful vitality. It glowed like polished silk. Ash-blonde she always called it, but the mixture contained silver, as well as ash, with the occasional russet streak. The prevalent shade was that of the palest of pale gold.

Her figure had a natural elegance, tall and slim and, at this moment, tense with a suppressed energy. She was dressed in jeans that moulded to shapely thighs, a halter top, the straining material barely containing breasts that were both generous and firm. The top, lavender in colour, cut into the sparse golden flesh of her midriff and reflected light back into her eyes, turning them an even deeper blue, almost violet.

She sighed again and ran her finger along the narrow window ledge. Then, cupping her breasts in both hands, she examined the dark cleavage with a detached interest. Perhaps the time had come to put the two beauties to some use. She looked from one lavender covered tit to the other. Donnie had said there would always be a job waiting for her at his club...

At that moment voices floated up from the yard below, deep gruff male voices. Two of them. Jo let her breasts drop and leant out of the window. Two men were walking across the yard. Both dark, one curly headed, the other with practically no hair at all, it was cropped so close to his skull. Both wore large rings in their ears and, startled, Jo saw that one was brandishing a long and heavy staff, the other clutched a whip. She felt her heart quicken at the sight. Who were they? Where had they come from? Could one of them be that strange young man the boss had mentioned?

She had seen no sign of them previously. They must be stable lads. Except she was pretty sure they were no horses in the stables.

"We're here for the summer, Troy was definite about that."

"He's heard from the Big Man, has he?" The one with long curly hair nodded. "But will he let us get on with it without interruption?"

"Ay. He's away, won't be arriving for a couple of weeks at least. Troy's delighted. He likes this place. And there's plenty of room, well hidden away."

The close-cropped head nodded in agreement. And the two men, broad-shouldered, narrow-hipped, and with muscles rippling under close-fitting shirts and jeans, disappeared round the corner of the stable block, whip and staff clutched tightly in large fists.

Jo blinked. They had gone. Laughter ringing round the cobbled yard was the only sign she had not imagined them.

She stared into the empty space. She was intrigued. The Big Man, who could he be? Was he the owner? Who was Troy? And, most interesting of all, who were they, those two hunky looking men? The boredom and unhappiness that had engulfed Jo at the thought of returning to her poky little flat flew. Here was something interesting. Something she would like to know more about.

She had done a little bit of exploring during the few short days she had been at the house and knew that the path the two men were following led through the apple orchard, across some fields and down towards the stream. It was still a lively bubbling brook at this point in its career, and, although she had not been that far, Jo had seen that it fed a lake. She had noticed the glimmer of a large expanse of water shining between the branches of the trees when she first arrived.

She had been left to leave whenever she felt like it, so long as she left her room clean and tidy. She glanced quickly round. The bed was stripped, the surfaces cleared. Her few bits and pieces were stowed in her hold-all. All she needed to do was grab her jacket, slip on her sandals and she was ready to go.

Jo clattered down the two flights of stairs. The ones leading from her little attic bedroom were narrow and bare, plain unvarnished deal. The next flight, were more palatial and of the finest polished oak, and they echoed to the clip-clopping of her sandalled feet. She yelled over the bannister on her hurry down.

With a week's wages stuffed in the back pocket of her jeans, Jo dragged open the heavy front door, sad to be leaving this lovely old place, never to return, she supposed with a sigh.

She loped round the side of the rambling old house towards the stable yard, towards the path that would lead her after those two very interesting young men.

Jo stood on the edge of the orchard and screwed up her eyes. Halfway across the field, shoulders swinging, the two men strode towards the wood. Jo strode after them. Her blue hold-all bumped against her bare shoulder and she hoisted it higher. She slid dark sunglasses over her eyes and a grin, puckish and mischievous, curled her pink painted mouth. Something was going on and she was not about to let the chance of adventure slip from her grasp.

The clinging denim protected her legs from the many thistles nestling unobtrusively in the grass, but her long toes, bare except for her best mules - plum-coloured leather, and the favoured item of her meagre wardrobe at present - were pricked and stabbed painfully as she hurried after the men.

Her long strides, careless and eager, turned from a hasty walk into a frisky run. She did not want to lose sight of these two when they entered the copse that bordered the stream.

The coolness of the trees after the warmth of the sun made her shiver, and goose bumps prickled over her body. Her nipples puckered, and thrust against the thin material of her halter top. There wasn't a sound. Surely the two of them, both big and with a heavy tread, should be making some kind of noise she could follow through the trees? Jo wanted to see where they were heading, but to her intense disappointment it looked as if she had lost them altogether.

"Damn." She stamped her foot and twigs snapped loudly under her sandal. They must really have been moving. She was quite out of breath. She dropped her hold-all to the ground and leant back against a tall beech tree, pressing her back, hot and sweaty, against the cool smooth trunk. In the dim light of the wood, she removed her sunglasses and they dangled from her damson-tipped fingers.

The narrow path ahead wound between the trees, the sun slanted through the branches high up above the ground. Although the light was low, it was obvious to Jo that her quarry was nowhere in sight. Annoyed, she swore quietly to herself.

And just then, a voice spoke softly, only inches from Jo's right ear.

"Now, just what do you think we've got here?"

She screamed in surprise and tried to dart away from the figure that loomed over her, but arms, thick and brawny, wrapped round her slender form, and a body, hard muscular and very masculine, pushed up against her hips, pressing her firmly back against the entrapping tree trunk.

"Would you have been following us, darling?"

The voice, still soft, was close and, looking wildly to her left, Jo realised that the second man, the scalp-headed one, was lounging on her other side, her blue hold-all swinging from his long fingers.

"Following you?" Jo gulped hard as she tried to think of a reasonable explanation for her behaviour. "No - that is - yes - well - not exactly following, no." She stuttered to a halt, smiling brightly.

"And do you think we would object if you had been?" The big curly-headed man stood back grinning, his arms falling to his hips as he thrust strong thumbs into the waistband of jeans, jeans that were old, dirty, and so tight Jo could feel herself redden at the unmissable sight of the prominent bulge straining the weak and loosening zip.

She looked from one to the other. Both of them were grinning. Their teeth gleamed whitely. The one with the curly hair sported a luxuriant moustache, the other a scar, pale and very thin. It cut through the natural swarthiness of his cheek, running from below his left eye socket and disappearing behind an earlobe punctured by a large golden ring. Yet they didn't seem to be unfriendly.

Jo began to relax. She decided to come clean. "Okay, yes." She smiled broadly, her best, and friendliest smile. "I was following you, but I didn't realise you'd seen me."

The scalp-headed man laughed loudly. Jo's face screwed up in dismay. "I mean, I just wanted to see where you were going." She felt she owed an explanation. "I've been working up at the house," she indicated over her shoulder. "I've only been there a couple of days and now the miserable job's come to and end - and - well - you looked like you might be interesting people to get to know." Again she smiled, bright and brave. "I've nothing lined up and I can't face going back to town, not for the summer. I thought, if you were local, you might know of some work going round here."

She paused for breath and fell silent, and the only sound was that of a cuckoo, hidden amongst the misty green of the branches overhead, intent upon producing his repetitive and doleful cry.

"There's work, sweetheart." Scalp-head spoke for the first time. His voice was deep and throaty. Cigarettes and booze, thought Jo. The sound of it sent a shiver through her loins. "We're here for the summer." He glanced at his companion and then his eyes swivelled towards her tensed body and he looked her over slowly. "We could do with some assistance. Not that there'd be any wages or anything, just your keep. But - if you're looking for something exciting, something just that little bit different - well - you could do worse than come along with us."

Jo's legs had turned to water at the sound of that throaty voice. And the way he had looked at her as her spoke. She writhed her hips against the tree trunk, lifted her mane of ash-blonde hair with both hands, flicked the heavy tresses away, tossed them over her shoulders, revealing the full curve of those breasts surging against the flimsy material of her halter top.

"Troy said blondes, didn't he Nico?" The curly-headed man grinned at his companion.

"And this one's full of spirit. She'd be willing to learn a trick or two. Would I be right, darling?"

Jo gazed at them both. A tingle of excitement tickled inside her tummy and she licked lips that had gone dry. "I'm certainly willing to give most things a go. What exactly is it you're offering?"

The one called Nico, the scalp-headed one, the one who turned her legs to jelly whenever he spoke, pointed down the path that wound its way between the avenue of beech trees.

"You come with us, darling, and we'll show you. And I think a girl like you will love everything we have on offer." He grinned at her. "By the way, what do you call yourself? I'm Nico and he's Seth." He nodded towards his friend, who now stood, legs parted, curly head thrown back, revealing a thick neck and heavy shoulders, The powerful arms that had recently pinned Jo to the tree were now folded across a stomach, flat and firm, strong as a sheet of granite.

Jo suddenly felt accountably shy with both men examining her so intently. She lowered her eyes. Her hair fell forward concealing the rosy blush on her cheeks, but she answered in what she hoped was a cool and clear voice."My name is Jo, Jo Tra..."

"Jo," Nico's voice interjected sharply. "That's enough, we don't stand on formality here, Jo. There's few of us use more than one name - except for his lordship, Dapper Troy Dempsey. But then he thinks he's someone of importance - and we let him carry on thinking that way, don't we, Seth?"

But Seth was already striding off down the path, whistling sweetly and swinging along through the trees, the staff in his hand ringing out as he thwacked it hard onto the path in front of him.

Jo looked after the muscular figure disappearing into the distance, shifted against the trunk of the tree, and a firm grip fastened onto her bare arm. Nico was standing next to her and she shivered uncontrollably at the closeness of him. He must have felt her body tremble for suddenly his arm was round her and his hand grasped hold of her breast squeezing and manipulating her right nipple until it hardened to a rock-like firmness and bulged through the fine material of her top.

"Shall we be going then?" Nico's face, almost on a level with her own, grinned encouragingly at her. The scar, white and slightly puckered at the edges, gave his face a lop-sided, rather raffish look when he smiled. "My hand," he leant forward, brushing her cheek with his lips, "my hand seems to be full of one of the bounciest juiciest tits I've had the pleasure to fondle for many a long day."

Jo felt weak at his touch.

"Do you think we should be getting along Jo?"

The strong arm wrapped round her body was a comfort. The feel of those virile fingers twisting and pulling at a nipple, engorged and sensitive, more than ready to be sucked, convinced her that she had no desire to turn back now. She didn't want to return to the big house, nor back to the city, not to her horrible little flat. Whatever it was these two rather adorable blokes had on offer, and Jo was not at all sure what it would turn out to be - well, she wanted some of it, she was quite convinced of that.

To Hell with the cash situation. Board and keep would do.

"Let's go." Her voice was breathless. "I'm game for almost anything. And if it's something new and unusual - that's just up my street."

Laughing at her enthusiasm, Nico held her closer, and together they strode down the path, between the trees. She glanced quickly round. Seth was definitely out of sight. "He's gone. We're alone," she whispered in Nico's ear. A pulsating energy filled her body. The touch of the man's fingers squeezing her breast, manipulating the nipple, trailing hard fingers over the delicate flesh beneath her halter top, was sending shivers of delight up her spine.

Nico did not reply. His arm pulled her close, secure. Jo could feel the muscles, rigid and iron-hard, beneath his shirt.

The whip, still clutched in his left hand, fascinated her, she could hardly take her eyes off it.

She licked her lips and pressed her body closer. His tongue shot deep inside her mouth, his free hand slid beneath the skimpy lavender-coloured top, slowly easing it up, then, with a sharp tug, yanking it over her shoulders. Her long golden hair caught in the folds of material, but a vigorous shake of her head made it tumble free, cascading down the hollow curve of her naked back, arousing and erotic.

Jo shook her freed breasts in Nico's face. Jo's breasts - only just held in place at the best of times by this particular outfit, now swung full, long and heavy, the tips graced by blushing nipples transforming the golden mounds into visions of giant peaches, luscious and ripe. Generous and plush, the flesh plump and perfect, they cried out to be nipped by the prick of sharp teeth. The bursting flesh begged to be nuzzled, for lips and tongue to clutch and savour, draw in the succulent flesh, suckle the nipples until they seemed ready to dissolve, for juice to flow like honey, sweet as nectar, onto a probing, questing tongue.

Nico slid the whip through a leather holster hanging from the belt slung round his bony hips. With both hands free he grasped hold of her breasts. "Nice titties - spectacular even." He appeared thoughtful, not talking to her, just about her. He dropped back, held her at arms' length, stared at her. From the waist up, his gaze roamed over her naked body, and then from the waist down, over the swell of her hips, the long slim legs, encased in jeans of a washed out blue, jeans that clung to every nook and cranny of her delicious-looking body.

Jo waited for him to say something. He leant towards her, weighed the breasts in his hands, bounced the heavy flesh in his palms, dug stubby fingernails into the creamy skin and tweaked the nipples with hard fingers until they felt so tight Jo thought they would explode. She knew he liked what he saw - and how he felt about it. The solid looking rod jutting at his crotch told her all she wanted to know. He was keen and so was she, but did she have the nerve to ask? Would he let her take control of that whip? She could not bear the thought of letting this opportunity pass her by. Jo took a deep breath and wriggled her body closer to the dark, stubble-haired gipsy.

Her fingers, inquisitive and itching to experience the texture, touched the glossy handle where it was tucked, snug and secure, into the black leather holster strapped round his waist. She shivered at the feel of the warm wood, thrilled as she imagined the strength of that leather thong cutting across firm unblemished flesh. Tingling all over, she rubbed her breasts against Nico's muscular chest and ground her generous hips hard onto the spare flesh of his stomach. She took a deep breath, pressed her face against his, looked over his shoulder and could see no sign of the other gipsy, the long-haired one - Seth.

They were alone, she and Nico, here beneath the beech trees. Her heart thudded, loud and insistent. The feel of that whip had sent tremors of excitement surging through her. It was now or never.

She stared into Nico's eyes. They were small, coal black and deep set. The brows were heavy, the expression unfathomable. Jo thrilled at that expression. She felt hungry for him. Hurriedly, she kicked off her sandals, unzipped her jeans, slid them down over her wide hips, wriggled her bottom free of the constricting material and let them fall to the ground.

Nico did not utter a sound. Jo was surprised. She cocked her head on one side and grinned. "You certainly are the strong silent type, honey. But I like that in a man. You're strong, but are you strong enough?" The question dried on her lips and she decided she would have to try again. She lowered her eyes and saw the jeans lying in a pale blue heap at feet. If she was going to get anywhere, now was the time to display herself completely.

She stepped free of the discarded clothes, kicked them to one side and stood, long legs parted, arms akimbo. The narrow string of her panties, the merest sliver of nylon and lace, jet black and more decorative than useful, cut across the crest of her belly, contrasting vividly with the creamy skin, before disappearing between her thighs, cutting deep into the cleft of her bottom.

She jutted her naked mound towards Nico. No hair adorned it, it was smooth and silky and Jo liked to keep it that way. Her whole body appeared sleek, the colour and texture of buffed and gilded satin: the fine hair on her arms and legs were of the palest blonde, almost invisible.

She watched Nico watching her and hooked nimble fingers under the thin black line of the panties. She slid her finger beneath the material, tweaked and plucked at the skimpy garment.

"If I were to slip these off, like a good girl, would you do me a very big favour?"

Her voice was husky and she lowered her eyes. Jo knew that the long curly lashes flickering over those high cheekbones usually got her whatever it was she wanted. And, at last, he did respond.

"And what kind of favour would that be, sweetheart?" The gipsy stood, arms folded, the tip of the whip's handle jutting out over his hipbone.

"Well - could I hold that delicious looking object hanging from your waist and possibly, just possibly" she looked up a coquettish smile dimpling her cheek, "well I really would enjoy the opportunity to stroke that long leather thong over those darling tight little buttocks of yours."

His face was expressionless. Jo decided to carry on. A surging energy was taking her over and she could feel the dampness between her thighs. With an elegant wiggle of her hips, a sideways dip, a slinky straightening up of her nubile body, she was naked. She looked directly at Nico. Her eyes, hugely dilated, the colour of rain-soaked violets, swam with desire.

"I'd perform the deed like this," she said. The black G-string dangled from the fingers of her right hand. Dappled light filtered through the branches high overhead, painting patterns of light and shade on her dewy flesh. She fondled her breasts with both hands, squeezed them close together until the nipples touched, she rubbed them, one against the other, and they grew, stiffened, lengthened and firmed. She glanced from beneath her long lashes at Nico. At last she had his full attention. Jo bent forward, her tongue shot from between moist lips and she twirled it long and pink and wet over those nipples, shuddering with desire at her own touch.

Nico stared silently at her. His hand played over the handle of the whip tucked into the leather holster at his waist. Jo felt excitement grow in her loins and goose bumps shivered up her thighs and arms, the fine blond hairs glistening in the streaks of sunlight.

She saw his fingers tighten on the handle, the polished sheen glimmering beneath the coarse fingers. She saw it slowly, very slowly slide out of its snug home. With a fervour of excitement growing in her belly, she watched him loosen the long leather leash, brush the tips of his hard fingers along the snaking cord. Euphoric at what she had achieved, Jo stretched out a hand to touch the leather - crisp - lively - stimulating.

Shaking with tension, her fingers quivered only inches away from the powerful switch, when, with no warning, strong arms from behind her wrapped round her naked body. Hot breath tickled the back of her neck and a lock of hair, black and curly, slipped over her bare shoulder.

She shouted out, shock and surprise surging through her. Those arms, locked beneath her breasts, hugged her close, immovable, and her feet lifted from the ground. She kicked and screamed, legs flailing wildly, hair flying in every direction. All she could see was the grinning face of Nico, and that beautiful whip raised above his bristled scalp. Her gaze followed the sliver of hissing leather as it snaked skywards. She saw it twist and turn, coil and curl, snapping the ends of twigs, whistling like a bird in the still air. She saw the curving writhing leash descend and then felt it, sharp and merciless, on the soft white flesh of her inner thigh, and she moaned, tears pricking at the lavender blue eyes, wide with amazement, bemused and unsure, wondering what she had let herself for.

"Smart action, Seth. You just saved me from a fate I don't like to contemplate." Nico's teeth gleamed white against the dark skin of his face.

"What would that have been then, Nico? This looks a tasty piece of flesh to me right enough." Seth squeezed tighter, bulging her breasts until they looked ready to spring away from the rest of her.

"Tasty enough maybe, But this particular young madam had the idea that she might just use this darling piece of singing leather on my backside, would you believe?"

The second gipsy, Seth, who had returned so quietly and now clasped her to his wide chest, shouted with derision at this news. "She's a little vixen then, is she? A vixen - vermin, and we know what happens to vermin, don't we sweetheart?"

He dropped Jo from his arms. let her fall to the ground with a heavy thud. She lay where she fell, the breath knocked from her body, the tall muscular Seth standing menacingly over her. "She doesn't seem to have much to say now, Nico. Do you think I frightened her or something?"

Snorting, Nico strode over to where Jo lay helpless and winded on the ground. He grabbed hold of her by the shoulders, wrenching her body, pushing her face hard into the ground, placing a foot in the small of her back. "Now there's a lovely sight, Seth. A big white blooming bum staring at me."

"To be sure Nico, it would be improved by the addition of a few red stripes scorched over that peachy skin."

"I'll oblige you there, Seth." Nico raised the whip, twirled it skilfully above his head, cracked it loud and brought it down, fast straight and accurate. Jo squirmed, tried to wriggle away, but the weight of the foot on her back pressed hard, pushing her into the soil, squashing her breasts and bruising the crests of her hip-bones.

"From the look of those cunt lips, Nico, this particular piece is ready for plucking."

"Fucking, did you say, Seth? Oh, yes, she's ready for fucking all right, aren't you sweetheart?" Nico pushed Jo with the tip of his boot, rolled her body over so she stared up at them with her large lavender eyes.

The whip sang again, lashing Jo's opulent breasts, slicing, cutting, tracing patterns of scarlet over the soft white mounds. Jo groaned. She wriggled her bottom, hot from the whipping, into the soft earth. Her legs spread, her fingers clawed at the air. The stroke of the whip on her own body entranced her. If she was not allowed to do the whipping, she was exquisitely happy to receive the tender kisses.

Nico dropped between her spread thighs, unzipped his jeans. His cock sprang, hot and ready, juice oozing from the tip. Jo gazed in awe and admiration. He played with the solid shaft, sliding the skin, shimmering and silky, over the vibrant head.

"Yes, Nico, yes please. I want, I need -" A sound behind her caught her attention. Seth was standing at her head. Her spreading hair was trampled into the soil by his feet. His long legs towered over her and his cock was also waving free. Gulping, Jo glanced from one to the other. Two cocks, both full, both ready. Her body quivered. She moistened her lips. opened her mouth, spread wet pussy lips with trembling fingers, revealing dark and intimate secrets and inviting Nico to seize and enter her.

"Come on then boys," she whispered. "Come on. I'm ready. Fill me up, the pair of you."

They approached her together. Seth sank his cock into her mouth. Her cheeks bulged, her tongue licked and kissed, her lips sucked hard.

Nico squeezed her shaven pussy, stroked the wet lips, rubbed the tip of his cock over her aching clit, then sank, deep, hard, insistent, into her waiting body. Both men thrust. Jo jerked between them. She longed to cry out but her mouth was full of cock. Sweet tingling sensations urged her onwards. Her pussy softened, moistened, spasmed. Nico shot hot and long into the heart of her. Seth lunged, his balls hot against her breast. Her throat gulped and swallowed, she writhed under the pressure of the two male bodies.

Jo lay weak and exhausted. She would have liked even more but they had withdrawn from her. She tried to get up. She was delighted by her new experiences. But the men hadn't finished with her yet.

Seth pushed her back to the ground. "Shall we tie the hands, Nico, that would stop the little varmint trying to get away from us. Am I right?"

"And ankles, Seth, and ankles."

Seth nodded in agreement. They both zipped up. Seth retrieved his staff which had fallen to the ground when he first grabbed hold of Jo. "My pole, Nico, that's what you do with vermin, you tie their limbs together and sling them from a pole."

"And then drag your prize back to the camp, Seth, for everyone to see. That's what you do with vermin."

The two men unfastened their belts. One knelt at her head, the other her feet. Jo squeezed her eyes shut. She didn't understand what they were planning, and she didn't want to see whatever it was. She could feel well enough. She felt her arms being dragged above her head. Felt the warm leather of Nico's belt as he wrapped and tugged it round her narrow wrists. The buckle was placed between her palms and the roughness of the surface cut into the tender skin.

At the same time her feet were lifted from the ground, ankles crossed. A constricting tightness bound the ankles together, the ankle-bones bumped one against the other, bruising. Then the staff, the one Jo had noticed in Seth's hand when she had first seen him in the stable yard.

Could it only have been a couple of hours ago?

Her ankles were fastened to the staff and a rope from round Seth's waist was fixed between her hands and feet. They lifted the pole from the ground. The leather belts cut into her wrists and ankles. The two gipsies removed their shirts, each made a pad for a shoulder, and, on these, they lodged the pole ends.

They moved off slowly. Jo swung helpless between them. Her hair hung, touching the ground, her body stretched helplessly. Annoyed at this treatment after such a wonderful experience, she shouted, but this only seemed to amuse both Nico and Seth. They strode off through the wood, Jo shouting and oscillating wildly between them.

5: Daisy And CJ Meet

Daisy was dreaming of an old gipsy woman who trapped her in a ginnel - there was this man - black eyes, so intense - sexy - she woke up feeling randy and blinked into wakefulness.

As she came to she gazed around with a mixture of alarm and excitement. She wriggled, tried to twist, but her body was caught. She realised with a lurching certainty that she was still bound. Her arms were fastened tightly behind her back, her ankles strapped firmly together. A rope lashed her waist to a solid upright wooden stake. Golden hair, loose and bedraggled, hung about her bare shoulders and her breasts, large and milky white, were sore, the exposed skin tingling in the soft evening breeze.

Dazzled by the lowering sun, muddled and disorientated, she squeezed her eyes shut. When she opened them again she could scarcely believe the sight that lay before her. She was trapped in some kind of corral with other girls, and each and every one was as naked as she was.

Silken-skinned bodies gleamed with the health of regular exercise, and chattering voices rose, fell and swooped around her, befuddling and amazing her. They giggled and called across the grassy area chatting to friends. They smoothed an eyebrow, exclaimed about a scagged fingernail. They swung their arms and shuffled their feet. They smoothed disarranged hair, and what was obvious even to Daisy's startled eyes, was that the shades of that hair varied from the shiniest of silvers to the deepest of burnt auburns. Every gradation of blonde, gold, sand and rust was on display, but not a single dark-haired girl could she see.

Daisy felt as if she had opened a mysterious treasure chest and discovered it to be full of precious coin. What she saw displayed before her eyes was a collection of glittering sovereigns and glinting crowns, shimmering, flowing and swaying in the low sunshine of evening.

She shook her head in disbelief, closed eyes that ached with surprise, counted to ten, slowly, and snapped them open again. She was not dreaming. She really was here - in a corral - surrounded by these naked girls. The sun was setting, the sky was streaked crimson, cerise, ochre and deep purple and the faintest glimmering of the first stars of evening flashed in the rapidly darkening sky. Cool grass tickled between her toes. Her ankles and wrists hurt, her breasts and pussy were sore, with a soreness that Daisy had never experienced before, a longing for more sort of soreness, and her tummy lurched uneasily, the rope searing into the gentle flesh.

How on earth had she ended up in this place? Daisy's head swam as she tried to recollect what had happened to her. She tried to concentrate, to think hard. But Daisy never found thinking easy, and her head reeled, her body ached and she really would have preferred to sit, or if at all possible, lie down. A vision of her own room came to her, small maybe, poky even, but with its big soft bed in one corner, her strawberry pink duvet, cosy and ready to snuggle under, a radio to listen to, a box of chocolates to nibble. The picture was very clear in her mind, so clear that she was almost convinced that all this around her was not real - could not be real. The chattering voices receded, became muffled. She felt sleepy. This was still a dream about an old gipsy woman - and the man - the man -

And then it all came flooding back!

JEM!

She heard an anxious voice behind her. "Are you all right?"

Daisy turned and saw a girl, much shorter than herself, but about the same age, whose elfin face, framed by curls of coppery red, was smiling up at her.

This girl was also completely naked, tightly bound, and chained by the neck to a post. Her wrists were fettered behind her back, her slender ankles manacled. Brown freckles sprinkled generously over a pale creamy skin and gathered between her small breasts in a deep V of dense colour. The nipples were large, and reminded Daisy of strawberry ice-cream cones. And, she noticed with a blush, between the red-head's slender legs, curls of deep bronze were trimmed into a neat little heart shape, leaving the pink slit nestling beneath clearly visible.

"Are you all right?" the anxious voice repeated. "You look a little queasy." The girl gazed at Daisy and her face, freckles dusting her nose, broke into a friendly grin. "By the way, my name is Cassie, but my friends call me CJ. I'm a bicycle-ist!" That seemed to amuse her greatly. Then she cocked her head on one side and surveyed the blushing Daisy with intense and unnecessary interest.

I'm fine - I think." Daisy looked round. "Where are we? What are we doing here?"

"Well, I walked here. On my own two feet, like an idiot. Me, who always thought she was so sophisticated and street wise. I got taken for a real lemon. But he sounded so plausible -"

"He? Who? Was it Jem?" Daisy could feel her nipples rising, tight and hard, and her pussy began to drool at the thought of his cock - the memory of that had suddenly become very clear, shaking her to her roots.

*   "Jem? I haven't met anyone called Jem. My downfall was brought about by two louts called Davy and Damien, twins, apparently. Not that you'd think so to look at them." She looked thoughtful and a smile played about her lips. "Mind you, I did see you arrive. It was quite a sight I can tell you."

"What do you mean?" Daisy stooped closer. She wanted to hear what this girl had to say.

The two girls huddled closer. As she bent forward Daisy's pendulous breasts brushed the top of Cassie's arm, so close were they, and her nipples stiffened to hard knobs at the touch of warm flesh.

"Well," Cassie said, "to be honest, I was here, all by myself to start with. These other girls weren't anywhere in sight. I don't know where they all came from. They just appeared in dribs and drabs. They seemed to know what they were doing - which is more than I did, I can tell you. I simply couldn't believe what I was seeing. You arrived on horseback. Most spectacular."

CJ's bright curls bounced excitedly above the freckled face and her green eyes shone, brilliant with excitement.

Daisy stared at her new companion, her face a blank. Slowly she brushed finger tips, the nails ragged and broken, over her eyes, she touched her bruised mouth, rubbed arms left reddened by the rope.

"It's true, it's all true, I wasn't dreaming, it actually happened, the clearing, the fucking, the horse." She shook her head in disbelief. "It's just that when I opened my eyes - and saw - all this - it looked and felt so - so -" Daisy ground to a halt.

"Unbelievable. That's the word you're looking for," said CJ helpfully. "Believe you me, if I wasn't talking to you, could see and touch you knew that you were real, well - I'd think I'd gone stark staring mad." The grin widened. Her teeth gleamed and her nose wrinkled prettily. "Mind you," she said, turning her head and squinting into the darkening distance, "mind you, by the sound of it, there's someone who doesn't sound too keen on the idea of being rounded up in here."

All the girls in the corral stopped talking. The chattering that had filled the evening air, ceased. A noise, strange high-pitched and piercing cut through the failing light. It was the voice of a girl, but it had peculiar pitch, slightly strangulated and muffled, but for all that, still roaring at full pelt.

"Put me down you bastards. Put me down. I'll walk, I promise. I'll come quietly, but just put me d-o-w-w-n-n." The plea ended on a long drawn-out wail of despair.

The gate of the corral opened and two men, one with long shoulder-length curls, the other, his head shaven, a scar slashing his cheek, strode through the opening. They were bare-chested and their muscles gleamed in the fading light.

"Wow", breathed CJ, "did you ever see anything quite so hunky in your life? But what on earth is it they're carrying?"

Depended between them was a strange object which slowly defined itself as a girl. Her ankles were bound to a long pole slung between the massive shoulders of the two men. The rope that bound her ankles also bound her wrists behind her back. She hung upside down. Shining sheets of hair, silvery in the fading light, brushed the grass. Her breasts, long and pendulous, swayed, and the large rosy nipples swooped from side to side. With ankles bound and arms trussed, her body hung, taut and rigid, but it was from her mouth that the noise, the shouting, the bellowing that echoed round the campsite, was emanating.

"Wow," breathed CJ in awe. "If only I'd known, I wouldn't have come so quietly. Obviously, in this place the more of a stink you kick up, the more likely you are to be handled by the professionals." Greatly agitated by what she had seen, her nipples perked and the heart-shaped cushion of curls nestling between her legs dampened. "Something tells me I've been doing things all wrong since I arrived in this demi-paradise."

They watched, enthralled, along with the other girls in the corral, as the wailing bundle was lowered to the ground, the bonds released, the pole discarded and a leather leash fixed to a manacle round the long slender neck.

"Hey," said CJ jumping up and down with excitement. "They're coming in our direction - uh, gosh, I'm sorry, but I don't know your name?"

"Daisy," said Daisy gloomily. "They may be coming this way, but neither of those is Jem."

"Neither of them is Damien or Davy either, but I'm not complaining. This place seems to be full to bursting with dishy young men." CJ grinned happily. "I wonder if any of the ones we've seen so far is the boss. If these are the minions, I can hardly wait to meet him. But I'm not complaining. What better way could a girl ask for to start a long vacation?"

The new arrival was led to a post only a few feet away from CJ and Daisy. Tethered by the leash round her neck, face crimson with rage, she stamped her foot and shouted after the retreating backs of her two captors. "You wait, you bastards. I'll get my own back, you see if I don't." As she shook her head in impotent disbelief, a sheet of silver hair flew in bright streaks across her angry face.

"Well, well, Daisy, I wonder what happened to her? She seems to have had a similar experience to yourself." CJ sighed. "I feel terribly cheated. In this place, to get the best treatment, you obviously have to push yourself forward." She smiled thoughtfully into the gloom. CJ had never had any trouble getting herself noticed in the past, and she had no intention of not being noticed here either.

If she had any say in the matter, that notice was going to be taken soon and it would have to be by someone of power and importance.

6: Chained In The Corral

Men had entered the corral about an hour ago; Davy and Damien, Jem, Nico and Seth, laughing noisily, joking, teasing one another, ignoring the girls but for the occasional slap. The girls, still fettered and chained, had been herded into small groups, three or four girls to a group. Hungry and thirsty, they had been promised refreshment later - after the men had had their own fill of food and drink, and had enjoyed an evening's entertainment seated round the campfire.

Around each small group of shivering girls the men had erected hurdles, roughly woven sheets of hazel bound with willow, lashed them together with ropes, and constructed roofs of branches and canvas, rough shelters of sorts for the night - a dark and starry night - and the naked girls huddled where they were chained.

They chattered or dozed. The experienced ones, tired from the day's training, murmured amongst themselves, exchanged gossip, examined new lash marks acquired during the day. Some, if length of chain allowed, gained warmth from the body of another. Some dozed where they stood, still leashed to posts. The new recruits, the ones gathered that day, bemused and bewildered by their predicament, tried to settle to their new and strange environment.

"Can't you just smell that food from here." CJ wrinkled her nose, the freckles feathering the ridge, dancing with each fresh pucker. "I'm starving, aren't you, Daisy? I can't remember when I last had anything to eat." CJ rolled her big green eyes, excited by the anticipation of food. Chained to a post, her movements restricted, she still managed to peer through the gaps in the rough hurdles, and stare up the slope towards the camp fire where the flames leapt and flickered, incandescent against a dome of blue-black sky.

She could see the silhouettes of people moving about. Loud shouts of laughter and raucous cheering floated down the field towards her.

"They certainly sound like they're enjoying themselves. I don't think they're planning to come back with our suppers very quickly!"

Daisy glanced up, her eyes blank. She made no effort to try and see what CJ was staring at so intently. Her pink and white complexion shone in the gloom of the shelter. Her breasts waxed like two full moons in the dim light. "I'm not hungry, not at the moment - not for food anyway." A sad sigh wobbled her breasts, and her shoulders heaved in sympathy. Long tendrils of blonde hair brushed over her face, the twisting curls falling into her dejected eyes and she shook her head in despair.

"What's up Daisy? What *are* you hungry for?" CJ found her new companion beguiling.

There was another big sigh, and Daisy replied softly: "You saw him, just now, when they came and fixed these shelters!"

"I suppose you mean that evil looking bloke, the one with the hooded eyes? Was that Jem?"

Daisy nodded. Her blonde hair glimmered. "Really, I'd like another fuck - like the one I had this afternoon - that's what I'd like - and -" - she reddened as she struggled to frame the sentence - "and I think I'd like to be tied to the back of that horse again, and feel Jem's belt on my bottom." The words came out in a tremendous rush. "It was so - so - thrilling." Memory of that afternoon's experience flickered in eloquent spasms over her voluptuous features.

Staring hard at her companion, CJ had to suppress a giggle. She bent her head so Daisy would not see the silly grin spreading from ear to ear. This girl was certainly a strange one. Whoever would have thought to look at her that she spent all her time thinking about her last sexual adventure and longing desperately for the next one.

"I suppose it takes all sorts." The third girl in the shelter spoke for the first time. The voice made CJ jump and woke Daisy from her sexual reverie.

"What was that?" CJ, arms still strapped tightly behind her back, turned carefully and looked directly into the face of the other girl.

This was the girl who had created such a row earlier, shouting and carrying on when she had been carried in, upside-down, suspended from a pole. On arrival she had been fettered to the post next to CJ. CJ had smiled, said hello, but the tall slender girl, with hair the colour of spun gold, had taken no notice of her, had turned away, ignored her. But CJ had caught a glimpse the red stripes scoring the pendulous breasts and criss-crossing the round and peachy backside.

Her lithe body, slim and elegant, was tied by strong ropes lashed round her middle. Her arms were bound at elbow and wrist, her legs at knee and ankle.

Pleased that she wanted to join in the conversation at last, CJ grinned at her. "Hi! I'm Cassie, but my friends call me CJ, and that," she nodded towards the dreamy Daisy, "is Daisy, my sex-mad sidekick. But who, if you don't mind me asking, are you, and how did you end up here?"

The tall girl peered at them in the dusky light. She didn't answer CJ's question immediately, but neither did she turn away. CJ considered this to be a good sign. An oppressive silence continued for a several seconds. This silence was too much for CJ, who had great difficulty in keeping quiet under any circumstances. "I couldn't help but notice - when you arrived - you didn't seem very keen on the idea of joining us. Am I right? And are those lash marks on your tits and bum?" Cassie was unable to keep the eagerness out of her voice.

"What if they are?" The tall girl's tone was sharp. "Is it any of your business - Cassie?"

Cocking her head on one side, CJ regarded the girl with interest. She was very prickly, but CJ was not easily snubbed. "Don't mind me, I've always had a big mouth. But - in this situation," she nodded towards her own and Daisy's straps and chains, "what with all these ropes and chains and stuff, well, we're all much in the same boat. And to be honest, it all seems pretty interesting to me. And Daisy's certainly been enjoying herself - so far. I think we could all end up having a good time - if we play our cards right - but it's always a good idea to have friends, someone to share your troubles with. Isn't that so, Daisy?"

Daisy was staring hard at the tall girl's breasts.

"Daisy - Daisy - for goodness sake girl, do try and listen to what I'm saying."

"I am listening," said Daisy petulantly. She smiled at the other blonde girl. "I was wondering, those marks, the ones we saw on your boobs and bottom when you arrived -"

"For goodness sake, Daisy, I knew you weren't listening. I just asked her about those."

Daisy took no notice of CJ. "Those long thin marks on your b-bottom - did he - did he - whip you?"

The new girl and CJ both stared at Daisy. Her big grey eyes were wide, her mouth trembling, and her tongue flitted and flickered over her bottom lip.

"There, you see," said CJ, beaming at the new girl. "I told you she was sex mad. But we both want to be friends with you. Daisy's quite thrilled about Jem. And, from what I've seen of the place so far - especially the blokes - well," CJ looked thoughtful, "I certainly like the look of *some* of them. Though I think we've probably only met the riff-raff so far." She smiled in the new girl's direction. "I'd love to know who's in charge here. But at this moment I need something to take my mind off my empty stomach.."

The tall girl shook her head in disbelief. "You two, don't either of you object to the idea of being tied up in here."

CJ grinned. "It's not really a question of not objecting, sweetie. We none of us seem to have had much say in the matter. What's our name by the way?"

Jo. I just lost my summer job at Dropwell Park. And as to all this whipping and stuff, am I really the only one who would rather it was all the other way round?" She blushed, lowered her head, and seemed glad of the cover of darkness. For Jo was not even willing to admit to herself how much she had enjoyed this afternoon's events.

CJ wriggled in her bonds, enthusiasm shining from her face . "You'd like to do the whipping and the tying up! Now there's a thought! But I can't see it coming off - not here - not easily."

"And after what happened this afternoon," sighed Jo, lowering her eyes, unable to look the other two in the face, "neither can I. But that doesn't mean to say I won't have a go at every opportunity that comes my way, you see if I don't."

"Great, fine, do your own thing," said CJ. "Meanwhile, we all seem to have ended up here. But today is a day I shall never forget. And believe you me, I can hardly wait for tomorrow to get under way."

7: Troy and The Hutch Bunny

"Maggie! Maggie! Where the devil has that girl got to?"

Troy Dempsey's voice bellowed as he stood, hand on hip, before the blazing fire. Grease smeared his chin, and in his right hand he clenched a long mug of cider. His clothes were immaculate. The shirt, the same shirt that had brought about Maggie's beating that morning, now rippled in silky folds over the bulging muscles of his shoulders.

It billowed softly over his wide chest and, open to the waist, disappeared, neat and precise, into the band of a pair of snug-fitting breeches. These were bronze in colour, shiny, the belt holding them in place, wide and buckled by a lion's head made of brass. The breeches clung to the iron-hard column of his thighs and were tucked into a pair of knee-length boots, buffed until they shone with the gleam of burnished chestnuts.

"Since that no-good bitch isn't here, someone else will have to take her place."

Troy stood by the fire in the middle of a circle of men and girls. The men, satiated by much food, roared with an excess of drink. Behind them, waiting for the next command to serve, were a dozen or more girls.

Troy pointed at one of these kneeling girls. "Come! You look as if you could do the job adequately."

The girl looked up, uncertain whether the leader of the camp could mean her. After all, she was a mere 'hutch bunny', a camp follower, one of the young and supple gipsy girls who accompanied the caravans. Dark-haired and sloe-eyed, they lived in old circus animal cages called 'hutches', eager to serve their masters, willing to learn and be punished. They were here to serve men and take orders from everybody, always available, known only by numbers.

The hutch bunnies were brought to the camp fire at night, ready in case anyone needed them. They knelt naked in the shadows, and the flickering firelight danced over their young bodies with a radiant luminosity, their chins held up by the wide collars they were made to wear.

"Yes, you girl."

Her eyes, large with rapture, gazed back at him. He waved his glass again in her direction and the golden liquid slurped onto the grass. "Come here," he roared. "Wipe my chin!"

The bunny, only recently released from her hutch, stood up slowly, her sylph-like body shaking with nerves. She edged towards the master who commanded her attendance, treading cautiously. Her collar forced her to stare straight ahead, and her bare feet had to feel each careful step. She stumbled over a discarded ham-bone. Gruff shouts and jeers filled the air, and Troy Dempsey, watching with amused contempt, bristled with relish. But she recovered and progressed cautiously onwards, arriving without further mishap in front of Troy.

He thrust a cloth into her quivering fingers and slowly she lifted it towards the grease-covered lips. She dabbed at his face with light fluttering strokes, and when the task was complete, lowered her eyes, her hands dropping back into position over her belly. She waited, meek and submissive, not daring to move until given the command to return to her place.

A dozen or more swarthy men watched every trembling moment with delight. They lounged on the grass, some still eating, others swigging large quantities of drink. Some were gossiping and smoking, enjoying this interval, but eager for the entertainment to start.

The dancing girls were late, but the men were here to relax and enjoy themselves and if there were no dancers - well, Troy enjoyed performing in front of an audience.

Troy gazed round at them and could see they were exhilarated, aggressive, waiting for his next move. He stared over their heads and saw that Maggie and Shorsa had arrived. They were standing behind the circle of kneeling bunnies, awaiting his orders, waiting to throw themselves with abandon into their dancing. He gulped down the remainder of the cider and threw the empty mug on the grass. The evening was balmy, heady, the girls had arrived late, and Troy Dempsey was in a mood to teach Maggie a lesson.

Maybe she was a good lay, and maybe she did look after his clothes well, but she had become lippy lately, too lippy for her own good. Troy smiled, a sardonic sneer twisting his handsome features. He was going to make sure she understood just what her position was in this training camp, that to him she was a minion, a mere scullion. He decided to demonstrate that fact to her, and now was as good a time as any.

He felt strong and vigorous and knew this evening was going to be enjoyable. He glanced down at the girl kneeling at his feet. She quivered, bound, gagged, subservient. She would provide a stimulating start to the evening's entertainment. His cock was already rigid inside the tight breeches. The girl would welcome a lesson on how to pleasure an important personage. *The* important personage, Troy Dempsey, leader of the training camp.

Someone threw a large branch onto the fire and it crackled and spat and sparks shot high into the dark night, a splutter of scintillating colour.

Men shouted and banged their fists on the ground. The girl at Troy's feet started, the sudden noise sending a shiver of apprehension, or was it anticipation, through her naked body. Shadows played over her flesh. Her dark hair, long and loose, hung over her narrow shoulders and shimmered in the light of the glowing fire.

Troy, delighted by the theatricality of the setting, held up a hand for silence. The men, realising the action was about to commence, shifted their positions, made themselves more comfortable, lit fresh cigars, filled their glasses, and waited. They settled, and the only sound was the cracking of the burning wood.

Assured of their full attention, Troy approached the trembling girl and placed a conciliatory hand on her right shoulder. She looked up at him, her large black eyes glittering, her fingers fluttering nervously over the bush of hair curling thick and black at the base of her belly. He caressed her upper arms, his fingers delicately tracing the crest of bone from shoulder to neck. He stroked the hardness of the iron collar beneath her chin. He spread inquisitive fingers, he massaged her quivering flesh, and brushed cool finger tips over her palpitating breast.

He raised his eyes and saw with satisfaction the face of Maggie, white against the darkness of the night, watching his every move.

Pleased with what he saw, Troy concentrated on his own enjoyment. He gazed at the flawless mounds of number three's breasts, plush beneath the palms of his hands, the skin delicate and dewy. The nipples, two dark buds, perched, alert and hopeful, plump and firm to the touch. Grabbing both tightly he rubbed them between thumb and forefinger. The girl moaned, her fingers scrabbled uselessly at her bush, her eyes filled with desire and she gazed at Troy with a gloating wonder.

"Shall I give her a taste gentlemen? I think this little bunny is on heat."

Fists thumped the ground in reply.

With a pinching roll of the thumbs he pulled her closer by the bulging nipples. Her mouth was now only inches from his rigid crotch.

"Did you enjoy that, girl? Those little titties of yours seem to have got bigger and rosier from my attentions. Do you think you could get a taste for being trained by me, girl?"

The hutch bunny stared up at him from where she knelt, her eyes dilated with longing. She tried to nod in reply but the collar cut into her chin and the only sign she could give was the lowering of her head until her glowing cheek brushed the bronze and bulging material of Troy's breeches. Urgently, she rubbed her gagged mouth from side to side, up and down, expressing her enthusiasm in the only way she knew how.

With a flourish worthy of the creature, Troy unzipped and let his massive organ swing free. An enthusiastic cheer sprang spontaneously from his appreciative audience. It was a prick of magnificent proportions. It swayed, it throbbed, it glowed, thick and long, the purple tip glossy. The girl wriggled her bottom and tried to move in closer. Grinning, Troy acknowledged the slow hand-clapping of the crowd and again stared over their heads straight at Maggie.

This would teach her who was boss, show her what happened when she became too brazen. She was his bond-maid it was true, and had been a novelty when she first arrived in the training camp. But it was at his say-so, as leader and chief trainer, that she remained only with him.

He could do as he wished. Give favours, take new girls, use them, discard them - gipsy girls, hutch bunnies, the new recruits. This was an enticing thought. The new recruits, the glittering ones gathered for the Big Man's inspection. Tomorrow he would choose one for personal training, but tonight, tonight this untried bunny would pleasure him, and Maggie could watch. This pleased him and his cock surged upwards.

He leant forward and his prick thudded against the bunny's face. She jiggled and wriggled, trying to nudge at the thrusting cock with her nose. Laughing at her efforts, Troy unfastened the collar and held it up for everyone to see. They whistled and cheered. He threw it onto the ground. Clasping tight hold of his cock, he jabbed it towards the girl's gaping mouth. Her tongue flickered with anticipation and she lunged. Entranced, the crowd watched in silence.

Small pink and darting, her tongue trembled over the glistening head. Mobile and ready, she licked, kissed and sucked, her touch light and dancing. Her lips absorbed the bloated tip, licked softly then drew back. Delicate, soft as thistle down, her tongue ran in long sweeping strokes down the full length of the shaft. When she reached the base her small mouth opened wide. She balanced the hanging balls between those soft lips, sucking first one and then the other.

Exquisite shafts of lust throbbed through Troy's loins.

He pressed firm hands onto her shoulders and dug hard fingers into the slender flesh. He pulled her body, slight and with a light-boned fragility, resolutely against his sturdy thighs. He clasped her close, her body was hot against his skin. He could feel the rapid thumping of her heart beneath her breast. The head of his cock slid into her mouth. Tense with urgent need, sensitive and oozing creamy juices, it touched the back of the girl's throat. Her muscles vibrated, spasmed, and she gulped as he pushed hard. She shivered at the pressure. He spread his mighty thighs and pushed again. With hands cupping her small breasts, he saw how swollen they were, the nipples full and firm, a rosy blush spreading over the milky flesh.

Troy intended this girl to work hard for her pleasure. Sweat beaded his forehead. He wanted the episode to last and for Maggie to experience each exquisite moment. He lunged, thrust deep, then slowly, with a languor that bordered on ennui, withdrew. The whole prick, moist and red, slipped from the swollen lips of the willing girl.

A groan rose from the crowd. Their faces, red from drink and the heat of the fire, gazed in disbelief. Surely Dapper Troy intended to see this through to its conclusion? They need not have worried. Troy was enjoying himself - and so was bunny number three.

Looking up, Troy saw Maggie's face, sharp with dismayed anger. What a jealous bitch she was.

The bunny was good and Troy was convinced he had almost gone beyond the point of control. Then she surprised him. Her sharp white teeth nipped the silky skin, the lightest of pettings, more of a kiss than a bite. Troy's whole body juddered from head to foot. With soft lips, and strong cheeks she kissed and nibbled, sucked and licked, fast, fast, faster. She was playing with his body and he was using hers. They moved in perfect harmony - man and girl - master and slave.

The audience stood, waved and cheered, they stamped their feet overwhelmed by the magnificent and awe-inspiring performance. They encouraged the girl with shouts of "more!" and she moved in closer.

She wriggled and writhed and set about her final task with a will.

Flames leapt high into the starry darkness and the fire roared as logs fell in on themselves. With hands planted firmly on the girl's swollen breasts, Troy shoved her away. She unbalanced and tumbled heavily to the ground. Dark eyes bright, shining in the light of the fire, she stared distraught at Troy as jets of hot white fluid arced from his body. The juices spurted into her face, smothering her cheeks, her mouth, her chin. They lay sticky on the sleek skin of her slender neck. The force of his ejaculation had spun glistening droplets through the air and they landed on the round plump breasts that were swollen with longing.

Troy bellowed, pleasure flooded through him. He stared at the discarded girl, grinning as she shook uncontrollably in an agony of frustration. He pushed her away with his foot. "Go back to your place, bunny, but not back to your hutch, not yet. You never know," he leered down at her, "I might need a clever bunny like you to pleasure me again later."

Bunny number three pulled herself to her hands and knees and crawled reluctantly back into the shadows, a smile of thrilled triumph lighting her impish face.

Troy pushed his prick back inside his breeches, clapped his hands and yelled, "Back to your seats everyone. It's time for the real entertainment." He beckoned to the dancing girls. "The performance, gentlemen, you've all been waiting for. I apologise for idling my time away in such a selfish manner."

Gipsy laughter trumpeted round the clearing. Troy grinned, delighted with their response.

"But it is definitely time for our two beautiful dancing girls, Shorsa and Maggie."

He spread his arms wide, inviting the two girls to step forward into the light cast by the glowing fire. His hair, disordered after his exertions, he swept back into place with a damp hand. His teeth gleamed white, his smile was sardonic and mocking.

Shorsa strode forward. She bowed, she smiled, she flicked the flounces of her skirt, revealing her naked pussy. She stamped a bare foot and turned to greet her partner. Slowly, Maggie emerged from the shadows. Her hands were clenched, pressed hard into the billowing skirt, her face was grim her brow puckered, her mouth twisted into a grimace.

"Maggie, Maggie, delight of my life, this is no way to start a performance. Your heart should be light, your face sunny, your feet ready to spring over the soft grass." Executing a clumsy pas de deux, Troy skipped to where Maggie stood on the edge of the clearing, and held out a hand in welcome. Her reluctance was obvious. He grabbed her wrist and whirled her into the light. The gold and emerald outfit shone, the tassels swung from nipples that were dark in the half-light. Releasing her from his grasp, Troy slapped the breasts jutting over the tight-fitting bodice and gestured for the girls to begin. A guitar strummed in the background. Maggie raised her arms above her head. The audience shuffled on the grass and the atmosphere was electric.

Shorsa eyed her companion, her own feet ready to effect the first steps of the dance at a sign from her partner. Maggie, her petite body straining, rose onto the balls of her feet, flung back her head, arched her spine, but instead of twirling and twisting in the age-old movements of a traditional gipsy dance, she sprang at Troy. With nails flashing gold she leapt, her natural animal grace combined with the anger and jealousy of a betrayed woman.

A cat-like fury seethed beneath her dusky breast, and her fingers clawed at her smiling and supercilious master. He had humiliated her and she was going to punish him. He had betrayed her in front of all the gipsies. This man, who she adored with an all-consuming passion, had taken another girl - a hutch bunny - when he knew she was watching.

Anger enveloped Maggie. She had to punish him. She would scratch that smirking face, gouge that bared chest, cut those arrogant thighs and, with this raging fury burning within her, tear the very balls from his treacherous and cheating body.

THE MORNING AFTER

8: Maggie Suffers Further Humiliation

Maggie crouched, each muscle aching, every joint stiff. Her head drooped, her eyes, two pools of pitch, stared directly at the crushed grass, and her mouth gaped where a gag, hard and rigid, forced her lips wide. If she tried she could raise her head, but the chain linking neck to wrists strapped firmly in the small of her back, pulled, tightening, scorching into the bruised flesh of her forearms. Her bare toes scuffed on the ground. She shuffled her feet trying to ease her position but the chain, heavy and dragging, attaching her to the underframe of Troy's caravan, clanked at the slightest move.

Last night, after the thrashing he had given her, he had left her here. This was not new. But to be left all night, for Troy not to have needed her, this was new. Maggie was in despair. She listened for the slightest sound from overhead, anything that would tell her Troy was awake. There was no sound. She was alone. Shafts of early morning sunlight pierced the thorn hedging behind the wooden van, and a cockerel crowed far far away on the other side of the wood, wakened by the rising sun, cheerful and full of his own importance.

She turned her manacled neck slightly to the right, squinted, and could see the embers of last night's fire. She could smell the smoke still heavy in the morning air and longed to be up and doing, getting things ready for Troy's breakfast.

What a mistake to attack him! It had been incredibly foolish, but the sight of another girl simpering and sucking, licking and lascivious, and enjoying *her* man - her man, Maggie's man! - it had been too much for her.

It was the girl she should have assaulted, not Troy. Troy was her lord and master of this camp, Troy could do no wrong. Bitter tears flooded her eyes, ran down her grubby cheeks and fell onto the broken blades of grass where she knelt.

A sound, a voice, floated towards her on the clear morning air. Maggie's ears pricked. Somebody was approaching the van from the rear.

"Troy, you lazy dog, it's morning. Are you awake yet? The sun's up and we've got business to attend to."

Two pairs of feet, both in boots, one pair following doggedly behind the other, stopped just in front of her. The first pair, the smaller and neater of the two, leapt up the steps and a loud banging made the whole van rock and shake. The visitors had to be Davy and Damien, the brains and the brawn, you never saw one without the other.

Davy banged and shouted and a heavy thud immediately overhead told Maggie that Troy had woken, tumbled out of bed, and was now stumbling towards the door. The creak of the brass latch, so familiar to her after all these months of shining it with a song her heart, made her stomach lurch. Then his voice - her beloved master - mumbling, the sleep slurring his words, drifted down to where she squatted beneath the van, and she strained to hear what he said.

"Davy, whatever time do you call this? And where's that good-for-nothing slut of mine. She should've got the fire going by now. And brought me my coffee."

"You had too much cider last night, Troy. It's addled your brain. The hussy -" Davy stooped, and the next thing Maggie knew his grinning face was peering at her "- the hussy, Troy, is neatly chained, gagged and trussed, just where you left her - all of five hours ago! And I can't see her making a run for it. Not after the way you padlocked all those chains together in the small hours. Don't you remember?"

"OK, OK, so what in thunder do you want?"

Davy's face disappeared from view and was replaced by the leering moon that was Damien. Teeth crooked and discoloured, stubble shading his heavy jaw. Maggie flinched at the sight. A shiver of revulsion rippled through her. He was so close, and she had nowhere to retreat to, she could not even wriggle slightly out of his way. Maggie could smell the odour of drink on his breath, sour and stale from a heavy evening.

If she screwed her head round, pulled in her chin until the metal rasped against her jaw, and opened her eyes wide, Maggie could see Troy's feet and ankles. Standing on the top step, she knew, he would be wrapped in his favourite robe, hugging it to that taut and tanned torso. The robe she had embroidered herself, the one of royal blue silk, soft and silky, dragons of red and gold leaping, flames belching from their flaring nostrils. Maggie yearned to kneel at his feet and beg his forgiveness. But she knew no such opportunity was going to come her way - not this morning.

"An idea, Troy, an idea I have. Are you ready for it?" Davy sprang back down the steps, pushing Damien out of his way. "Or shall I send Damien for a girl - the bunny from last night maybe? Start some coffee brewing?"

"Sure. Give me five minutes and I'll be with you."

The door slammed. Davy gave Damien a kick, and Maggie saw his lumbering body amble away towards the hutches. A gnawing ache hollowed her stomach. Was he going to get that bitch from last night, that number three? Would *she* be the one to brew her own darling's coffee this morning? Black despair filled Maggie's heart. Her fingers clutched at the air and her nails, long and sharp, dug into the palms of hands resting on the swell of her buttocks, bound and shackled by her master's chains.

Davy sat on the steps of the van. He whistled softly, sounded cheerful, cocksure. He reminded Maggie of the cockerel, the one she had been listening to a few minutes before. She saw him draw a knife from the cuff of his boot and begin to carve at a piece of wood. She had never trusted him, had always thought him brash and sly. He was arrogant and had no respect for her, even though she was Troy's woman.

Davy glanced under the van and grinned at her. "This'll make interesting listening for you, Mistress Maggie, very interesting listening indeed. You're too damn conceited for your own good. A haughty baggage, that's what you are, too haughty by a mile. You were, but not any more I reckon." His sharp pixie face smirked and he waved the white wood of the stick he was whittling in her face. "Troy too, rates himself, don't he?" He spat contemptuously. "Well, we shall see, we shall see about that when the Big Man arrives!"

Maggie shook her head in bewilderment. She didn't understand what he was getting at. She knew the Big Man was coming, and that Troy would be on trial as Chief Trainer, but this had little to do with her - or Davy. Could there be anything Davy knew that could hurt Troy? Maggie doubted it.

"Ah-ha, here's Damien, back again, quick as a flash. And with a pretty little thing bouncing along behind him, neat and tidy, fresh for the morning. Do I recognise her? Well, well, I think I do. Could it be the same one Troy had his bit of fun with last night? Do you think she can make coffee as well as she sucks off, Maggie? But I forgot, your mouth is full and you can't give me an opinion. And anyway, here comes Troy."

Maggie heard the click of the latch again and saw Troy's feet, this time neatly shod in the cream pig-skin, her favourite of his shoes. They cleaved close and he stepped lightly past Davy, striding towards the remains of last night's fire.

Davy stayed where he was, glancing from Troy to Maggie. "We gentlemen will soon be enjoying our breakfasts, Maggie. That dear little bunny looks like she knows what she's about. You may have to stay there a long time."

Maggie moaned.

"We-ell, perhaps, if you're a good girl, I'll have a word with Troy. See if we can get you out of there." He winked at her.

Maggie's shoulders shook with frustration. The heavy chain drooping from her collar shuddered. The hasp locking it to the metal under frame rattled and banged against the iron bar. She wanted to get out of here, prostrate herself in front of Troy, demonstrate her sorrow at the way she had behaved. The fire was crackling already. That little slut had laid, lit, and got it going in double quick time. Soon the coffee would be brewing.

Troy was devoted to his morning coffee. Maggie always prepared it to perfection. Surely that miserable creature, surely she would make a mess of such a delicate operation. She must! Despair flooded Maggie's trussed and aching body. She knew she was fooling herself. Catering for the men's needs: food, drink, fucking: the girl would already have plenty of experience. She would know what to do.

Davy threw the stick he had been carving, delicate cuts making the sap bleed from its centre, onto the ground only inches from Maggie's eyes. Still whistling, he sauntered to where Troy sat, hunched, fresh shirt gleaming, the cord of his breeches curving over narrow buttocks, a wide belt, cream pigskin the same as the shoes, fitting snugly round his waist. His long black hair was tied back from his face in a shining tail secured at the nape of his neck.

"Sit down, Davy. Sit down." Troy sounded relaxed, confident. "You haven't had breakfast yet, have you? Good? We'll have eggs, bacon and mushrooms, freshly gathered this morning, and as sweet as anything you'll ever taste. Would like that, Davy?"

"Couldn't be better. And is this girl going to do it all? Wouldn't you rather see young Maggie serving? All done up in her chains, the lash marks still fresh from last night?"

Troy snorted.

"There'd be no need to remove any of the fetters Troy, and there's plenty of chain on the capstan. It's long enough for our needs. We could loosen the linking chains between wrists and ankles slightly, then she can go about her business serving us. And the bunny could cook, if you prefer." Davy leaned closer to Troy, lowering his voice. "And maybe, Troy, if you're intending to punish her properly, this could be the last time she'll serve you for some time."

Troy looked up, his expression sharp.

Nervous anticipation made Maggie pee onto the grass. Please let Troy agree. Surely he would. She must get out of here. If only she could get close to Troy again, she could soon demonstrate how much better she was than that bunny bitch. That number three, she needed to be sent back to her hutch, and quickly.

"Okay, Davy."

Maggie breathed a sigh of relief.

"Get her out. But make sure the cow keeps that gag in. I've no wish to hear any of her lip this morning. But she does brew a wonderful pot of coffee."

Jumping up quickly, Davy strode towards where Maggie knelt, cramped, confined - and damp. She stared up at him, her eyes large and luminous.

"Come here, Maggie, light of my life. Your master wants you."

Davy unwound some of the holding chain from its capstan. It groaned and rattled and slowly released the heavy chain link by link. When there was enough, he locked it back into its static position and extracted her from beneath the van. Her dark eyes flashed in the bright light as she was dragged from the semi-darkness and, eloquent in her desperation, they pleaded for her to be allowed to serve her master.

With his back to Troy, Davy winked at Maggie. "We'll just loosen these feet a little bit here." He knelt down, unfastened the padlock, loosened the chain by a few links. He winked. "Just enough for you to take some dainty little steps."

Maggie felt the tightness binding her ankles ease. She stretched her toes and wriggled them in the cool grass.

"That'll be enough of that, Missy." He slapped her legs and she felt his fingers, thin and bony, creep up the soft roundness of her thigh. "Next, we'll get rid of this." He yanked at the chain linking her wrists to the collar. "We'll move these nasty scratching fingers round to the front, lay them over your belly." He tipped her onto her back.

Now her wrists were weighed down only by metal bracelets, her arms and hands were free. Maggie spread her fingers, easing the numbness that had spread from her shoulders to the tips of her fingers during the long cold night.

"Ah-ha, I can see those little devils would soon be put to use again if I left them like that so I'll just snap a bit of chain to those two bracelets, so nice and shiny and just beggin' to be coupled together." A piece of chain dangled from his fingers. "Once that's clipped into position, all nice and snug, you'll able to carry the victuals all right, but there'll be no leeway for any histrionics on your part, sweet Maggie. And the gag stays where it is - Troy's instructions. We don't want any interruptions squealing into our conversation, Mistress Maggie. And we all know you've got too sharp a tongue on you for your own good."

Davy stood up, towered over her, his legs straddling her chained and gagged body. He signalled to Damien, who was hovering in the background: Damien, who all this time had been standing transfixed, his attention divided between ogling the girl preparing breakfast and observing Davy trussing Maggie.

"If you think you've got the time, Damien, could you give me hand? The young lady wants to approach her master in suitable style."

Damien shambled towards them. Maggie stared up at the twins. Damien, arms folded, leered down. Davy skipped around her prostrate body. Excitement was oozing from her every pore. She knew Troy had watched the whole episode. She longed to walk towards him, head held high, erect and proud, dark eyes blazing her devotion. Her breasts and bottom glowed with the stripes administered last night. Her nipples protruded, sore and sensitive, the loops of thin leather Troy had bound round them cutting into the tender flesh. Her legs were weak with cramp, but she was willing. These two, however, Davy especially, seemed determined to humiliate her further.

"Well, Damien," Davy grinned at his brother. "The collar is still in place and we've plenty more chain. Shall I fix a lead rein to her? Shall we lead her on all fours to her master, Damien?"

Damien nodded, licked his lips, and sniggered.

"Would you like to turn her over onto her belly, Damien?"

Damien nodded vigorously.

"Yes, I thought you'd like that Damien. OK. So, once I've secured the chain, I can lead and you can bring up the rear - and a very pretty view of a darling little rear you'll have Damien."

Damien guffawed loudly at his brother's joke. He rubbed sweaty palms down his bulging thighs and swung his arms towards Maggie.

She closed her eyes, obliterating the vision of his face, coarse and unwashed, approaching hers. She felt his palms, warm and clammy, slide under her. He flipped her onto her stomach. The same sweaty palms clasped the well-striped buttocks and he wrenched her bottom into the air. His hands stayed put.

"Ah-ha, Damien," crowed Davy. "I see you have your own ideas on how she should crawl to her master. Hands and knees not good enough for you, eh, Damien? You want to see her perched on tippietoes and finger tips do you? And would that be because that position will expose those juicy folds and especially that dark little rosebud of her bum to your inquisitive eyes? Would that be the reason, eh Damien?"

Not a sound came from Damien, but Maggie could feel her bottom cheeks spreading as he separated them and stroked the tight flesh hidden in the dark dell with a stubby finger.

Troy said nothing, made no objection, and Maggie's heart sank.

The journey would not be a long one, but it would be slow and difficult. Keeping her bottom stuck in the air, balancing on toes and finger tips, with chains linking ankles and wrists, everything would combine to make this an agonising excursion. Maggie steeled herself, glad to do it for Troy's sake.

Damien's hands closed her bottom. Davy yanked on the lead chain, her head jerked up, and slowly, very slowly, the small procession made its way towards Troy who sat, arms folded, legs crossed, smiling and aloof.

Her fingertips scrabbled at the soil. Her toes slipped and slithered on the grass. She stared straight ahead as Davy pulled her by the neck. Her bottom, silky and full as a round moon, wriggled and writhed under Damien's gaze and Maggie, naked, quivering with nerves, crawled, inch by faltering inch, towards her master.

A slow hand-clapping greeted the group as they stuttered to a halt in front of Dapper Troy. "Well done, Davy, well done. A very pretty picture."

Maggie was exhausted. She longed to flop onto the grass. Her legs were weak, her arms crying out with stiffness. But when Davy came to a halt he pulled hard on the chain and she had no choice but to remain in the same position. She lowered her head, meek and submissive, but not before she had noticed a cold gleam in Troy's eye. She must not make a mistake now.

The other girl was still cooking breakfast, only the coffee remained for Maggie to prove herself by. She would do it just the way he liked it. She would serve him crawling on her belly if that was what he wanted. There was no way she had any intention of sacrificing her exalted position in this camp to some upstart hutch bunny.

"You liked that, Troy?" enquired Davy. "Yes, yes, of course you did. This is your woman, and you've trained her. I can understand your satisfaction in seeing her perform so well." Davy unhooked the chain from Maggie's collar. "Now she can make the coffee and serve our breakfasts which have been cooked so beautifully by the hutch bunny, eh Troy?"

The bunny simpered, standing by the fire, frying pan clutched in her hand.

"Yes Davy, she can. That other bitch can return to her hutch now. Damien can take her. You and I have got business to attend to, it seems. Be off now, Damien, there's a good lad."

Damien's face fell. He looked from his brother to the bunny.

"Do as the master says, Damien. Get her back to her hutch."

The bunny glowered and slammed the frying pan onto the ground. Maggie's heart glowed.

"No sulking now Damien. Bunnies don't only serve, they need servicing regularly, isn't that right, Troy?"

Troy nodded, his assent.

The bunny looked up brightly.

Damien, already aroused by the sight of Maggie's rump swaying in front of him earlier, grinned at his brother, unzipped his jeans and thrust the bunny to her knees. He pulled her bottom high, parted the tight dark entrance with poking fingers, and plunged his rigid cock deep inside the narrow hole. The thrusts were short, sharp and urgent and he grunted as his juices spurted, bathing the tawny rear and trickling down the backs of the bunny's thighs.

The bunny, hair hanging to the ground, breasts wobbling, wiggled her bottom at him. Her sex lips hung plump and inviting, fluttering in Damien's direction. Damien, ever-ready, massaged his cock to an iron-firmness and jammed it hard inside the willing bunny. Her bottom slammed against his thighs, he penetrated deep and solid. He snorted his pleasure as his prick shot a second load, and the bunny squealed her delight at the double fuck.

"OK Damien. Very good. I think we all enjoyed that. Now, off you go." Davy's voice rang out clear across the field.

Damien turned and shook a joyful fist into the air.

"It doesn't do to upset young Damien," explained Davy. "He's mighty strong and with a quick temper if he gets taken the wrong way. But, you know, Troy, you could make more use of him than you do. You saw the way he handled the bunny? Some of these girls, well I know he could prove very useful in certain aspects of their training."

"I think that's for me to decide, Davy." Troy frowned and flicked a speck of ash from the one immaculate knee. "I'm the one in charge here. The one the Big Man will hold responsible if things aren't up to scratch."

Davy lowered his eyes and twiddled his fingers. "True, very true. And it's about the Big Man I want to have a few words. But shall we get this young Maggie to go about her business first? I don't know how you feel, but there's something about the sight of a tricky young madam, all chained and gagged and poised in such a difficult position as that, well, it seems to have given me monstrous appetite."

Troy stood and strode towards Maggie, back bent, body straining, waiting for her master to give his orders. His hand thundered onto the tautly drawn skin of her thighs. He ran long fingers over the red welts administered last night. They creased the cheeks of her bottom, and he squeezed, pinching and prodding at the sore flesh.

"Yes, this bitch has to learn some manners. She's been spoilt all these months. I shall have to think of a way to bring her smartly into line."

"My thinking exactly, Troy. Great minds, great minds."

"Ha, you're a sharp one Davy. But don't you try getting above yourself." Troy grabbed hold of Maggie's hair and pulled her upright. "This one is mine to punish - or dispose of. And now I say off you go miss. Go about your business. The fire's lit and the food is cooked - no thanks to you - but the coffee still isn't made." He twisted his fingers in her dark curls.

Tears sprang to Maggie's eyes. He was still angry with her. And for all his bravado, she knew Troy was weak. Davy would twist him round his little finger with his weaselly words and puffed up praise.

With chains dragging on her limbs, she shuffled towards the fire. She would prepare a pot of coffee the like of which Troy had never experienced. But she intended to keep her ears open, learn the details of Davy's plan and, if it involved being separated from Troy, and the opportunity arose, she would scupper it - and Davy with it. She realised he was intent on improving his own position, his and nobody else's, except Damien's, possibly. Her good, Troy's future and the fortunes of the camp, these were of little or no interest to the likes of that cunning and shifty Master Davy.

9: - And Meets Her Match In CJ

Even before daybreak men had returned to the corral.

A mist, rising from the stream in the valley below, was making the girls shiver in their bonds. But the men removed the night shelters and exposed the huddled groups of girls completely to the bite and chill of the morning air.

With the shelters dismantled and the hurdles laid to one side, they began to divide them into groups. A finger would point and girls would be detached from the cluster in the corral. Once unleashed and a rein fastened round their slender necks, they were tethered in small or pairs. Ropes of uniform thickness bound them one to the other. Fine chains were snapped round wrists and ankles, and the girls clattered through the open gateway accompanied by the whistle of whips and the roar of threatening cries.

For some of the groups a more elaborate arrangement was supplied. A yoke, heavy and polished by much use to the shine and smoothness of glass, would string three girls together, maybe four, weighing down their shoulders, forcing their necks to bend and their heads to droop like so many tired and overblown blooms in July. Reins, long and supple, in a variety of colours, some merely black or chestnut, but others of brightest golds and greens, scarlet and azure, hung from their throats, hanging between and drawing attention to breasts that were a delight to behold. Some were full and melon heavy, with nipples of palest rose, others small, tight, firm and jutting, capped by miniature helmets of shining bronze.

The reins recognised no distinction and cut between both ample and petite alike. The strips of leather nestled brightly against plush skin, brushed over softly moulded bellies, swayed between thighs taut and tanned from weeks of outdoor life. The loose end, dragging on the earth, hung waiting to be grabbed, pulled back hard between the parted thighs; waited to split the swollen lips, to rub, to stimulate and moisten susceptible flesh, to massage and stroke the tender folds until each girl moaned and wriggled her hips in an ecstasy of anticipation.

Once fully satisfied of the attention of his entire team, the male drover would tighten the reins in his fist, jolt them with a brusque flick of his wrist, and the girls would lift their feet high, or as high as the fetters allowed, raise their proud heads and, lively with the willingness of lust, bear the weight of the yoke on narrow shoulders. With much shouting of orders, swishing of whips and crack of riding crops, giggling and sighing, the group would then trot from the enclosure, away across the meadow into the pearly light of dawn.

Eventually the new girls, Daisy, CJ, and Jo were left alone in the empty corral. During that long night each one in turn had drifted off into a light and fractured sleep only to be jerked awake by the cutting of rope when either legs or neck had buckled and the dreaming captive was startled back into the reality of the encampment. Now dawn had arrived, a cock had crowed, and shafts of early sunlight were setting the dew-spotted grass aflame.

"CJ, CJ, there are some men are coming back." Daisy shook the tiny sagging figure roughly by the shoulder.

CJ, who had only been dozing lightly, grateful to forget her empty stomach and cold wet feet for a short while, started with surprise at Daisy's frantic shaking. She opened her eyes and rubbed the sleep from them. A smell of wood-smoke drifted over the field, accompanied by the aroma of freshly brewed coffee and frying bacon. She sniffed appreciatively. Her two companions were wide awake. They looked much brighter than she felt, and were staring, transfixed, at something behind her shoulder.

CJ shuffled round, anxious to see what they were seeing. Two figures had left the circle of Romany caravans and were walking, swiftly, purposefully, towards the three girls chained in the corral.

Twisting her head round, CJ stared at the approaching figures. "If I'm not very much mistaken, those two heading this way are Damien and Davy, my two heroes from yesterday." She grinned, surprised at how pleased she was to see them again.

"Oh, bully for you," scoffed Jo. "I can see from here that it's not Nico and Seth, far too civilised looking, far too agreeable."

CJ collapsed into a fit of giggles. "Civilised! Damien! Look at him. He looks like something Frankenstein might have created on a bad day." Her russet curls shook as she giggled at her own joke. The tip of a pink tongue brushed over the fullness of her lower lip. CJ always liked to look her best when meeting any half-fanciable bloke, but, under these circumstances, okay would have to be enough. "Now Davy," she said, her eyes narrowed in thought. "Davy - well - he's another barrel of worms altogether. Somehow, there's something about him I find rather dishy and attractive. I think it's that he's cunning - cunning and sharp. I like that in my men."

A long low groan distracted the two girls and their attention was brought back sharply to their companion.

"Whatever's up Daisy, sweetheart? You sound like you've just been mortally wounded, or had your fanny goosed at the very least."

"Oh CJ, CJ," she wailed, "neither of them is Jem." Tears trickled down her plump pink and white cheeks.

"Never mind, Daisy," CJ cooed, winking at Jo. "I'm sure he'll turn up soon. I've noticed that the men in this place don't seem to be able to keep away from this enclosure. But," she added, green eyes open wide, tongue flickering, "that wonderful aroma of bacon and eggs seems to be hurrying along behind them, and it's reminding me that I am ab-so-lute-ly ravenous."

"Good morning, ladies, good morning. Is that hunger I see in those gorgeous green eyes?" Davy had entered the corral alone. Damien remained outside.

CJ nodded and smiled at her hero from yesterday. Would he be her saviour today? Was he about to take them food-wards? Davy was close now and looking all three up and down with an appraising eye.

"You, I do know, you little darling, but as for your friends - I don't think I've had the pleasure." He smiled a sharp and foxy smile at Daisy and Jo. "I'm Davy, and that large gentleman here, that is my own twin brother, Damien. Now I just know we're all going to get on fine, and isn't this a bright and beautiful morning, to be your first in these wonderful surroundings."

"Where, where are we, Davy?" interjected CJ.

"Why, The Dropwell Training Grounds. Did you not realise that this is *the* place to be for all young ladies who wish to undergo the rigorous and stimulating education that is available *free* to any suitable recruit? And if I may say so, you three look willing, ready to take instruction, work hard and obey orders. If I'm right, we shall all enjoy ourselves."

"What about some breakfast?" CJ raised an eyebrow. "I don't know about anyone else, but I could eat a horse."

"There won't be any call for you to do anything so drastic, sweetheart. But -" he signalled to Damien, who started towards them - "but, it's you I've come for, you little red-headed darling" As he spoke, he detached CJ from her post. "I've been outlining a very interesting plan to Dapper Troy Dempsey - he's the boss round here, in case you didn't know, and he wants to have a look at you. So the sooner we get back up the slope to the camp, the better."

CJ, with arms and legs still bound, was stiff and cold. She eyed the approaching Damien with apprehension. In his right hand swung a lasso. Whatever kind of plan did Davy have in mind? She'd never set eyes on this Troy Dempsey, but apparently he was the boss of this set up, and that was interesting.

Damien was getting closer by the second. Now, he was only ten yards from the little group of naked girls, shivering there with trepidation. None of them could take their eyes off the lumbering gorilla.

He halted. His massive body swayed on legs as thick as small tree trunks. His shoulders heaved under the grubby white T-shirt. His arms swung. The rope curled, first lazily, then faster and faster, until it screamed through the air above his head. It flailed, it span, it began to drop, its movements so rapid that she who blinked missed its speedy progress.

CJ screamed. Her friends stared open-mouthed. The rope encircled her body just below her breasts. It cut into the meagre flesh covering her ribs and struggling was pointless. She felt the lasso tightening round her body, tightening until even breathing was an effort.

Damien grinned at his brother. His misshapen teeth shone dull yellow, his bulky face was thick with stubble.

CJ trembled.

"Yes Damien, I know you're pleased with yourself, but Troy is waiting. This little lady could be my key to an exciting future, Damien, so let's be off."

CJ felt herself being pulled, slowly, inexorably away from her friends. Damien had the other end of the rope clutched tightly in his fist. Leering all the while, he dragged her, feet scraping over the rough surface of the field, towards the open gate.

"Whoa, Damien! Stop!" Davy's tone was brusque. "If we're going to have the slightest chance of getting her up this slope in one piece, we'll have to unstrap her ankles."

Damien's face fell.

"I know, I know, you prefer her like this, but I expect Troy will have his own ideas on how to bind her when she arrives. Our job is to get her there as quick as we can."

"What about the others?" gasped CJ, the breath jolting from her as they started off once more. Damien merely glanced over his shoulder at her and grinned his broken-toothed grin.

"Damien won't answer any questions, Cassie. I do the talking for both of us. I'm the brains and he's the brawn. We find it suits us that way."

As they zig-zagged up the slope, CJ caught a glimpse of her two friends, still tied to posts in the corral. She'd known them for less than twenty four hours, but even so, would have preferred them to all stay together.

"Will *you* answer my questions then?" she panted. "Are we leaving the others behind?"

"Yes we are. I've got no use for either of them myself. The one's too meaty, too lanky the other. It's you that holds an exciting future in those pretty hands and tight cunt."

CJ coloured. Her normally pale face turned beetroot. She always blushed easily when embarrassed and she was embarrassed now. She decided not to ask any more questions. Whatever it was he had in mind, she was going to find out soon enough.

Damien climbed the hill at a great pace, dragging CJ ignominiously behind. It was a long ascent but he coped with ease. CJ's legs were weak, her knees about to give out completely, when a smart thwack on her bouncing backside jolted her back to life. Davy was not going to allow her to collapse. Strength returned to her limbs, and she clambered gamely on.

When they reached the summit, CJ knew it was only because of Damien keeping tight hold of her lead that she managed to remain upright. She was breathless. The rope round her ribs prevented her filling her lungs. She longed to lie down on the grass and gulp in fresh, reviving air, but the other two had no intention of pausing at all. Damien was off, striding towards the encampment, Davy skipped along behind, tapping her bare bottom, encouraging her onwards. The sweat dripped from her brow, into her eyes and down her cheeks. Her hair felt clammy and CJ was convinced she did not make a very pretty sight.

They entered the circle of gipsy caravans. Empty plates were strewn about the grass. Mugs, some full, others drunk to the dregs, were scattered round the well-trampled sight. Plumes of smoke, puffy as cotton wool, wound lazily upwards from the remains of the fire, the logs were charred, but the centre glowed deep crimson, proof that one blast from the bellows, lying discarded a few feet away, would set it roaring into life.

The caravans, which previously CJ had only glimpsed from a distance, glowed in the morning light. Their paint was fresh, their windows sparkling. Spruce gingham curtains, some red, some blue, some yellow, fluttered rakishly at open windows. Everything was clean and bright. Even the wooden steps leading to the entrances, she noticed with amazement, were whitened to the blinding glitter of freshly fallen snow.

Panting and blinking, trying to catch her breath, her attention was caught by the man seated near the camp fire. His face was swarthy. His hair long and straight, brushed back and tied neatly at the nape of a strong neck. His shirt was fresh, his breeches sharply creased. He looked - divine. CJ fumed. There had been no need to truss her up like this. She attempted to struggle under her ropes, opened her mouth ready to voice her annoyance, tell Davy all this had been wasted effort, she'd have come willingly, when something caught her eye, something the sight of which made the words dry in her throat and almost choke her.

Beside the largest and smartest caravan, the one made of varnished elm and decorated in gold leaf, motifs of horses, trees, flowers and dancing girls coating its surface, standing beside this van was a contraption, a large contraption. Solid wood and polished metal, it swayed and jangled gently in the still morning air. It was tall, this contraption, well over six feet high CJ estimated. And it needed to be. A girl, wrists chained to the cross bar, head thrown back, pussy thrust forward, legs splayed and with ankles bound, firm and immovable, swung between the smooth warm wood of the polished uprights.

This girl's mouth was filled by a round gag, her arms stretched high above her head, and her small body, taut and extended by the pressure of the chains at wrist and ankle, swivelled very gently. The only sound was the rattle of the shackles.

A mass of curls, similar to CJ's in their unruliness, but black instead of chestnut, drifted over shoulders drawn and distorted by their bonds. Curls, similarly dark and rebellious, coated the base of her belly, covering but not concealing the pink beneath the mat of pubic hair.

CJ cried out, she couldn't help it, and the girl struggled in her chains, hauled her head up, straining the muscles of her slender neck, stared at the newcomer with gimlet eyes. The eyes showed no fear or pain, but burnt with a profound and furious anger.

Somehow CJ knew that had the girl been in a position to put her thoughts into words she would have been spitting venom, piling obloquy on insult, invective on derision, and all in her, CJ's, direction. How was it possible to have aroused such fury in a complete stranger? CJ shivered at the sight of this girl. Her body tingled, a mixture of alarm and elation enveloping her at the sight of such burning hatred.

"You've noticed young Maggie, then?" The voice was slow, lazy, with a hint of humour bubbling beneath the surface. "What do you think of her?"

CJ, still tightly roped, her arms numb from the cutting bonds, dragged her gaze away from the suspended girl. It was the seated man who had spoken. He was waiting for her to say something. CJ felt a glow spread from her freckled cheeks, flame her breasts and belly and, for once in her life, she could not think of anything to say. She was dumbstruck. The sight of the girl, bound, chained and gagged, with only her eyes free to express her inner thoughts, had turned CJ's tummy to water.

The men watched her watching the girl, and to her utter astonishment CJ discovered that she found this rather exciting. Until yesterday she had never even considered that being bound by ropes and chains might be - interesting - but now...

"Are you going to answer, Cassie? The man asked you a question and Mr Dempsey expects a reply." Davy's eyes were bright and eager. CJ could see that he was desperate for her to say something. She stared once more at the girl still swaying gently in the frame, took a deep breath and looked Troy Dempsey directly in the eye.

"I think - I think -" her mouth felt dry and she knew she was trembling. Her nipples had swollen and were tight and tingling. The words blurted from her mouth. "I have to say that I think she looks absolutely stupendous - wonderful - marvellous - but I feel confused." CJ, gazed at Troy, her green eyes large and bewildered. "Why does she seem to be so angry with me?"

Troy Dempsey pushed himself up off the low stool. He towered over the diminutive CJ and, stretching out a finger, caressed the firm tip of her swelling breasts. "You're right, Cassie - it is Cassie, isn't it? She is angry, but then, so am I, and it's all her fault. I'm angry with her, and she's angry with you. She's there to be punished and to witness the engagement of her replacement."

"Replacement!" CJ looked round. "What replacement? Who's going to... Who do you mean? *What - me!* That's why she's so upset? You mean *you* want *me* to replace her - replace her where - why? What does she do?"

"She's my woman. But she's misbehaved. She is to be relegated to the hutches. She will have a given a number, and she will become one of the bunnies."

CJ stared open-mouthed at Troy Dempsey. What kind of place was this? She had to find out more. "Will the same thing happen to me?" She was nervous and the question was almost whispered.

"Not if you're a good girl, Cassie. The blondes and the red-heads, they're different. We have a contract. You are all here for special training, not like these dark-haired gipsy whores. They are just for our own use and pleasure." Troy grinned down at her. "But the extra special girls, the ones that are small, tight-cunted and willing, and with nipples like fresh strawberries," he rubbed his palm over her alert breast, "if I can train one of those to perfection -"

"Don't forget, Troy," said Davy, his face bright and animated. "Don't forget it was my idea, and it was me that recruited this one, yesterday. As soon as I saw her, I knew she would be just right for the Big Man. Together, we can train her up, and when he arrives, you can let him know that it was me brought her here."

"Okay, Davy, I haven't forgotten. But just why you're so keen he should know it was you, I can't imagine. Do you think he might be willing to grant you some kind of favour?" Troy snorted his doubt.

Davy did not reply, merely smiled, shook his head and picked up his half-finished mug of coffee, cold now and with scum forming on the surface. "I brought her here for you to train, Troy - put you in the Big Man's good books. She's got two friends down in the corral, both blondes. They'd make a nice pony pair. Shall I send Jem down to look them over? He's the man for understanding ponies."

"Good idea, Davy. We need to get on with the training. There's only a couple of weeks to the inspection. Time enough - but we ought to get on."

Davy glanced at Troy. CJ could see the glance was sly. "If Jem approves the two blondes, do you want them got up in all the gear?

Troy nodded.

"Shall I get Damien to fetch a bunny to assist Jem?"

Troy stared at Davy. "Why not," he said. "Why not! Tell him to take number three. She seems a likely sort, quick to learn. He can teach her how to apply body paint, do the pony make-up and the hair. I think she may have a future, that girl."

CJ watched and listened, desperate to join in the conversation, tell him all about Daisy and Jo. But her attention was caught by a rattling and shaking of chains. Raising her eyes she gazed at the angry girl suspended in the rack. But this time, instead of hatred seething in those pitch-black pupils, she saw desolation and despair. The eyes had turned into two dark, unfathomable pools brimming with tears.

Troy ignored the woebegone girl and turned to Davy. "You both go, you and Damien. You give Jem his orders, Davy, Damien can fetch the bunny. Tell Jem I want intensive training to start as of ten minutes ago."

"We're your men for that, Troy, aren't we Damien?" Damien nodded, his stubbled face beaming with pleasure. "But what about this young lady, Troy?" Davy touched CJ's auburn curls. "What do you have in mind for her?"

Troy leant forward, stretched out a hand and stroked CJ's breasts. "Oh, she's all right, Davy. This young lady seems quite keen on everything she's seen so far. A morning kneeling in chains will give her a good start in the understanding of discipline. She can stay on her knees and keep quiet while we discuss business."

"Fine, Troy, fine. But she's hungry."

"There's food left in the pan. When you and your brother get back, Damien can feed her. It won't do any harm for her to wait. She's here to learn it's our needs that come first in this place. But get along, Davy.

There's a lot to be done during these next two weeks."

Troy moved closer towards CJ and ran hands that were cool and appraising over her body, squeezing and pinching the fine flesh, delving long fingers between her thighs, massaging the wet pussy lips.

On the edge of the clearing Damien sniggered loudly and pressed his own massive hand over a crotch that bulged, large and obscene. Davy frowned and signalled to his brother to be quiet, to keep still.

"You're keeping Maggie in the rack, Troy?"

"She can stay there this morning. Then it's off to the hutches with her before midday. And this young lady can take her place. We could try some of the new equipment on her later, what do you think, Davy?"

Smiling his agreement, Davy nodded, signalled Damien to go about his business, and walked rapidly towards Jem's van. Damien shuffled towards the hutches to retrieve bunny number three.

CJ's heart swelled with pride. This very dishy man, the head man, wanted to train her, and dispose of that dark-haired bitch. She felt elated and thrust her mound towards his probing fingers. She was to become an integral part of this community and confidence surged through her.

"This equipment you mentioned," she breathed, "have you got it handy?" She glanced towards the rack. The girl was watching her closely. "This gear sounds awfully interesting." She thrust her small breasts at Troy. "And, to be honest, just at the moment, I feel ready to try anything, especially if you're involved." She rotated her hips and wriggled, a salacious and sensual squirm, on Troy's embedded fingers.

"You've a lot to learn, haven't you Cassie?" Troy withdrew fingers dripping with CJ's juices and thrust her to her knees. "When I said you spend the morning on your knees, that's exactly what I meant. You on your knees, Maggie in the rack. When she's relegated to the hutches, then we can see about trying the new stuff on you. You have to learn that I'm the boss and you're the slave. And slaves who have mouths that won't stop yammering, well, they soon find out that we've gags a-plenty to stop those lippy mouths."

Troy returned to his stool awaiting Davy's return. Cassie knelt on the grass, bemused but entranced. Maggie hung in the rack, limbs chained, mouth gagged, dejected at the sight of CJ obeying *her* man's orders, and the picture of bunny number three pleasuring him still sharp in her memory.

10: CJ Learns About Discipline

"That's enough talking, man. Let's have a bit of space. Clear all this junk away."

CJ, stiff from many hours kneeling in one position with her wrists and ankles bound, wondered just what Troy meant by junk, and whether she was included. She did not have to wait long to find out.

Davy and Damien leapt into immediate action. Davy cleared stools, picked up cups and plates, stamped out the ashes, still smoking, white and hot, all that remained of the crackling fire. He threw the heavier items to his brother who caught them with deft sallies and thrusts for one so large. Damien, stools tucked under his arms, cups hanging from beefy fingers, scuttled away heavily laden, dropping odd items as he went.

Troy Dempsey's long angular face, its natural dusky tone made darker by a life spent mostly outdoors, glanced at CJ kneeling at his feet. "Look at her eyes, man, the message is always in the eyes. She's learning discipline and wants to get started on the next level - and so do I." His own dark eyes glittered with a compulsion tempered by excitement and his lips were reddened by teeth that gnawed obsessively. "Tell Damien, when he's finished clearing up, to bring the new equipment."

"I'll tell him, Troy, I'll tell him. But the little minx, what do want done with Maggie?" Davy's eyes shone, his shoulders heaved and he flexed supple fingers.

"Take her down, Davy, take her down. She's off to the hutches, and that's where she'll stay until I know she's come to her senses."

"How long do you think, Troy, a day, two days - longer?"

"The way I'm feeling at the moment with this little darling, all willing and eager," he leant down and squeezed her CJ's freckled breasts, "it could be forever."

CJ could not stop herself. Giggling at the unlikelihood of it all, she glanced at her rival. Maggie was squirming and writhing, shaking her head and desperately trying to kick with feet that were firmly chained. Davy stood in front of the wriggling girl, his hands caressing the body that was trying to push him away with ineffectual thrusts of the hips.

"I'll get rid of her then." And without waiting for a reply, Davy unlocked the hasps that chained Maggie's ankles and wrists to the heavy wooden frame. She dropped to the ground with a muffled groan and curled up into a mournful heap. CJ could tell from the way she rolled on the grass that her legs and arms were aching and weak, but Davy was ready for her. A lead snapped onto the metal collar encircling her neck and, with the bare-arsed girl crawling on hands and knees, he dragged her away.

Where was he taking her, CJ wondered? Where were these hutches Troy kept mentioning? Carefully, not wanting to attract Troy's attention, CJ stared after the pair. Maggie was protesting weakly behind the large gag stuffing her gaping mouth. Davy was striding, confident and cocky, away from the gipsy caravans, dragging the reluctant girl towards a long row of low wooden animal cages huddled in the shade of the thorn hedge that edged the meadow.

Even from this distance CJ could see these cages were not exactly commodious. They appeared to be stoutly constructed of planks of wood, but the side facing onto the field, the one CJ could see quite clearly, was made of a fine wire mesh. If she screwed her eyes up and concentrated hard she could see that what initially she had thought were pigs or goats curled up behind the wire mesh, were were actually *girls*. So, inside those cages - or hutches as they seemed to be called - were indeed animals, but these were human animals, girls like Maggie.

CJ shivered, she had no wish to live in a cage like that. They looked very claustrophobic, and she made an instant decision that whatever it took to keep in Troy Dempsey's good books. Whatever demands he made of her, she would comply.

"You won't really leave her there - forever - will you?" CJ fluttered her eyelashes in Troy's direction. She had no wish to be the sole cause of another girl's punishment, especially one she felt had never done her any harm. "I don't want Maggie to suffer too much - not on my account. But, on the other hand, I don't want her brought back here yet either." CJ dimpled sweetly.

Troy threw back his head and issued a sharp bark of laughter, a laugh that to CJ's ears did not contain much humour. "She'll be all right. You don't have to worry about Maggie. She's angry, in fact she's furious, but a stretch of punishment in the hutches won't do her any harm."

His hand touched the top of CJ's head. His fingers twined painfully amongst the red-gold curls and a long-drawn out hiss of pleasure whistled between his clenched teeth. "You've got other things to think about, young lady. Davy and Damien will be back soon with the equipment, then we can commence the next round of your instruction - develop your interests further in the regime of training we specialise in here."

CJ cocked her head. This man was an enigma. She had no idea what he intended for her, so she adjusted her position slightly and grinned back at him. "Training - I keep hearing this word - training. It sounds -

intriguing. What am I being trained for?"

"Keep you mouth shut and do as you're told." His words were harsh and the flat of his hand stung against her pale cheek.

CJ felt the flame of hurt and embarrassment flash through her. She was going to have to be careful what she said - and who she said it to. Tempers were short here and hands quick to punish. Tears welled in her eyes, Her throat constricted. Her mouth, always too big for her own good, she clamped firmly shut. All her life her inability to keep quiet at the appropriate moments had got her into trouble. She bent her head forward. She had no wish for Troy to see the tears in her eyes or the tremble on her lip.

She need not have worried, for Troy's attention had wandered. He was looking out for his two henchmen, waiting for them to return, heavily laden and eager to assist in the next constriction and training of Cassie.

"We're back, Troy. I hope we haven't been so long that the young lady has had time to change her mind."

Sniffing back her tears, CJ glanced up, glad to see Davy's grinning face again.

"What have you been doing to her, Troy? The girl is weeping. That's no way to treat a lady, Troy, is it?"

The jolly expression and winking eye told CJ that the words he spoke did not reflect Davy's true beliefs, She began to feel a little uneasy. Was she about to be chained and strung up like poor Maggie? Cassie eyed the bulky equipment Damien was carrying.

"Is it all there, Davy?" Troy left her where she was and strode to where Damien stood, flushed and expectant.

"Of course. Would I let him leave an essential item behind? And, if by some terrible mischance we did forget something, well, Damien here knows this particular piece of equipment inside out - don't you Damien? It's his favourite, and this lot is brand new. He only put the final rivets into it last night, isn't that right, Damien?"

Damien nodded, proudly displaying the items he had so carried here so lovingly before Troy's critical gaze.

Troy stroked the leather straps hanging from the brawny arm, his expression unfathomable. CJ watched warily from where she knelt. Never in her life had CJ seen anything quite like this. Belts and buckles, straps and metal rings, swayed and jangled. The straps creaked with stiffness and had the delicious perfume of unused leather. They draped over Damien's arm, scarlet and silver, their warmth and brilliance flashing in the sunlight. The buckles and rings twinkled and shone from hours of polishing. CJ's stomach tightened at the sight.

"Right Davy, bring the girl here, out into the clearing where I can get a good look at her." Troy selected one item from Damien's collection and it dangled from his fingers. He glared at CJ, who trembled in front of him, her arm tightly clasped, Davy's bony fingers biting into her flesh. "Release her, Davy. I'm going to demonstrate what we expect of the girls in this establishment. Release her, and if she moves without instruction from me, she'll feel the flat of my hand on those pretty boobs and buttocks."

Davy unfastened the chains binding CJ's wrists and ankles. They fell to the ground with a jangle. She stood erect, her heart pounding, unable to control the trembling in her legs. Troy towered over her, and the shining scarlet of the leather hanging from his hands transfixed her gaze.

"Put your arms up, straight up in the air."

CJ did as she was told - immediately. The harness, for that was what it was, she now realised, slipped easily over the copper curls and rested on her shoulders. As yet unfastened leather, ringing with many metal joints and buckles, hung from her neck and fell about her body. The touch of metal, cold and hard, made her shudder, her breasts quiver, and the nipples tauten until they stood stiffly up like two over-ripe strawberries.

"She's excited already, Troy, you can see she is. And just from feeling the stuff on her skin. It's swelled her titties up nicely."

"Be quiet Davy, and give me a hand. Stop admiring and get the harness in place over those tits. It'll be a squeeze. The leather's new and there's not much give in it."

"Aye, but the tits are soft." CJ could see Davy's fingers could not resist the lure of her milky breasts, so startlingly white against the redness of the leather. He cupped brown hands beneath the gentle curves squeezing and fondling. Then fingers that moments earlier had softly caressed grabbed hold of first one breast then the other, roughly manipulating, pressing and pushing until both popped through two tight circles of leather.

CJ gasped at the sudden coarseness of his handling and tried not to look. She closed her eyes to what was happening, but her sense of his touch was electric. As Davy squashed and prodded at the front, Troy pulled and poked behind her back. Strips of leather that had hung loosely moments earlier were wrenched into position, buckled tightly, tested for firmness.

CJ opened her eyes. Her breasts, two bulbous mounds of snowy flesh, the shell-pink nipples bursting from the rounded peaks, bulged before her. She stared, amazed at what she saw. Never in her wildest dreams had CJ thought her small but pretty breasts could be made to look so generous. She beamed - then gasped for breath. The buckle Troy had fixed in place dug into her spine and the straps were made fast over her slender shoulders and bound around her ribs and cut into the sparse flesh with each breath she took.

"Now there's a pleasing sight." Troy gave one final tug to the harness fastened across her back. "The scarlet of the leather and the whiteness of the flesh, oh yes, yes -" His hands stroked the flare of her hips.

Troy strode round in front and stared at CJ in her harness. His eyes were dilated with desire and his fingers stretched towards, and stroked the straining breasts. "The arm cuff next, Davy."

"Right you are, sir." Davy clicked his fingers, and with eyes wide CJ saw Damien spring into life, dart forward, a long red tube of leather held out for Troy's inspection.

Davy smiled proudly. "He's done a good job, Troy. You see the lacing? It's all been hand stitched and the thongs soaked in brine. It's tough, really tough."

"And she's got such fragile looking arms." Troy picked up CJ's hands and gazed at the fine pale skin dusted with freckles.

CJ could not stop herself. She snorted with laughter and the words simply tumbled unbidden from her lips. "Fragile! Me! That's the last thing I am. Tough as old boots, me."

Troy's right hand slapped hard onto her tight little breasts. "You've forgotten what I said already? Don't move and keep your mouth shut."

He grabbed her wrists, pulling her arms roughly behind her. CJ could feel the grip of the leather tube first slipping over her fingers, then pushing together the palms of her hands, pressing her wrists hard, one against the other. The flesh was squeezed by the leather. Her arms compressed, restricted from varnished nails to distorted shoulder; the two became one until all she could do was wriggle her finger tips very slightly. The lacing certainly was tight and her shoulders were forced up and back thrusting her already bulging breasts even further forward. The top half of her body was trapped, her legs free, but for how long?

The tightness of the costume on her ribs and arms made her hot and uncomfortable. Her breasts hurt, her nipples tingled so much they stung. So why, CJ wondered, why in the midst of all this apparent pain and suffering, why was her pussy soaking wet? Why was she longing to part her legs and feel fingers stroke and nuzzle her aching crotch?

She stared at the three men gathered round her. A deep well of desire had grown in her loins. She felt on fire with the heat of it. At this precise moment any one of them, even Damien, would have brought welcome relief. But did she dare to put her longing into words?

"Look at those sodden curls, Troy, the little darlings. Her cunt must be streaming." Davy stepped forward, hand outstretched. Without thinking, CJ parted her legs.

Troy's arm thumped heavily across Davy's chest, bringing the him to an abrupt halt. "She's mine, Davy," he croaked. "She's mine, not yours - not yet."

"Of course, sorry." Davy retreated and CJ bit her lip. She had seen the look in his eye and knew he wanted her. But Troy had intervened, he was the boss, his word was law. She turned her full attention towards him.

CJ stared at his wide shoulders, his long arms, his narrow hips, the cord breeches hugging the taut muscles, and her jaw dropped. How could she not have noticed? She had been so intent on what was happening to her. The breeches clung all right. They clung not only to the hip bones and muscular thighs, they outlined in precise detail, stiff and ram-rod straight, a mighty cock, a prick to be proud of, one that filled the front of those immaculate cords to bursting point.

The blush, the one that always betrayed CJ's innermost thoughts, swept over her body. A flush of deepest rose spread from her engorged breasts to the tips of her ears. She wriggled her hips and licked her swollen lips.

"The pole, Damien!"

Damien nodded and waved a pole, white, thick as a man's arm and about a yard in length, high in the air. CJ looked at him. What on earth were they planning to do with that pole? The one in Troy's breeches looked long enough to do the job she had in mind. Her eyes widened with alarm as Damien approached, pole extended.

"Quickly, Damien," Davy ordered. He sounded anxious, his tone was abrupt. "Can't you see Troy's ready. He wants to get on with the girl's training. Get it in place - between the vans - you've done it before, haven't you?"

Damien looked from his brother to Troy, from Troy to CJ and then at the pole in his hand. A smile of enlightenment spread across his face. Dropping everything else to the ground, he trotted towards the caravans.

CJ watched every move. She intended to keep an eye on that pole. With relief she saw him lodge one end on the hub of a wheel, between the spokes, about three feet from the ground. He lodged the other end on a neighbouring wheel. From his pocket he extracted a length of rope and began, with careful precision, to both ends of the pole into place, then, smiling, pleased with himself, he turned and looked at his brother.

"Shall he fix the girl in place, Troy, or do you want to do that yourself? It would please Damien to be trusted with such an important task." CJ could see the glitter in Davy's eye. She glanced from Davy to Troy and an air of expectant tension hung over the little group.

"You do it Davy." CJ noticed the self-satisfied smile on Davy's face when Troy made his decision. "Damien can watch, perhaps another time he can do it, but with a new girl - I want to be sure it's done properly."

"Okay, Troy. Give me some of rope, Damien."

Damien obliged, grinning and whistling softly through his teeth. Grabbing hold of the rope in one hand and the leather sheath binding CJ's arms in the other, Davy marched her towards the caravans - towards the pole. With no way of balancing, her arms were bound so tightly, CJ stumbled, her ankle giving way when she trod on a knotted tussock of grass. Davy stopped her tumbling to the ground, pressed her close to his wiry body, she could hear the pounding of his heart, loud and rapid, under the white T-shirt.

"Pick your feet up girl," his voice hissed hot and soft in her ear. "If you're going to be any use to us, and not offend his lordship, you'll have to learn to balance when you're nicely trussed up." And she felt his cheek, harsh with stubble, press into the silky bounce of her auburn curls.

She heard Troy and Damien laughing. Ashamed there was an audience to see her amateur fumblings, CJ regained an awkward balance and tottered clumsily towards the pole. It gleamed in heavy shadow, white in the dimness between the vans. Aware the only thing keeping her upright, was the steady grip of Davy's fist, she marched proudly, head held high, breasts thrust forward, loins burning with desire.

Davy tugged her to a halt and CJ looked at the pole, then at Davy. She longed to ask what the next move would be, what was expected of her, but knew, in this place, she should keep her mouth shut.

Damien had provided Davy with rope and she could feel strands, dangling from his fingers, tickling the backs of her thighs. Damien had given him plenty. And now, as they stood, man and girl, in front of the pole, he let go of her bound arms. Without his support she swayed unsteadily. Her body, swathed in breast and arm harness, brushed against the white pole. It was metallic and cold. It touched where the gentle swell of her belly caved into the narrowness of a slender waist and that touch was electric. It delivered an unexpected charge of sparking anticipation. A foretaste of what she hoped was to come shivered from her bulging tits to her curling toes.

"Spread her legs, Davy. Spread them wide as you can. Tie those ankles to the rim of the van wheels."

"Right away!"

He knelt down behind her and CJ felt the rough unshaven cheek rest on the apple smoothness of her bottom. Then steely fingers caught her ankles and drew her legs wide. A low cry of alarm was stifled in haste as her body plunged forward, she was falling. The pole caught at her waist. The cold metal dug into the flesh of her stomach, the round balls of her breasts jutted over the metal rod and a cloud of flaming curls tumbled, smothering her face.

Rope wound round her ankles, scaly against the fragile delicacy of her skin. Davy tugged and the rope burnt, abrasive and harsh, dragging her feet towards the van wheels. With thick tough knots he tied those small feet firmly against the wooden wheels, locking her in position. The cold of the metal, the heat of the ropes, the tightness of the harness, CJ felt both bewildered and excited by what was happening. This was all new to her. The words Daisy had spoken in the enclosure last night, returned. This was the kind of thing she had been talking about. Although the circumstances were different, this was very similar to the experiences she had related.

CJ understood now why Daisy had spoken with such fervour, why she was so keen to meet her Jem again. Wriggling her bottom and flexing her pussy in anticipation, CJ waited, nervous but exhilarated. Was Troy planning to fuck her? Take her from behind, like this, rooted to the spot and helpless? CJ hoped so.

She could feel the heat of his body before he even touched her. His hands, large and hot, cupped the cheeks of her bottom, squeezing and pinching the downy flesh. Then his fingers were jabbing into the dark and narrow cleft. CJ gasped with surprise. Hot fingers pulled her cunt lips wide, digging and exploring with a sensual inquisitiveness and dexterity. They dug deep inside her, poking, rubbing, massaging and manipulating. CJ moaned but a stinging hand slap on her bare rump reminded her to hold her noise.

This was going to be difficult. Normally, she was a noisy lover. If this was really all part of the training ritual she was going to prove a difficult pupil. The fingers retreated, she wriggled her bottom in enticement. Her shoulders ached, her breasts felt ready to burst and she no longer had any sense of feeling in her encased arms. All sensation was concentrated in her pussy. It throbbed, it burnt, it sizzled with a deep and unquenched fire.

The thrust when it came was long and deep. The cock was full and hard and knew its business. The weight of the plunge thrust her hips forward. Her belly slapped against the pole and the harness cut under her breasts. The cock, crammed into the tightness of her pussy and, having started, seemed to have little intention of stopping. Troy's cock pistoned inside her with deep and questing thrusts. She could feel his balls slamming into her crotch. She gasped for breath as he pounded, unrelenting and determined. Tears welled up in her eyes at the joy of it. No longer was she a mind within a body, she was all sensation and that sensation was concentrated in the engorged and dripping centre of her sex. The plunging prick ploughed on and it was at this point CJ lost control. Screams of ecstasy and cries of elation rang from her throat.

With pussy juddering uncontrollably, she clamped the pulsating cock firmly between its sodden lips. The white hot fluid jetted deep inside and she spasmed beyond control. She would have fallen to her knees had the ropes, the pole and the hard body of her seducer not held her where she was, held her bound, straddled and helpless between the wooden wheels of those two impassive gipsy caravans.

Breathless and elated, CJ hung over the pole, glad of its support. Troy withdrew, stepped back, stroked her soggy lips. Was he planning to take her again? CJ wriggled her bottom in anticipation. But a noise, harsh and insistent, interrupted this delicious dream. Troy snorted, slapped her bare bum, left her where she was, and leapt up the steps of the larger van, the one decorated in gold leaf. He had left her like this just to answer the demanding ring of the telephone. CJ was devastated.

11: Gathering Fuel Leads Shorsa Into Trouble

With a doubtful expression clouding her pretty face, Shorsa looked at the pile of firewood she had gathered. It wasn't a particularly good morning's work, not even for one person working on her own. She was standing near the trees down beside the stream. She looked up the sweep of the hillside, in the direction of the gipsy camp. From the position of the sun she could tell it was already after midday.

She pushed back her mane of hair, black as a crow's wing, from eyes that were dark and limpid. She pursed her lips, folded her arms, and tried viewing the heap from a different angle. If only Maggie had turned up to help, as promised, it would have been a more presentable pile by now.

She sighed again, tetchily, leaned forward and pushed the heap a little higher, adding another small branch to the top. How could a girl be expected to do such heavy work on her own? Especially on a day like today. She looked up. Invisible overhead, larks were singing, and the sun, high in the sky, was at its hottest.

Shorsa sighed once more, stretched her arms and spun round on her toes. Her naked breasts, full, lush and tipped by nipples of dark mahogany, swung heavily. Her skirt, torn and dirty from the morning's chores, swirled about her ankles. Her feet were bare, the long toes brown from sun and soil. She clutched the hem of the ragged skirt, lifted it to wipe the sweat from between those luscious breasts, and enjoyed the touch of a lively breeze tickling over the damp black curls of her naked pussy.

Exhausted from her exertions she sat down, settling her bottom onto the wood pile. Work, she had to admit, was not her favourite occupation. Not work like this. Perhaps not work of any kind. From where she sat she could just reach the stream with her feet, and she bathed them in the cool and refreshing water that gurgled over large flat stones, bubbled and broke over hidden rocks, and disappeared, tumbling and burbling, beneath the hanging willows.

Despondent and annoyed, she kicked her heels against the logs and tried to smooth the tangles from her wind-blown hair. Damn Maggie! Why didn't she turn up?

The heat was making her sleepy. She turned towards the sun, felt its warmth on her face and on her bare breasts. The burbling of the water, the singing of the birds and the scent of bluebells smothering the woodland floor behind her, cast a spell over her black and slanting eyes. She was some way from the camp, and although eventually someone would wonder where she was, Shorsa was never one to turn down an opportunity to doze in the midday sun. Her morning's task was, she judged, almost complete. It wasn't her fault she hadn't managed to gather much.

All around was the buzzing of bees gathering nectar, never stopping, forever busy, always working, their furry little bodies weighing down the heads of the meadow flowers. Just listening to their interminable humming made Shorsa feel sleepy. She stood up, stretched, yawned widely, and rubbed the indentations made by the rough bark of the logs from her bottom. She gave in to torpor, flung herself full length onto the warmth of the sloping meadow and prepared to doze, undisturbed for ten minutes, or maybe fifteen.

Once rested and refreshed, she thought drowsily, she would start the long uphill journey back to the encampment to ask for help. And give that Maggie a sound piece of her mind.

There could hardly be a more idyllic and peaceful picture: a girl, tall and striking, hair, long and black, fanning out like silk around a fine-boned face, her eyes shut, the black lashes curling over, and shadowing, the delicate blue-smudged skin below each socket; the nose long, straight and proud, the lips full, moist and crimson, and this beautiful but indolent face was delightfully rounded off by a chin that dimpled softly.

Her slender body, the breasts quite naked, skirt rucked round her hips, lay cushioned in grass of deepest green growing lush beside the waters of a stream that chattered and gurgled incessantly. Dusted by the pollen of wild flowers, those generous breasts splayed amply, dark-tipped and succulent. Her flat belly rose and fell to the rhythm of approaching sleep and the long legs, folded at the knee, revealed dark and secret crevices, damp and musky.

Sleepily her fingers stroked at the moist and slippery slit. Agile and expert, they rubbed and fondled and, with little effort, a tension grew between her thighs. Shorsa did not cease her strokings. With legs spread wide, her hips heaved from the ground, her fingers slid faster and faster, massaging that point of joy to a quivering ecstasy. With eyes closed, mouth wide and shouting, paroxysms of bliss surged and tingled, turning her whole body into a quaking heap of solitary rapture.

Relaxed and content, Shorsa slumbered.

Slumbered, that is, until into this dreamy landscape an unwelcome noise intruded. A voice, loud and authoritative, called out orders, and several pairs of feet thudded and pounded the earth. Shorsa heard the creak of wheels turning and the sharp crack of a whip applied to taut and straining flesh.

Was she dreaming? She rolled over lazily on her grassy bed. There shouldn't be anyone coming this way. Only she and Maggie, as far as she knew, had visited this dell since the group arrived here a couple of days ago. Disappointed by the intrusion, Shorsa yawned and stood up. Shading the sun from her eyes, she stared up the hill in the direction of the unexpected sounds.

She could see people on the ridge, high above her, silhouetted against the brightness of the noonday sun. Squinting her eyes, she could make out the outline of a cart. Between the shafts of the cart were fixed two girls, harnessed and wearing bridles and reins. A man held the reins of the nearside girl. Even from this distance Shorsa could tell it was Jem. The easy arrogance of posture, the sway of his shoulders as the whip curled above his head; the continual flicking and swishing at the flesh of the trotting girls, only Jem was so insistent on perpetual flagellation.

Had they seen her? Shorsa decided if they hadn't they soon would and it would be for the best if she made the first move. She rubbed her palms in the damp soil at the edge of the stream, streaked her face with dirt, tangled her hair and stood, hip jutting, one hand supporting the small of an aching back. Raising her other hand to her mouth, she inserted two fingers and whistled, a long, loud and penetrating blast.

The cart drew to a halt. The group wheeled round and looked in her direction. Shorsa waved an arm high in the air, cupped a hand round her mouth and shouted: "Can you give me a hand? I need some help with the firewood." She indicated the pile at her feet. She wasn't sure if the words would carry so far, but knew they had seen her.

Jem wouldn't leave without investigating, not now. Not now he knew she was there. His need to be in charge, to have girls obeying *his* orders, was overwhelming. She smiled to herself. Now the logs could be carried back to the camp, and she could hitch a lift in the cart herself. The whip cracked and the little cart turned. Two bobbing heads pointed in her direction and man, girls, and cart started the descent towards where she waited in the narrow valley, lush and cool, by the bubbling stream.

The group descended the slope at some speed. Soon Shorsa could see clearly the unexpected splendour of the ponies. They gleamed, they shone. Decorations of gold and silver adorned their straining bodies. Whorls and curlicues delved and rippled over every inch of naked flesh, swirling and leaping like flames. With every step they lifted their thighs high, the movement elegant, encouraged by the sting of Jem's whip.

The ponies galloped bravely. They drew close and Shorsa gazed, openmouthed, at the extravagance of the decorations. The painted breasts were splendid in their elaborate adornment. Each pair, magnificent in its own right, was enhanced to perfection by the touch of glittering body paint. They bounced, they swayed like gold and silver moons tipped by nipples picked out in splashes of luscious scarlet.

The leading girl, the left-hand of the pair, was broad and strong and Jem controlled her every move with swift tugs on a bridle that sat deep in her mouth. Golden hair haloed her head. Curls the colour of rich butter dressed in ringlets, plaited with scarlet ribbons, cascaded, bobbed and spiralled prettily with every nod of her lively head. Her eyes were grey, flecked with brilliant blue. Streaks of shadow, amber and aquamarine, enlarged and enhanced the already glittering orbs. Excitement quivered through this pony.

The other one, the one tethered to the right, although similar in height, was of more slender build, but with breasts that matched the first pony's in their generosity. Her hair, shining with natural health, was scraped away on one side from a cheek blushed with exercise. It was pinned high behind her ear, the lobes of which hung heavy with silver rings. A flower of sweet purple lilac, a perfumed plume, was fastened to the pinned-back hair, and nodded proudly in the dazzling light. The colour of the blossom was only matched in freshness by her sparkling eyes, bright and watchful, clear blue lavender, ringed with sooty black, and made gaudy with shadow of purple streaked with silver. Brows, dark and straight, added strength and character to a proud face and those brilliant eyes focused Shorsa's attention with their piercing stare. Her mouth, thickly outlined with paint the colour of crushed elderberries, had a determined look and, even though dragged open by the pull of the bit, still managed to convey a certain sullenness of temper.

With a sharp tug on the reins, Jem brought the little group to a halt only yards from where Shorsa stood. The two ponies stopped, not quite in unison. They could only have started their training that morning.

Nervously patting the ragged folds of her skirt, Shorsa felt soiled and dirty beside all this splendour. When the girls' breasts stopped shaking and the wooden cart ceased swaying, she noticed for the first time that there was a third girl with them. A hutch-bunny. She was tethered at the rear, a studded collar round her neck, and, hanging from it, a chain attached her to the floor of the cart. She was small and dark and her hair swung in a thick plait down her back.

Shorsa relaxed slightly. So this was a bout of intensive training. Pony drilling and hutch bunny discipline combined. Jem would be so full of his own importance he probably wouldn't notice the task she had allotted herself should have been completed hours ago. As Jem calmed the agitated ponies, Shorsa stared at the bunny. Normally, to her, such lowly trade all looked the same. You'd seen one hutch bunny, you'd seen them all. But there was something familiar about this one, something of significance. She was sure she must have seen her recently, but where?

"And just what have you been up to all morning, Shorsa? It's well past noon!" Jem's mouth curled in a thin smile as he glanced up towards where the sun hovered high and hot. "Any task you were given should have been completed by now."

"It's all these logs, Jem," Shorsa dimpled prettily at him. "I've collected too many to get them all back on my own." She sighed heavily, exasperated by the predicament in which she found herself. "But, to be honest, all this would have been finished hours ago if that no-good layabout Maggie had turned up like she should."

A laugh, short sharp and sardonic, grunted from Jem's throat. "If it's Maggie you're waiting for, you've a long wait. She's been hutched. Didn't you know that?" He looked at her quizzically. "I'd have thought you would've have heard when you went for your orders. The decision was made early this morning."

The expression on Shorsa's face gave her away. Hutched! Maggie! The shame. The ignominy. Troy's woman, to be tied up in one of those old animal cages!

"You really didn't know?" Jem was staring hard at her and Shorsa twisted her fingers together, nervous that he would soon put two and two together. Uneducated he might have been, but Jem was not stupid. It would not take him long to realise that nobody had given Shorsa any orders that morning. Nobody at all. That she had slipped away early. True, she had gathered mushrooms first, piled them by the remains of the fire, ready for cooking. She had been busy whilst the rest of the camp slept. But before anyone was awake, she had slipped away and come here, to laze away the morning, with her friend. But Maggie had let her down, and now Jem would want to take his revenge, punish her for her indolence.

"It's not like you're thinking, Jem!" The excuses were bursting from her. "I - I knew that Troy would want the fire kept well up. That he'd be needing all the wood." She swept her arm round to show Jem just how much she had gathered. "Troy always likes to keep the f-"

The whip zinged through the air, the tip cut across her heaving breasts. "Shut up!" Jem growled. "Do you think I'm interested in your pathetic excuses? You've been sitting on your lazy backside all morning, that's what you've been doing, hoping that nobody would think to look for you. Well, I may not have been looking, but I've certainly found you, and now it's up to me to ensure that it will be nigh on impossible for you sit on that sluggardly bum of yours for the next few days."

The whip sliced through the air once more and Shorsa's skirt, only ever held in place by a single button, dropped to the ground. The larger of the two pony-girls tried to open her mouth as if to speak, but Jem was having none of it. His hand dragged the reins, pulling hard on the bit nestling inside her soft mouth. Turning abruptly, he led the pair away, cart and bunny in tow, towards a willow leaning crazily over the water. He lashed the reins to the trunk. The two ponies shivered in the shade. Their decorated flesh glimmered and shone. Side by side, they pressed shoulder to shoulder, their eyes huge with excitement, the little cart quivering behind them.

Detaching the hutch bunny from the cart, Jem caught hold of her collar, and dragged her towards Shorsa. Shorsa stood, tummy fluttering, wondering just what punishment he could have in mind for her. Jem thrust the bunny in her direction. She slid on the damp grass, bumping into Shorsa. Shorsa jumped back. She didn't want to feel the touch of bunny flesh. The thought of it made her shudder, and she trembled for her friend incarcerated in a cage.

The two gipsy girls stood close, the one short and energetic, the other tall and languid, both wondering what would happen next. Jem, displeased with the way the cart was dangling at an untidy angle, hurried back to the pony girls. Shorsa and the bunny watched him go, dark eyes darting after his every move. Neither intended to be taken by surprise, but one of them decided to take advantage of this unexpected interlude.

"Psst."

Shorsa jumped at the unexpected sound.

"Psst, long shanks, are you deaf?" A pointed finger dug sharply into Shorsa's ribs.

Amazed by the sheer audacity of the creature, Shorsa realised the voice could only be that of the hutch bunny quivering next to her. Hurriedly she glanced at Jem. He was engrossed in the arrangement of ponies and cart, adjusting positions, stroking hair into place, testing the harness cutting between each pair of ripe breasts. So engrossed was he, Shorsa lost her wariness, relaxed slightly, and decided to put this bunny in her place. The cheek of it, thinking she could address someone of Shorsa's status without first being given permission!

"And just who do you think you're talking to, runt?"

"A piece of cunt, just like meself, and it's number three is all I am." The impish face grinned unabashed. "You're no different from the rest of us. Neither you, nor that stuck up bint who calls herself Troy Dempsey's woman."

Shorsa glowered at the girl. "What do the likes of you know about Dapper Troy? He wouldn't have your sort anywhere near him."

The girl glanced at Jem, eyes narrowed, assessing the likelihood of his attention returning to herself and Shorsa within the next few minutes. Satisfied he was engrossed, she fell to her knees, put her hands behind her back, opened her mouth at the level of Shorsa's bare crotch and imitated the licking, sucking and kissing of a large and urgent prick.

Shorsa's eyes widened in recognition. "You! It was you last night! It's your fault that Maggie is where she is now!"

With a movement so swift the kneeling girl did not see it coming, Shorsa's leg kicked out. The ball of her foot planted firmly in the centre of the other's chest, against her breasts, and sent the mimicking, taunting creature bowling over and over, shoulders, bottom, pussy all appearing and disappearing in a tumble of hair and limbs. She floundered on the grass and her spinning body came to a halt only inches from the rushing waters of the stream.

Shorsa leapt after her, hands outstretched, fingers spread, nails ready to gouge skin and flesh from that jeering face, those bouncing tits.

"You little cat!" she hissed. "I'll tear you into little pieces and feed the bits to the fishes in the stream - if they'll have you." She hovered over the girl, who instead of having the grace to look frightened, lay there, giggling, her mouth still working, pretending to mould itself round an imaginary and demanding cock. She even had the cheek to slip deft fingers between her own cunt lips, pull them wide, slide the tips lovingly in her flowing juices, lift her hips, and spread wide, waggle her pussy as if in welcome at the approach of a massive and engorged thrust.

Fury overwhelmed Shorsa and she lost control. She fell on the girl. Her nails scraped the dusky skin, her teeth sank into the soft and pliant flesh of the girl's breasts. She pounded on the laughing belly and swaggering limbs. She was lost in anger.

A cut like clawing brambles blazed over Shorsa's thighs. It came, again and again, slashing the soft flesh, cutting between the cheeks of her bottom and stinging the tender and sensitive folds nestling between her legs. Powerful arms wrapped round her waist and, kicking and screaming, jeering obscenities at her foe, she was dragged her off the squirming bunny. Jem threw her to one side. She fell heavily and the breath was knocked from her lungs.

Then the whining tip of the whip sliced over Shorsa's exposed breasts and belly. He dragged her upright by the roots of her hair, lashed both wrists together, and secured them in the dimpled hollow of her back. He positioned the hands so the tips of her fingers brushed the fine-bloomed flesh where it split into a dark and narrow dell, softly parting and separating the two heavy half-moons of her pear-shaped bottom. With an oath and a blow to her cheek that bruises her pride more than her flesh, he shoved her to her knees, and with her face aflame with discomposure, she pressed it thankfully into the cool grass.

Jem's attention turned to number three. "And you're no better," he shouted at her. "I'll soon wipe that smirk off your face."

Hearing these words, Shorsa felt encouraged. She manoeuvred slowly, not wanting to grab Jem's attention yet, and stared at the bunny. One glance was enough. The episode with Troy last night had emboldened this girl. Far from being disconcerted or unnerved by Jem's threats, she welcomed the attention, was provoking him on purpose. She wanted to feel the cut of the whip and the bite of the rope on her slender arms.

She certainly got what she wanted!

The whip circled round her buttocks, incisive and precise. It traced patterns of scarlet over her back, thighs, breasts and belly, and the girl scarcely flinched, kept on smiling all the while. He bound her arms behind her back, fastening them at wrist and elbow, and launched her towards Shorsa. She landed on her knees next to her rival, mouthing ridicule all the while.

Shorsa longed to attack again. But this was neither the time nor the place. They both knelt, faces pressed to the ground, bottoms waving skywards. The two pony-girls, who had not made a sound during the fight and the punishment that followed, shuffled their feet, and a whimpering groan from the larger one made Shorsa glance sharply in her direction.

What she saw brought a smile to her lips. The pony making all the fuss was staring with tears in her eyes at Jem. He stood, whip in one hand, breeches unbuttoned, cock waving splendid and erect. The tip glowed glossily red, the shaft was thick and strong. The pony with the scarlet ribbons gazed, eyes agog, at the magnificent prick. But she was not to benefit from its thrust. Jem was heading towards the two gipsy girls.

He swayed in front of the bunny. She cocked her head and grinned. A flash of irritation clouded Jem's features and he slapped that cheeky face with the flat of his hand. The bunny opened her mouth in protest and the glistening prick slid between her pouting lips. Her eyes rounded with excitement and she rocked on her heels, thrusting towards the delicious object until her whole mouth smothered and devoured it.

Shorsa and the two ponies watched, entranced. The bunny wriggled and squirmed. Her breasts wobbled, the dark nipples grew thick.

Shorsa licked her lips and envied the bunny that touch of cock. Her own pussy was glowing. The excitement of the fight, the feel of soft woman flesh ripping under her nails, the sight of rampant cock thrusting and lunging down bunny throat, all these exquisite preliminaries had charged Shorsa's belly into life and she glowed with lust. A tingling anticipation of pleasure to come burst her nipples into life and they stood, full and throbbing, the tips hot and rosy.

With eyes glazed and slender body quivering, the bunny licked and sucked with enthusiasm. Jem flicked the whip over her back and she shook at its touch. He stared at Shorsa, his expression sneering. Shorsa bit her lip and felt a jealous heat burning at the sight of such obvious ecstasy. She opened her mouth, curled her tongue and licked the tip of her nose with a gesture both sinuous and sexy. Jem watched with lustful eyes, and with a final thrust down the bunny's throat, his cock glided from between the crimson lips and bunny number three gurgled her satisfaction.

Without a backward glance, he hurried towards Shorsa. She knelt on the grass, wet, watchful and alert, but he immediately disappeared behind her. No sooner had he gone than she felt the silky tip of his cock first nuzzle, then split apart the dewy lips of her pussy. He drove it home. Long, and hard as iron, it slithered expertly against the throbbing walls of her cunt, the base of the shaft vibrated her clit, rubbing, massaging, burnishing it to a pitch of uncontrollable urgency. Her fingers squeezed into fists behind her back, the muscles of her tummy tightened, and her pussy softened, warm and slippery. Waves of joy sliced into the depths of her loins, lanced through belly and breasts. Jem bellowed and liquid, thick and hot, pumped fiercely inside her.

With bodies twitching and squirming with satisfaction, Jem hauled both girls to their feet. Shorsa's knees felt weak. Number three was smirking. With his one hand on her collared neck, and the other gripping Shorsa's tousled hair, he dragged them to where the pony cart patiently waited.

When they reached it, Shorsa stared in amazement. One girl, the one with scarlet ribbons plaited into her curls and the strong broad shoulders, had tears running down her cheeks. Her eyes, full of a frustrated sadness, were gazing at Jem with unfettered admiration. Shorsa snorted. That girl was in love - what a fool. She was a fool like Maggie was a fool. The one imagining herself in love with Troy - and look what had happened to her - the other, for some God forsaken reason, going gooey-eyed over Jem!

The bunny giggled at the sight and, impatient to be off, Jem reattached her chain to a ring embedded in the floor of the cart. A second chain, manacle dangling open, was lying next to it. He snatched it up and snapped the metal fetter into place on the collar around Shorsa's neck. Flicking the whip expertly over the painted backsides of the two ponies he shouted orders and they lifted their heads, strained their shoulders and pulled, until the wheels of the cart ground slowly into motion.

"The firewood, Jem, what about all me firewood?" Shorsa was dismayed that her morning's hard work was to be abandoned in such a cavalier fashion.

Jem snorted and lashed with enthusiasm at the trotting bottoms. "Forget that, Shorsa. Save your breath for the climb back to the camp."

"But it took me all morning -"

The whip lashed across her back. "I said, forget it. There's already plenty of wood in store, as you well now, and anyway, you can come back for this lot tomorrow - pulling the cart yourself."

"I don't pull carts!" Shorsa was truly shocked.

"You do now. Your behaviour needs some curbing, and I'm the man to do it."

"But the training, Jem!" Shorsa's words came it in broken little gasps as she struggled up the slope. "You've all the new girls to train. Like these two." She nodded at the two puffing ponies.

"Plenty of time Shorsa, plenty of time. The Big Man isn't due here for a couple of weeks. Now shut your mouth and stop dragging on the cart."

Shorsa grunted. Furious at Jem's dismissive tone, she felt anger surge up in her breast. This anger grew when she saw the hutch bunny grinning cheekily in her direction.

"Plenty of time, Shorsa," mimicked number three. *"Plenty of time.* There's always plenty of time in Dapper Troy Dempsey's training camp for extra disciplining of the inmates. I would have thought someone of *your* superiority would have known that." And, kicking up her heels, the hutch bunny trotted effortlessly after the jaunty little cart.

Puffing and blowing, Shorsa stumbled behind her. It was true, there was always time for plenty of extra training. And with the Big Man's imminent arrival, no doubt the intensity of that training was about to be increased.

12: Commotion In The Camp

Jo's heart was thumping loudly and rapidly. Being a pony-girl was no joke!

The painful climb had been both long and slow. At first she and Daisy had trotted gamely upwards from the stream, pleased to be on their way back to some rest, shade and refreshment. After the initial climb up a slippery slope, a long flat grassy path had brought welcome relief to their bare feet. They galloped gamely along this pleasant ride but however hard they tried to please, Jem's whip never ceased to flick and swish, whirring and sighing over their naked bottoms. Always dissatisfied with their efforts, the tip of the whip cut into the tender flesh at the backs of their knees and they lifted their thighs higher in immediate response.

At the end of the grassy path they rounded a rocky corner and the soft and easy ground gave way to a stony corridor winding beneath a rugged cliff face. Boulders jutted through the thin soil. Jo remembered this bit from their journey down to the dell, that delightful little valley of coolness and shade. Mentally, she winced at the memory. The stones underfoot were sharp, jagged and plentiful, her feet, already sore, suffered extra torture on this return journey. The wheels of the cart were well-oiled and it bowled along easily, but the additional drag of the extra gipsy girl they had just acquired, and who seemed so intent on causing trouble, was adding considerable strain to the young and inexperienced shoulders of Daisy and Jo. Getting home was proving much harder than the outward trot.

Now they were climbing to a ridge and Jo knew once they were over that ridge it would be downhill once more. She glanced at her fellow pony. Daisy's face was red with effort, the formerly bouncing curls lank and lifeless. The summit was approaching. When they breasted it, right legs raised in unison - the training was having some effect - a delightful vista was spread before their eyes.

A stream, the same stream they had stood by earlier, but narrower and livelier here, tumbled through the valley bottom. Naked dark haired bunnies were crouched over the water, some washing pots, some rinsing clothes, and others, upstream, collecting the cool clear water in tall pitchers, which they heaved onto shoulders that sagged under the great weight. Hauling themselves up off their knees, they staggered unsteadily past the corral, empty now. They reeled and swayed their way back towards the vans, drawn up on a small plateau backed by high hedging and shaded by tall trees.

No words passed between Daisy and Jo and it was an involuntary decision on both their parts to pause at the same moment, take breath and survey the busy scene. And busy it was, surprisingly so. At first Jo had little suspicion that everything was not as it should be. After all this was only her second day here. But the camp, which at this time of day, she imagined would be quiet, with tables set out under tall trees, food laid, glasses filled, men relaxing, and from what she had learned of this crowd, girls quietly serving with obedience and alacrity, was not in evidence. A strangled cry from Jem's throat startled them all.

"Whatever is the matter, Jem?" From the rear of the cart, Shorsa's voice called sharp and wary.

"Whatever is the matter, Jem?" mimicked bunny number three.

Shorsa and the bunny eased their way round the edge of the cart and peered over Jem's shoulder.

Jo gazed at the scene. There did seem to be a considerable air of confusion she had to admit. Men strode hurriedly about the encampment and a clamour of voices, men and girls, floated up to the group perched on the rocky crest above the camp.

Jem swore quietly to himself. Taking no notice of Shorsa's suggestion, he shoved her and the bunny back into position. His whip sang as he spun it through the air. It landed with practised ease on Jo's shoulder. "Get going, you lazy bitches. I've not given you permission to stop!"

The two ponies sprang into life at the touch of the whip. The way down the slope was steep and Jem ordered the two gipsy girls chained at the rear to act as brakes. The descent was taken at a good trot, and the cart dragged on Jo's narrow shoulders, the harness cut cruelly beneath her breasts, and the bit dug into the fleshy interior of her puffing cheeks. But for all this discomfort, she was fascinated. The camp, what she had seen of it, had seemed so well organised, and now, even to her inexperienced eyes, it was obvious that disorder reigned. Silently encouraging Daisy to keep up, she surged forward, for here was something of real interest.

Maybe these men, so superior and boasting, weren't the masters of their own destiny. Perhaps there was some other person pulling their strings. Jo felt elated. Someone had upset them. Whoever that someone was, Jo was on his side and her heart lifted at the prospect of encountering a fellow subversive.

Jem, not hiding his alarm at what he saw happening a hundred feet below, rushed the ponies onwards. Down, down, down, they galloped. The two gipsy girls tried hard to steady the wildly swinging cart. Their heels scorched the earth. The ponies, the wind blowing their carefully arranged tresses, their eyes streaming, pounded the soil. Jem's shouting and cursing encouraged them all onwards. Excitement surged through their veins. The ground levelled out and they were within shouting distance of the caravans. Jem grabbed hold of Daisy's reins, pulled hard, turned her head, and gradually, the whole careering outfit slowed to a sedate walk.

They reached the edge of the camp, calm and serene, the only indication of their precipitous descent, the flush on the cheeks of the ponies, and the limping and hobbling of Shorsa and the hutch bunny on bruised and battered feet.

Jo stared at the chaotic scene and noticed the small dark wiry man, the one who had snatched CJ away that morning, rushing towards them.

"Hey, Davy, is something wrong?" Jem grabbed Davy's arm as he hurried past.

You could say that!" And Davy rushed away, a list clutched tightly in one fist.

"Well, thanks for the information," Jem shouted after him. Anger and annoyance clouded his brow. "You lot stay exactly where you are." He tied Daisy's reins to a tree trunk. "Don't move. I'll be back."

The four girls watched him hurry across the seething plot and disappear into the throng.

Jo raised her eyes and looked round. The scene was one of considerable confusion.

"What do you think's going on, Daisy?" she whispered through her bit.

"I don't know," mumbled Daisy morosely. "But he's gone again." The painted mouth pouted, and she fidgeted in the shafts of the cart.

"Daisy! For goodness sake, can't you see something important's happened? Stop mooning over that useless piece of prick and put your mind to wondering what's going on."

The cart shivered behind them. "Huh! From what I've seen of her, that fat article could hardly add two and two, let alone work out what's going on here."

Stuck in the shafts, Jo could only just turn her head. But the voice which had spoken was light and lilting and she was sure it belonged to the small, cheeky girl. The one with a number and no name. She strained to turn as far as she could, tried to get a good look at her passengers. "You two are part of this set up," she said from the side of her mouth. "Have you ever seen it in this kind of uproar before?"

"There's a new moon tonight." Shorsa spoke the words quietly.

"So what?" said Jo in amazement.

"New moons affect some people - and those who live in the open air and sleep under that stars can be affected more than most."

Jo snorted her disbelief. "Believe me, honey, this ain't nothing to do with no new moon. This lot of bozos are acting like someone's just put fleas up their arses - but who? That's what I'd like to know."

"*He* knows." The other three all looked at Daisy in surprise. She was staring into the distance at Davy coming back, Damien loping by his side. "He must know. But he was so awfully rude to Jem just now. Not telling him when he asked so nicely, I don't want to speak to him."

The bunny crowed with laughter at Daisy's little speech. "*Don't want to speak to him.* My, my, pig-face, you got any brains under all those slushy curls?"

"Don't you know how to be polite?" Jo defended Daisy angrily.

"For goodness sake, shut up all of you." Shorsa interrupted. "Let *me* do the talking. Even if I am chained up with a bunny slut for company, I'm still the person with the most clout round here."

"*Bunny slut, bunny slut,*" mocked number three. "What about Maggie then? She's a bunny slut *now*." She giggled and hiccoughed and gasped for breath when Shorsa kicked her hard on the shin.

Mutinous but aware that Shorsa spoke sense, Jo decided to hold her tongue. Any minute now, Davy would be within calling distance. Perhaps this girl really did know what she was talking about. For all Jo knew, she was Queen of the May in this set up.

"Davy, Davy, light of my life, can you spare us a moment of your precious time?" Shorsa's voice wheedled and Jo cringed at the obsequious tone.

"Shorsa, Shorsa Colquhoun, is that you?" Davy drew to a halt in front of the ponies and peered over their shoulders to where Shorsa stood still chained by the neck to the cart. "I never noticed you lurking there. And what nonsense brought you to this pretty plight?" The pixie face was grinning and, without his coffle of girls in tow, and with Damien by his side, Davy seemed more relaxed. His eyes devoured the whole set-up. "Now there's a charming picture. Four delightful young ladies all tied and chained ready to perform with the cart. It'll warm the cockles of Troy's heart - and at the moment he needs something like this to cheer him up."

"Why Davy? Has something gone wrong?"

"Depends what you mean by wrong, Shorsa. To me, well, what with the clever little plan I've been hatching inside my head just recently -"

"If I could get over there, Davy, I'd kick the balls off you!"

Jo could have cheered. She stared at Davy and from the agitation in his twitching face, recognised the truth was about to come spilling forth.

"All right, Shorsa, all right. Hang on to your titties - it's a big surprise for everyone."

The four girls held their breath.

"There was a phone call, what, not more than an hour ago, sometime after noon anyway. After Miss Maggie had been sent to the hutches but before -"

"DAVY." Four voices yelled in unison. Two of them slightly muffled because of the bits in their mouths.

"All right." Davy's face glowed with excitement. "It was a phone call from the Big Man himself. No, that's not strictly accurate." His eyes twinkled at the four frustrated expressions turned in his direction. "If I'm going to be honest, it was the Big Man's assistant, let me see, what did Troy say his name was? Andrew? Anthony? Antoine? No, no, it comes to me now, it was Antonio, that's what it was, Antonio."

He seemed to relish the sound of the name as it tripped off his tongue. Seemed to enjoy the sound of it so much, he was forced to pause, reassemble his thoughts and regain energy, before he could continue.

"And what did he want?" asked Shorsa through gritted teeth. She would have stamped her foot had it not been so sore. "Is there a change of plan?"

"You might say that!" grinned Davy. "Indeed, you might just say that!" Taking a step back, he surveyed the four girls, all breathless with anticipation, and inspected the cart, the harnesses and the chains. Damien echoed every move he made and the two of them sauntered round the abandoned team.

Although Jo had no idea who this Big Man was, or what his plans were likely to be, she could tell from the gasps and twitterings of the other two that they knew all right, they were only too well aware of the significance of this message.

"The Big Man," Davy continued, "wanted Troy to know there had been a change of plan. Some other scheme of his had fallen through; he would be arriving here earlier than anticipated. In fact," he spun round on his heel and Damien had to step smartly out of the way, "in fact he would be arriving here on Saturday and he hoped, without putting Dapper Troy to too much trouble, he hoped he would be able to have everything ready for him by then."

Screams of surprise from behind made both Daisy and Jo jump in the shafts.

"Saturday!" screamed Shorsa.

"Saturday!" sniggered the hutch bunny.

"Why, it's Tuesday now!" exclaimed Shorsa. "Oh, how I would love to have been here, to have seen Troy's face when he received that particular piece of information." The little cart began to rattle and shake and Shorsa collapsed into a fit of giggling.

Jo longed to ask just what was going on, but felt cautious when any man was hanging around, whip dangling from his waistband, and anyway her mouth hindered by bit and bridle, was sore. Every time she tried to get her tongue round any words the piece of metal rubbed her lips so much, she winced at the discomfort. But she could still use her eyes and ears. The hubbub was tremendous. A discordant air, boisterous and turbulent, filled every inch of space.

"There's Troy!" Shorsa's breath rasped between her teeth.

Jo stared at him with interest. She had heard his name mentioned so often during the last twenty-four hours, but this was the first time she had set eyes on the chief. She was impressed. He was tall, neat, good-looking. Jo felt her tummy tighten slightly at the sight of him. Her hips wriggled in a movement she would not willingly have admitted to.

Troy was striding towards them.

"He looks so cool." This time Shorsa sounded disappointed. "I expected him to be - untidy - at least."

"Davy! Here, Davy! What have you got?"

"Some trainee ponies, Troy, a hutch bunny - number three in case you're interested - and Shorsa, for my sins."

"So, where were you earlier this morning, Shorsa Colquhoun, when I sent orders for you to come to my van?"

There was no reply.

"Right. Well, I'm too busy to give you the beating you deserve - but later, my girl, later."

"This lot aren't really mine Troy. Jem brought them."

"Shut up Davy. I've other work for Jem. I'm not interested in what was what or whose was whose. All plans have changed. This lot," he consulted the list clasped in his hand, "this lot - or I should say, the two new girls, they're to go to Nico."

Jo's mouth fell open at the sound of that name.

"I shall want their harnesses left here, but you can keep their arms sheathed. Nico can decide on that one."

Davy nodded.

"The other two," Troy consulted his list with a frown. "Shorsa - take her to the end of the main drive. There's a group there with" - his finger ran down the list, searching - "with Seth in charge."

Shorsa groaned.

"What about the bunny, Troy?"

"She comes with me."

Davy's eyebrows rose in a query of disbelief. "Are you sure Troy - a bunny?"

"The bunny, Davy, *that* bunny." His finger pointed directly over Jo's shoulder, and she heard the soft tones of the bunny muttering: "*That bunny, Shorsa, did you hear that? That bunny. And that bunny is me.*"

Jo had no time to ponder the intricacies of the rivalries between the gipsy girls. Davy had already unfastened both her and Daisy from the cart. The constriction and weight cutting into her shoulders for the past few hours, lifted. He removed her bridle. The only restriction now was the arm sheath. This he left in place.

"It's you two luscious darlings for Nico, then. Ah, to be in his boots. He's a lucky man." Davy stroked both bottoms lovingly, poked a finger deep inside Jo's arse, and with what seemed to be an air of genuine reluctance, fitted collars and leashes and handed the two girls over to Damien. "Now, you heard what Troy said, didn't you Damien?"

Damien nodded, his thick neck creasing, his yellow teeth exposed by a wide grin.

Jo stared at him with distaste.

"And, Damien," Davy's finger prodded his brother's bare chest, "you are to come back and find me, pronto. No hanging about, no gawping - understood? And if you're not back in half an hour, I'll be up there looking for you."

Damien shuffled awkwardly.

Hoping his brother had got the message, Davy slapped both ponies on their rumps, and the little group set off. For their own reasons, neither Daisy nor Jo wanted to go. And as Damien led them further away form the little cart, Shorsa and number three still tightly chained, Jo could see Daisy's head craning in a desperate search for Jem. She herself kept her eyes skinned, flickering in every direction, scanning the area, looking high and low for a first sight of Nico. He had humiliated her yesterday, and the way things were going, it looked like a similar opportunity was about to come his way today.

13: A Surprise Find Beside The Lake

"Jem, get two of those bitches out of there. All bunnies are to be out and training. Now!"

Maggie trembled when she heard the anger in Troy's voice. From where she huddled, crouched in the close confines of a bunny cage, she could see very little. What was visible was a mass of scurrying legs. Only inches from her nose feet thundered past. She pressed her naked body hard up against the wire of the heavily padlocked door and felt miserable.

Maggie had never been incarcerated like this before - such punishment was not intended for the likes of her - these were for the dross, the lowest of the low, the bunnies. Now the ones left there were agitated, uncertain like herself, perplexed by the uproar that had taken over what was, at this time of day, a normally well-organised and sleepy camp.

"I'll get a couple out Troy. Give me the keys."

Jem's voice roared only a few feet away from her. She could not see him, but she could smell him. He was nervous. The odour of dry sweat filtered into the cage and Maggie wrinkled her nose in distaste. She hoped Jem would not come anywhere near her. Although she was embarrassed by her imprisonment, if there was to be any choice, Maggie would rather remain where she was, humiliated and scorned by the other bunnies maybe, but for someone of her status to be handled by Jem - it hardly bore thinking about.

The jangle of a bunch of keys falling to the ground caught her attention.

"Bugger!"

She could just see them, lying on the grass, only a few feet away, the early afternoon sun glinting from the shiny metal. They glittered with an ominous and worrying nearness. If Jem stooped to pick the up...

"Well, well, well, if it isn't Maggie!"

Jem's darkly hooded eyes glanced lazily over her cowering body. Maggie stared boldly back. There was no way she was going to let him see how much she feared him.

"Now let me see. Troy's instructions were to release a couple of you. And I think you will be my first choice." He scooped the keys into his palm, selected one of the shiniest, inserted it into the padlock hanging from Maggie's hutch, and the door swung open easily on its well-greased hinges.

"Jem, I -"

"Shut up. I'm following Troy's orders."

"But Jem, Troy would never have meant you to take me." More upset than she cared to let him see, Maggie's voice broke slightly and she had to gulp back the choking sensation constricting her throat.

He stared at her, his eyes narrow and darkly threatening beneath the hooded lids. "You count for nothing any longer," he sneered. "You know Troy's got a new woman. You haven't got any status. You're a bunny."

New woman! The words reverberated inside Maggie's head. New woman! No! It wasn't possible. *She* was Troy's woman. Jem had hold of her arm. He dragged her roughly out. With head lolling, bottom scraping, her toes caught in the wire of the door. It banged painfully against her ankles. Maggie was pulled from the cage, an ungainly, dumb-struck creature, bathed in misery. The news she had dreaded, and which Jem had just confirmed, soaked into her raging soul.

Jem jerked Maggie to her feet. His hands clasped both wrists and the skin burnt at the firmness of his grip.

"Ow, Jem, let me go. I'm not going to run." His fist punched and Maggie gasped for breath. "Troy doesn't intend me to stay here for long, does he? That other girl, the new girl, the small one with the carroty curls, she's only a diversion - isn't she Jem?" Her voice rose a couple of octaves as he twisted her arms up behind her back. Maggie stood on tip-toe, her feet scrabbling to gain purchase on the slippery grass.

"I said, shut up. What Troy plans to do is none of your business. You're coming with me. But I've still to choose another girl. Troy said to train a pair of you."

Maggie tried to regain her composure. If Jem was working to Troy's orders she'd have to go along with that. Troy would soon be bored with this other girl, probably was already. Maggie looked round wildly. If she knew Dapper Troy, he'd be missing her expert touch. There was no sign of him. He had completely disappeared. Maggie's heart sank. Troy must be very busy. Something of importance had happened.

"Take me to Troy, Jem," she begged. There was no response. His attention was fixed on one of the bunnies. One particularly bold girl sitting on the floor of her cage, legs drawn up, thighs splayed, eagerly fingering herself. She was dipping one finger after another inside her damp pussy, licking each one with relish, squirming her hips and gaping her slit for Jem's benefit. Maggie stared at the juicy folds of the cunt revealed in all their crimson glory.

"Jem," she pressed her pliant body hard up against his. She could feel the strength of his muscles beneath the black shirt. His body was hard and, after looking at the lascivious bunny, rigid with lust. "Jem, if you take me to Troy - now - he'll be pleased, I know he will."

Maggie's heart was thudding loudly. She felt desperate. If she couldn't distract Jem's attention from that slavering slut, they would both be servicing him in no time at all by the state of his jeans. The thought made her shudder.

Clutching her wrists in his fist, Jem strode towards the happily performing bunny. He dipped sideways, unlocked the padlock, hooked his boot behind a spread knee, and pulled number six from the hutch on his toe.

"You're coming with me." He yanked the beaming bunny up by her long dark hair. "As for you," he twisted Maggie's arms, pulled her face towards his and grinned. "I've told you, Troy's got a new woman. He said to train two girls and I follow Troy's orders. You're both coming with me, whether you like it or not."

Number six grinned and winked at Maggie. She seemed pleased to have been chosen. She opened her mouth and imitated the sucking and licking actions needed for servicing a large and demanding prick - news of last night's humiliation of Maggie by number three had flown round the camp - tossed back her hair, cupped pert dark-nippled breasts in both hands, nipple rings tinkling, and jiggled about in happy anticipation. Jem grabbed her wrists, chained them behind her back and fixed a collar and lead round her neck.

Maggie's eyes darted from side to side. There was still no sign of Troy. Only minutes earlier she had heard him give those instructions to Jem. The orders had left her subject to Jem's devious lusts, but he'd disappeared. Where to, she had no idea. But it was becoming obvious to Maggie that Jem was speaking the truth. Troy had abandoned her.

Maggie felt her heart was sinking and despair engulfed her. Jem had already fixed a lead to the bunny's collar and was now fiddling at her own throat. She was at his mercy. He held the lead tight, forcing her chin up. Her head and shoulders jerked back, her tits and sex thrust forward. From his belt, Jem detached two lengths of rope, black, silky to the touch, but tough and strong. He bound Maggie's hands, secured them in the small of her back. The tightness of the binding made Maggie's shoulders drag in their sockets.

He strutted in front them, cock rigid. He seemed pleased with his achievement. He pulled on the leads, dragged both girls' heads back, swung the crop high and it landed smartly on first one dusky bum, then the other.

"Get moving, you pair of no-good vermin." His voice was gruff with lust. "We're going to get some real training in for the pair of you. Training like you've never experienced, Maggie." He spoke with derision and scorn and snorted with pleasure. "There'll be no easy ride for you. In fact, the ride you're about to get is one you'll never forget."

The crop cut across Maggie's bottom and she winced at the sharpness of it.

"Now get going the pair of you. We've wasted too much time already. Get moving."

The reins tugged at two delicate throats and the girls sprang into action.

The bunny was in a hurry, her long legs striding. Maggie had to jog to keep up with her. "What - what - what's all the hurry Jem? Whatever is all the commotion going on here?"

"I told you to stop being so nosy. But I suppose there's no harm in you knowing. The Big Man's arriving sooner than expected."

"The Big Man? The circus man?"

Jem's crop cut across the tops of her thighs. "I just told you," he was breathing heavily. "He's arriving sooner than expected. Troy had a phone call this lunchtime. The man's arriving on Saturday."

Maggie was astounded. She realised how important this visit was to Troy. This was his first year in charge of the training camp. She had heard him making plans this morning with Davy, deciding which girls to train to please this important visitor. He had even said she and Shorsa could entertain him with their dancing. She had been looking forward to this special occasion. Now everything was going wrong. It was all the fault of that red-head - and bunny, number three.

Anger and despair welled in Maggie's breast. Hutch bunnies! Most things were the fault of these wretched hutch bunnies. Some of them were almost uncontrollable. She glanced at bunny number six loping along by her side, breasts swinging, the chains dangling from her nipples tinkling as she ran. They were all a nuisance. They should be made to suffer for upsetting everything they way they did.

Panting and with aching legs, Maggie decided to reason with Jem once more. "If something so important is happening Jem, Troy'll be needing me. You know he will." There was no reply. The man was not listening. He was intent on getting his pair of trainees through the crowd. They were weaving their way amongst the multitude of milling girls. Jem drove his pair with expertise and they soon reached the centre of the camp.

The ashes of this morning's fire glowed, a small heap. At this time of day it should have been roaring. It had been neglected as every single member of the camp, men and girls alike, was engrossed in the instant training necessitated by the unexpected bringing forward of this important visit.

They were approaching Troy's van. A girl was stretched on the rack - her rack. Her replacement? No! She was dark-haired. A long thick plait snaked down the straining back. It was a bunny - that number three!

The sound of the bunny by her side sniggering brought a blush of humiliation and fury to Maggie's face.

They trotted past Troy's van. The door was open. Heavy shadow enveloped the interior. But, with eyes straining, staring hard into that inky blackness, Maggie glimpsed something that made her stomach lurch, her heart flutter and her head spin. Within the dark interior, just visible, she could see the glimmering shape of a girl, pale skin, white against the velvety darkness. She could make out the shimmer of red-gold curls. But what made Maggie's heart feel as though it was sinking into the soles of her feet, was that the girl was roped, arms stretched above her head, legs spread, ankles lashed to floor fixings.

And, worst of all, kneeling between those spread legs, head buried in the depths of plump white thighs, was a dark head, hair brushed straight back, a small gold ring glinting from the lobe of his right ear - Troy - her Troy, sucking off one of the gathered ones, a new girl, the red-head Davy had brought to the fireside this morning.

Tears sprang into Maggie's eyes. The collar binding her neck felt tighter. Her throat gulped her misery. She longed to race over to the caravan, leap up the steps, scratch out the eyes of that red-headed bitch, claw that oh-so-perfect fine white flesh. Claw it until thin red stripes crazed that usurping body from tits to toes, from arse to ankle. She wanted to spit in her face, humiliate the bitch, humiliate her the way Maggie herself had been humiliated.

Within the last few hours Troy had betrayed her twice. Once with a hutch bunny, that alone was degrading enough, but now with this - this - *outsider*! How could he abuse her so? She determined to get her own back. But the sight of her lover sucking the cunt of another girl had started Maggie's own juices flowing. She wanted a screw, needed a screw, and needed it now. Jem lashed the pair of girls and they galloped harder. At the moment Jem was the only screw on offer. So be it. After what she had just seen, Maggie was willing, more than willing, to take him on board.

Jem pulled hard on her lead and the two girls wheeled to the left. They were taking the path which cut through the corner of the wood and soon they were under the heavy shade of the tall beech trees. Jem urged them on. Twigs caught in Maggie's hair, stones bruised her bare feet. The path was straight and short. They came through the trees and the ground fell away. Spread below them, curving into a deep and luscious bowl, was a smooth carpet of grass. It differed in every respect from the wild meadow where the gipsies camped. This was a lawn, well-tended and cared for. Its green was the green of an English garden.

"Whoa! Whoa!" Jem jerked the rein and Maggie felt the collar cut deeply into her throat. "I have to get my bearings." He wrapped the lead round his forearm and shaded his eyes with the other hand. "To the left. We move to the left. Get going you two lazy good-for-nothing sluggards." His crop bit into Maggie's shoulder. She tossed her head and glanced at her companion. The bunny was still grinning. Her teeth gleamed and the ragged tousle of curls bounced beguilingly about her narrow shoulders. She was keen to be off and her legs, much longer than those of the petite Maggie, bounded with long graceful strides, one stride to every two of Maggie's.

With Jem encouraging them from the rear, the two girls galloped across the undulating lawn in the direction he had chosen. Maggie's eyes were streaming. Her shoulders ached and her legs were tired, but she had to keep up with bunny number six.

They followed a path that swept in a wide arc across the lawn before disappearing through an arch cut into a ancient yew hedge. Once through the arch, a dimness, cool and green, settled over the galloping girls. After the brilliant sunshine of the open ground shade now enveloped them, soft and chilly.

The sudden change in temperature made Maggie shiver. She blinked away the tears that misted her eyes and gasped at the view that lay before her. A lake, large and luminous, lapped against a rocky bank, the water slate grey. Willows, gnarled and twisted, trailed tendrils smothered in new green leaf into the chilly depths. Brash and noisy, only a few feet from where they stood, a waterfall tumbled over a solid slab of rock. A glittering sheet of silver broke into mounds of spumy foam ten feet below.

The lake narrowed before reaching the falls, and a bridge, solid but elegant, arched over the water, echoing the roar of the falls. The bank on which the girls stood sloped gently, and grass, soft and damp, tickled Maggie's feet. Late daffodils stood in irregular clumps, the brilliant yellow of their trumpets, garish in the gloom.

"Get going, you lazy bitches!" Jem's crop cut across the back of their thighs. "You haven't got time to stare at the view. There's work for the pair of you."

Why had he brought them here? Were they going somewhere special? Maggie was eager to know. The image of Troy sucking the redhead, the bunny stretched on *her* rack - Maggie's nipples tingled, her belly was hot with desire.

"Fuck me, Jem! I'm desperate!"

Jem dragged the rein and pulled her head back towards him. His face grimaced down and Maggie saw anger mottling his reddened cheeks.

"I'm not kidding, Jem." The vision of Troy sucking red-gold pussy was vivid in her memory. She blinked prettily, her lashes curled sootily, brushing the dark perfection of her high cheekbones.

Bunny number six sniggered.

Jem glowered, but then what might have been a smile curved his thin lips. The hooded eyes narrowed and he pulled Maggie's head closer to his chest. He ran the hard leather of the crop between her breasts. "If it's a fucking you want Maggie, well that's a lucky chance, 'cos it's a fucking you're about to get. A real, hard, no holds barred sort of fucking. But first it's the crop. I've always been good with the crop."

The tip of the crop tickled over her flesh, tangled in her pussy and jabbed at the slit, damply parted, ready and waiting for the thrust of a thick and rigid rod.

"But we've a little further to go." His voice was brusque. "There's a particular place I have in mind." He loosened his grip slightly on Maggie's lead, absent mindedly ground the crop against her mound, thrust it quickly inside her. Maggie moaned and squirmed on the solid cowhide. Taking little notice of her longing, Jem withdrew the crop, thwacked the impatient backside of the giggling bunny, and they were off once more.

They trotted over the bridge. The boards of solid oak echoed to the pounding of three pairs of feet. The spray from the waterfall spattered the naked flesh of the girls. On the opposite bank a rocky path snaked between the gnarled trunks of old willows, disappearing behind a clump and reappearing, dark and mysterious, dank and shivery.

Still Jem urged them onwards. "We're going somewhere just a little bit special. Somewhere Damien showed me yesterday."

Wherever it could, the path clung to the edge of the lake. When they left the bridge Maggie noticed it was rough, natural stone, but gradually its texture was changing. Slowly the stones were becoming smoother, the pieces still small, but dressed paving, neatly laid, tapped into place with precision and dexterity. As the group progressed so the stones turned into slabs grew in size, larger pieces replaced the small, and the surface was smooth as glass.

This path was man-made and had a purpose. It was leading to something. The willows hung heavily over the water, moorhens skittered on the surface leaving whorls and eddies in their wake. Her attention distracted by these water birds, Maggie felt rather than heard the bunny catch her breath.

A temple! Was it a temple?

A flight of steps, six or maybe more, cut from the same stone as the path, curved upwards. They rose with an elegant grace towards a columned entrance. The columns were fluted, supporting an architrave, massive but well-proportioned. Maggie gazed with wonder at what she saw.

"It's beautiful, Jem. Are we going in? Will it be all right? I mean, perhaps it's a holy place!"

A short bark of laughter rang out. "It's a folly, you fool. Eighteenth century. See the date carved above the door - 1720 - built by the original owner of the house, I should think."

Jem thwacked Maggie's backside with the crop.

"Get up those steps. There's only one thing this particular temple's dedicated to, Maggie, and once you get inside you'll understand what that is. And when you next see Damien, you'll thank him for discovering it.

14: Jo Returns To Dropwell - And Daisy Is Left In The Stable

Damien's heavy body lolloped along, blocking the view ahead for Daisy and Jo.

Jo had been on her feet since dawn. Would she ever be allowed to rest? She was beginning to doubt it. She hadn't had much rest last night, either, tied up with Daisy and CJ in the corral. And just what had happened to CJ? She had been spirited away first thing and Jo hadn't set eyes on her since.

Daisy's face was beetroot, her ample breasts heaving, her shoulders drooping with exhaustion. The body paint, so carefully applied by the bunny number three, still glowed, splendid on the girl's ample curves.

"Excuse me," panted Jo. "Have we got much further to go?"

There was no reply. The lump of male flesh in front of them seemed to be deaf - or dumb at least. Jo was sure he understood every word spoken, but, for some reason of his own, chose not to answer. How much further was he taking them? The wood was on their right. The track they were following skirted the southern edge of the trees and now was beginning to curve northwards, then sloping upwards.

They rounded the bend, Damien in front, two bare-titted, bare-arsed girls on leather leashes following. Though bit and bridle had been removed, their arms were sheathed behind their backs, pony strapping crisscrossed their bodies, and a tight thong tugged between their pounding thighs.

Straight ahead stood an archway and on either side loomed imposing walls twenty feet high. The entrance through the archway was barred by tall wooden gates but as they approached the gates opened, slowly, heavily, creaking on their hinges, and Damien lumbered through. The girls trotted after him.

"It's Dropwell Park!" said Daisy excitedly.

No sooner were they safely in the courtyard, than the gates slammed behind them with a horrid finality. Damien tugged on the leads and the two girls drew to halt. Jo glanced at Daisy and saw with surprise that she was beaming with pleasure.

"I've always wanted to visit this place," she said.

"Well, you're visiting now. I'd much rather not be here at all."

Daisy frowned. "Why not, Jo? It's a lovely house and this was where you were working only yesterday."

"Exactly Daisy. That's the reason. Could be very embarrassing!"

"No talking! No talking!" came a new voice, low and menacing. "Haven't you ponies been taught anything yet?" The owner of the voice emerged from the shadows. Neither Daisy nor Jo had noticed him until he stepped from the darkness into the brilliance of the sunlit courtyard. Solidly built, not particularly tall but broad of shoulder, the man's jeans were tight, his shirt billowed. His hair was shaved close to the skull, and a scar cut across his cheek from eye-socket to ear-lobe.

"Nico!" gulped Jo.

"Hello again. How nice to be remembered by one so luscious." His fingers tweaked Jo's nipples. "But you really will have to learn to keep your pretty mouth shut." He turned to Daisy and glanced appraisingly at her near-naked form. "Well done, Damien," he said at last. "You've brought along a pair of beauties."

Grinning, Damien handed the leads to Nico, saluted, turned on his heel and loped back towards the gates, slamming them shut as he left.

Jo's heart sank. She may not have liked Damien, but at least he seemed harmless. Of Nico, she was not convinced.

They were in a courtyard positioned at the rear of the house. Although Jo had only been at Dropwell a few days, she had explored the immediate surroundings thoroughly. This was the west wing where most of the main rooms were situated: the drawing room, the ballroom, the library. The ground floor windows in this wing were tall and elegant, though none looked out over this yard. Mostly they opened to the south, allowing the light to filter into the cool depths of the old house.

Jo started. Nico had said something but she hadn't caught it. He grabbed their leashes and led the pair of them, Daisy excited, Jo full of trepidation, through another archway, similar to but smaller than the one they had just entered. This led into the stable yard. Jo recognised it immediately. This was the yard her bedroom had overlooked. This was the yard where only yesterday - she could hardly believe it - only yesterday she had first glimpsed Nico and his companion. It was from this very house she had slipped, full of curiosity, hurried across these same cobbles, in pursuit of those two men. Then, except for having lost her job, she hadn't a care in the world. Then she had been free. Now look at her.

Yesterday the stables had been just that to Jo - stables. But after her morning's experience as a pony girl, she looked on them with fresh eyes. Yesterday they had been empty, not a horse or pony in sight. Today things were different. Fresh straw lay heaped behind the half-open doors, and she glimpsed heads nodding in the darkness. But these were not the heads of horses. These heads were small, the hair glossy and the colour of ripe corn or berries in autumn. Here were girls, girls she had probably last seen in the corral. Now they were tethered and chained in stalls awaiting Nico to impose his training regime.

Nico ran rough fingers down Jo's stomach, stroked the smooth skin of her naked puss. "I have such plans for you," he said, and tickled the tips of his fingers into the folds of her cunt where the tight strap dug into her. "Wait there. I'll be back soon."

Keeping a firm hold of Daisy's leash, he slung Jo's over a post, tied it with one hand and tested the knot. Under no circumstances was this knot likely to slip. "I won't keep you long." His dark eyes glinted beneath the heavy brows. "This one," he pulled on Daisy's leash, "this one will be joining the others in the stables, but you I'm taking elsewhere." With a final squeeze of her sex that brought tears to Jo's eyes, he left her and strode across the yard, dragging Daisy behind him.

He opened the half-door to the stable. A sound of shuffling feet whispered from the straw-strewn stalls. Jo could see Daisy was reluctant, but still she followed Nico into the stable. He tethered her to an iron ring in the vacant stall by the entrance. Daisy turned big eyes on Jo in mute appeal, but what could Jo do? She shrugged her shoulders in a hopeless gesture and waited for Nico to return.

Nico seemed to have little interest in the girls in the stables. Firmly bolting the half-stable door behind him, he hurried to where Jo waited, looked her up and down, and smiled a slow and calculating smile. Releasing her from the post, he walked towards the house.

Was he planning to take her in there? Was even Nico prepared to contemplate something so bold? What if the housekeeper was still in residence? Jo shivered and felt sick. She trotted after him, arms tightly sheathed, eyes nervously scanning the building. Glancing up, she saw, high above her head, the window of her room, the room she had slept in so happily, and had called home for such a short period of time.

She eyed the house anxiously. Her tummy tightened and she tried to hold back. But Nico was too strong. He dragged her round the corner. They were approaching over the gravel of the drive, heading towards the main entrance. There, only a few yards away, was the foot of the grand flight of steps leading to the front door. Jo trembled with mortification. Her feet tripped unsteadily, the buckle of the sheath dug into the soft flesh above her elbows and the cunt strap dragged, pulling tighter and tighter with every reluctant step that took her closer towards that door.

Jo knew the house was empty as soon as they entered. It felt different. Relief washed over her. But the silence was oppressive. This house, which only yesterday she had been sad to leave, felt strangely threatening.

If she had not been so caught up in her own anxieties the strange sounds, scrabbling and tittering, that had tracked her progress from stable yard to steps, would have caused her concern. Now, suddenly, the sounds became unignorable. Voices giggled and whispered behind her. Jo tried to look round, but Nico had tight hold of her lead. All she could see from the corner of her eye, were two silhouettes, hunched shadows, dancing on the buttermilk paint of the wall.

Jo's nerves, already on edge, tautened. She quivered from head to foot. She wanted to run, to escape from this strange place with its weird noises, and return to the bright sunlight and fresh air. She opened her mouth to shout, "Run, Nico!" But no sound came out. She felt frozen to the spot.

Suddenly, two figures, screeching and yelling, cavorted in front of her. They skipped and screamed, scampered on either side, mouthed obscenities, gesticulated freely. And with energetic leaps and bounds a pair of bunnies threw themselves at Nico's feet.

"Hutch bunnies," gasped Jo. "It's only a pair of hutch bunnies." She wanted to giggle. Those damn bunnies seemed to get everywhere.

Prostrating themselves in front of Nico, their foreheads brushing the wooden floor which Jo herself, on hands and knees, had helped polish, they simpered and begged. "We're here, Nico. Please, Nico, how can we help?"

"A couple of willing helpers, I see," said Nico, glancing down at them. He stood, arms akimbo, looking from the bunnies to Jo.

What Jo was looking at made her blush. A pussy chain, hanging loose, attached to a hasp, nestled, bright, shiny and tantalising, in each bunch of black curls. The chain was there to be fastened, drawn tight, to drag the dangling lips close together, to bite into the soft and pliable flesh that hung between each bunny's legs. Fascinated, Jo glanced down at the inflamed flesh of her own mound. The cunt strap, fixed in place at dawn, had made her skin red, biting into the flesh, making it glow. Her own tender pussy lips gaped, a pink slash startling against the gleaming gold of the paint that decorated her belly.

"We will proceed," ordered Nico, his voice soft but urgent.

Giggling, the two bunnies stayed where they were.

"I said, proceed!" His voice was loud now and angry. He lashed out at the bunnies, booted one on the thigh, the other on her shoulder. As if this was the signal they had been waiting for, they sprang into action. With a wiggle of bottoms and waggle of shoulders, they crawled slowly down the length of the hallway, ankle and wrist manacles click-clacking as they went. They crawled past the door that led into the drawing room, past the door that led into the dining room. They ignored the library. Awkwardly they continued, only pausing, panting like two patient, well-trained Labradors, when they reached the door that led into the billiard room.

Nico's fist still firmly clutched Jo's lead. She looked from the bunnies to Nico and noticed his eyes had narrowed to slits. His throat vibrated, his shoulders lifted in a massive heave, a noise, more of a grunt than a snort, came from his mouth. The bunnies must done something right, thought Jo, for this was Nico smiling, laughing even. He was pleased with them.

Lifting their heads from the floor, the bunnies glanced over their shoulders. Nico nodded. "Okay, I've already sussed this place out, and you're right, snooker it is." He strode down the hall, the bare floor echoing to the thud of his boots. The whip dangled from his hip and the black jeans clung to the tightly muscled moons of his buttocks. With her sheathed arms bouncing against her own bottom, Jo hurried after him towards the billiard room.

The billiard room, the billiard room, there was something about the billiard room. She racked her brains. Why was he taking her to the billiard room, and why, Jo wondered, why did mention of the billiard room ring bells? Frowning, she concentrated hard, trying to remember what it could be. Of course! Yesterday! When her boss told her her services were no longer required - he had mentioned something about the billiard room, equipment being brought, something like that.

Nico was extracting a small key from the back pocket of those jeans. Jo stared. The key shone in Nico's palm. He turned it a couple of times.

The door of the billiard room swung open and light from windows, blinds half-drawn, flooded into the hallway. Jo blinked, but Nico was already striding through the open doorway, dragging her after him. Still giggling, the bunnies brought up the rear. The door slammed shut and the key turned in the lock. There would be no easy escape from this room.

It was large and surprisingly bare. The walls were dark, panelled in oak, the ceiling decorated with ornate plaster work. Billiard cues were stacked in racks on the end wall, and the centre of the room was filled by a table. It was huge. Its surface was smooth, flat and brilliant green. The wooden surround gleamed darkly with years of polishing. Woven pockets hung from each corner, two more dangled at the centre point of each side. In these pockets, curled waiting, were lengths of fine linked chain.

Jo looked more calmly at the rest of the room. The walls were panelled, and the wood was dark oak, but this time she noticed, set into the panelling, about four foot from the ground and at intervals of approximately ten feet or so, were rings, solid looking rings, made of iron, painted glossy black. Her gaze flickered from the rings to the chain. She shivered; a frisson of expectation tingled in her naked pussy. The rings and the chains were designed for each other. Those rings were intended for the chaining of girls.

The bunnies had scampered into the room behind her, and it was to them that Nico's attention now turned. First, he led Jo to one of the rings and secured her by the leash, then turned towards the two giggling girls. They squatted, thighs spread, displaying their moist and open sex, the pussy chain hung, brushing the wooden surface of the floor. Their hands dangled between their knees, their eyes sparkled and they watched Nico approach with delight.

His whip, no longer attached to the loop of his belt, was grasped firmly in his fist, his knuckles white with pressure. One bunny hung her head to hide the silly grin that spread from ear to ear. The other sniggered and wriggled her bottom. Two pairs of be-ringed tits, dusky-skinned, the nipples deep crimson, alert and perky, bounced and swayed. The one with the silly grin glanced at her companion, and snorts of laughter racked their supple young bodies.

It was the grinner that Nico lunged towards. Grabbing hold of her by the ear, he pulled her, squealing, away from her companion, and dumped her against the wall. She settled, inquisitive eyes following Nico's every move. She exuded an air of excited expectancy.

Jo watched enthralled.

Nico propped his whip against the edge of the table. His hand delved into one of the centre pockets. A length of fine chain hung from his fingers. Weighing it thoughtfully, he looked from the chain to the bunny. He smiled, a slow self-satisfied smile, and sauntered back towards her. The rings hanging from each nipple tinkled as the bunny took deep and steadying breaths. The chain in Nico's palm jangled. He leant towards the grinning girl, threaded the chain through the nipple rings, spun her round, and pulled her by the chain towards one of the wall rings. The bunny scampered after him. Unclasping the fetter on the wall, he slid the chain onto the open hasp and snapped it shut. The girl stood on tip-toe, half-suspended by her nipples.

Yanking her arms behind her, Nico snapped another piece of chain between her wrist manacles. He stepped back, regarded her critically, stepped forward and spread her straining legs wider with the toe of his boot. He picked up his whip and, using the handle as a cane, thwacked it onto the firm round split cleft of her bottom. The bunny whimpered softly.

If he could treat that bunny in such a manner, thought Jo, what treatment did he have in store for her? Her heart thundered in her chest. There was no way Jo intended anything like that to happen.

But the sight of the chained and punished bunny was having a strange effect. Her tits tingled at the thought of rings being pierced through them. She imagined such rings attached to something immovable, of her own nipples being stretched and distorted like those of the bunny. A liquid heat burned in the base of her belly.

A shuffling and giggling brought Jo back down to earth. Nico had hold of the other bunny. She was sitting on the floor, legs spread wide, her arms stretched above her head. Nico was busy securing her wrists to a wall ring. She sat there grinning, watching Nico with bright eager eyes as he extracted something from the rack of billiard cues. It was an iron bar, quite short but rigid. The bunny spread her legs wide and Nico attached the bar to ankle cuffs, forcing her legs to stay flat and gaping on the wooden floor. He knelt between her knees, the bunny gasped and winked at him as his fingers fiddled with her cunt chain.

Jo watched fascinated. He was shortening the chain, pulling the dangling lips closer and the holes piercing the moist crimson flesh stretched. The bunny caught her breath and a small tear ran down her olive cheek.

"What do you think of it so far, sweetheart?" Nico grinned at Jo, his gaze fixed on her breasts. He didn't need an answer. Jo's erect nipples were traitors to her thoughts. "You could do with some rings hanging from those stiff little teats."

Jo struggled and squirmed. Nico's breath was hot on her shoulder. He pressed close, squashing her ample breasts with the muscles of his chest. He pulled on the buckles of the arm sheath, loosening them, allowing the hard tube of leather to fall away. Jo's arms were free for the first time since dawn. Then he unfastened the remaining buckles. The pony strapping fell from her body. Slowly, he undid her leash. Jo was free. Blood pumped back into flesh deadened by the tightness of the costume. Her whole body tingled, her mind raced.

Without thinking too clearly, she decided to take this opportunity, make a run for it. Like a cat loosed from a cage, she darted away from Nico, ran round the other side of the table and grabbed a billiard cue from the wall.

Nico's face glowed puce with an incandescent rage. "You bitch!" He hurled himself round the table in hot pursuit. "There's no way you can escape from this room," he yelled.

"Oh no? Just try me, sunshine! Come any closer and I'll belt you with this." Jo swung the billiard cue above her head. The plume of perfumed lilac, previously so proud and pretty, now hung limp from its fixing in the strawberry blonde hair, it dangled, decrepit and discouraged, behind Jo's left ear.

The whip buzzed angrily in Nico's hand. It sang, it flew, and like an angry hornet aimed directly for Jo's tits. She leapt to one side. The whip missed by inches. She brandished the cue, strode towards Nico. Now, he was the only barrier between herself and the door, the door that was her only means of escape. She glared boldly at him. Her gaze was stern, her resolve firm, her heart fluttering.

The expression in Nico's eyes was disturbing. He was no longer chasing her. He almost seemed to be begging her to come closer. Jo gripped the cue tightly. No matter his attitude, she was prepared, ready to bring her weapon down with a mighty thwack on the shoulder that controlled that stinging whip.

Poised and prepared, she stepped forward. Her long legs shook under her, her bare bottom quivered. Stripped of all dignity, shivering at the enormity of what she planned to do, Jo only had eyes for her prey.

But she had forgotten the hutch bunnies.

In her determination to overcome her persecutor, to defeat once and for all at least *this* man, the one who had tied her up, humiliated her, brought her to this place, Jo forgot entirely there were others in this same room. Chained to the wall, yes, immobile perhaps, but keen initiates in the ways of the camp, Nico's compatriots, his assistants, his kinsfolk.

One, face pressed to the wall, was helpless - blind to what was happening. But the other, wrists chained, legs spread, feet jutting across the polished floor of the billiard room, was watching all the action. She had kept very quiet, her bright-eyed gaze following every move Jo made. And as the slender girl, blonde hair dishevelled, arms raised, eyes staring, the combined weight of the cue and melon breasts swinging in agitation, caused her to teeter, she made her move. She thrust her bottom hard against the wall, squirmed rounded hips in preparation and, with the inexorable momentum of a pendulum, swung feet into action.

The pole, rigid and straight, binding her feet apart, swept over the glossy surface of the floor, carried on sweeping until, swinging her legs with an animal energy, she caught Jo where the ankle joins the shin. With a yelp of excruciating pain, Jo tripped, she stumbled and staggered, unbalanced and caught off guard. The cue catapulted from her clutch, and with arms flailing, knees collapsing, and mind spinning with alarm, she tumbled, sprawled flat on her face, and skidded over the polished surface of the floor. Her naked body only came to a halt when the crown of her blonde head collided with the cap of Nico's well-burnished boot.

15: Training In The Temple

The thought of what might be inside the temple captivated Maggie.

Together, she and bunny number six bounded up the steps, their naked rumps glimmering in the pale and watery light. The heavy doors barring the entrance were slightly ajar, and when Maggie pushed with her shoulder, they swung open and allowed the girls to step into a surprisingly bright, circular interior. Light poured in through a glass dome high above. The floor was marble and cool to her bare feet, cooler even than the path outside. Her toes curled at the chill of its touch.

She gazed round in awe and goggled at what she saw. Statues of all sizes lined the walls. Life size figures in stone writhed in frozen ecstasy, and tiny ones, so small Maggie could have held them in the palm of her hand, nestled in niches or seemed to cling to ropes and chains dangling from the rim of the dome.

Many of the figures were female, all bound and gagged or restrained by implements carved in the stone. They crouched, they crawled, they strained in scaffolding or bowed low under the weight of stock-like frames. They varied in colour from the purest and whitest of marble to the dull grey of lead. Beautifully carved in intimate detail by craftsmen who knew their work, ropes and chains of stone twined round delicate ankles, bound narrow wrists and girdled waists that would never thicken with age. Each one was feminine perfection personified.

One in particular caught Maggie's attention. The figure was straddled over a bar. The bar cut deeply into the soft mound of her belly. The intricacy of her pussy was fully displayed, making Maggie gasp at the delicacy of the detail. She smiled to herself. This one reminded her of days with Troy, of her own frame, of the chastisement he daily administered. She longed to be back with him to feel his whip stroking her buttocks, her body responding to every lash with growing desire.

And then the vision of that bunny tied to her rack, and that red-headed interloper, intoxicating her man with her slippery cunt, flashed vivid and real in her mind's eye. Her tummy churned at the memory and her resolve strengthened.

Maggie stepped forward, dragging the bunny with her. "Just look at these darling little things, Jem. Did you ever see anything so sweet?" She indicated one of the small statuettes. It was perfect, a real girl in miniature. "Look at the face, the tits, the cunny. All there. Nothing's been left out. What is this place, Jem? Who does it belong to?"

"It's a folly, I told you. It belongs to the house. It's dedicated to the goddesses of bondage, flagellation and fucking, whoever they may be - and you two are about to be the latest offerings."

Jem hauled the two girls together and drove them towards the centre of the temple. A squat slab of marble, cold and hard, stood directly under the glass dome. Pillars supporting an arch of stone sprang from either side of the slab. They swept upwards, reaching towards the cupola, a filigree of carving decorating the upward sweep. Each carving represented a tiny figure, male and female, intertwined, bodies merging and melding, the flesh so expertly moulded it seemed almost to breathe.

Plump and glossy, these carvings entangled voluptuously, the delicate touch of a master craftsman evident in every detail. Each cunt was lovingly featured, every cock full, rigid and active. Maggie stared, entranced, at these erotic posturings. She licked dry lips and scratched sharp and tapering fingernails over the tingling flesh of her bottom. A moist heat oozed between her thighs.

Jem stroked the writhing figures. His grubby fingers prodded flesh that would never yield to his touch. With hooded eyes glazed, he turned and stared at the two girls panting on the ends of their leashes. His face was hard, the expression cold.

"You," he said, letting go of the bunny's leash, "you get up on the slab. And stand, legs apart, head up, here, underneath the arch." He patted the glassy coldness of the slab.

The bunny scrambled to obey, more than willing. She perched her bottom on the edge of the platform, pushed with her chained fists, and levered herself onto the smooth surface. Once on the marble, her dark tumble of hair contrasting vividly with the whiteness of the stone, she rolled onto her knees and pushed herself up gracefully.

Cautiously she spread her legs, toes gripping at the marble. Her eyes widened with alarm when one foot skidded, and she began to lose her balance. Letting go of Maggie's lead, Jem grabbed the bunny's ankle and steadied her, preventing her gliding headlong off the slab. Then he clambered onto the marble to join her. He grasped the lead dangling from her collar and secured it high up at the top of the arch.

"That should stop any more acrobatics." He tugged on the leather. The bunny's head jerked up and her breasts, dark-nippled and dusky-skinned, jutted proudly, desire plumping the nipples into firm, juicily dark cherries. The rings piercing each nipple pricked the puckered skin, and the gold chains hanging from them glittered in the dazzling sunlight pouring through the shimmering dome.

Jem sank to his knees and spread her legs, then selected two pieces of rope hanging from his leather belt and tied each ankle wide apart to the uprights of the arch. The bunny grinned and waggled her hips in his face. He slapped her belly and jabbed at the soft flesh nestling between the spread thighs.

Then he jumped to the floor, turning to Maggie. "Your turn. Up on the slab. Kneel between the other girl's legs. I want your bum sticking right up in the air. I want to be able to spread those cheeks wide." He pinched the dimpled flesh with his sharp fingers.

Maggie obeyed quickly. She wanted to demonstrate that if Troy thought he could drop her for another woman whenever he felt like it, he was wrong. She'd show him. She'd give Jem the best fucking of his life. She wanted him to fuck her, arse, cunt, mouth, she didn't mind where. By the time she had finished with him, Jem would not be able to stop boasting to the others how he'd fucked her, Troy's real woman. Fucked her so well, Troy would remember how good she was, and be sorry he ever let her go. She squeezed the cheeks of her bottom and flexed the muscles of her cunt. Her muscle control was perfect.

Maggie perched her bottom on the edge of the slab and pushed herself up, copying the bunny's method, taking the opportunity to display herself comprehensively. She was light and strong and was soon swinging her legs from the floor. She slithered her bottom over the slab and lay on her back, her shoulder blades contracting at the touch of the touch of the cold marble. She counted to three, "one, two, three - heave." Her body flipped over. Her breasts, warm and soft, squashed against the chilly stone surface and her tummy clenched at its touch.

Putting her forehead to the marble, her arms still firmly fixed in the small of her back, she slowly, very slowly, drew her knees forward. Her torso lifted, her bottom waved in the air, her face remained on the cold surface. But out the corner of her eye, she could just see one bunny foot securely bound to the base of the stone arch.

"Not quite where I want you." Jem lashed at her exposed and vulnerable backside with the crop. "Slide forward and spread your knees." His hand pushed hard on her bottom. "I want your fanny just this side of that other cunt."

Maggie shuffled her knees, and slid slowly into the position Jem demanded. She understood what he was after. She was going to be fucked while the bunny, suspended from the stone arch, her body stretched her legs spread, was about to be sucked - just like Troy had been sucking that red-haired bitch.

Maggie's determination grew. "Are you ready Jem?" she said, her voice low and seductive. "My cunny's fair streaming for the touch of cock."

Both girls were ready, awaiting Jem's attention. Jem was concentrating on their sweet young bodies. None of the occupants of the folly heard the door creak slowly open. They were too engrossed to notice a large figure hovering in the shadows, watching every move Jem made with fascinated interest.

Jem was standing to one side of the girls. When Maggie turned her head, resting her cheek on the marble, she could see him. His fingers were playing with the front of his jeans. The zip was tight over a massive bulge. He pulled decisively on the brass tongue and Maggie stared wide-eyed at the prick which sprang from within. It swayed and glistened. The tip was deep red. The shaft was thick and lay heavily in the palm of his hand. His fingers manipulated the silky skin. Maggie gulped and closed her eyes. Surely he didn't intend to make that monster grow to even greater lengths? But when she looked again, he had disappeared from her view.

"Wow," she heard the bunny's breathy voice say, "come on, big boy, suck me, suck me." This was the first time Maggie had heard the bunny speak. Obviously something extraordinary was needed to make that one express an opinion.

Jem's crop clattered to the floor. He was climbing onto the slab, joining the boldly displayed pair of girls. Was the action about to start at last? Maggie wriggled her bottom, thrusting it further up into the air.

She had heard about Jem's reputation when it came to fucking. Girls in the camp had testified to his speed. What Jem wanted he took, fast and furiously. He certainly had no intention of hanging around. He was kneeling between her thighs, his fingers stroking the split separating the cheeks of her bottom. The fingers spread over the silky flesh, pulled the cheeks apart, nuzzled deep into her furrow. Maggie gasped as one finger sank into her cunt, another squirmed its way through the rosebud of her bottom.

Jem worked both fingers hard, screwing them deep inside her. Maggie's juices flowed. Her eyes glazed, her belly had grown hot. Her breasts felt big, swollen with desire, the dark nipples, darker still, plump and lush. After one last thrust, Jem's fingers withdraw. Her heart was beating fast, her fingers, shackled in the small of her back, scrabbled at thin air, desperately feeling for him.

Where had that big cock gone?

Now it brushed the delicate skin on the inside of her thigh. It was hard, rigid, and hot and felt even bigger than when first she glimpsed it. His fingers grasped her gaping lips, engorged and succulent, and tugged and pinched the delicate flesh. She was wet, dripping with desire. The tips of her fingers, resting on the base of her spine, curled in anticipation. Jem's tightly muscled body pressed onto her back. Gladly, she accepted his weight.

"Suck me, suck me," hissed the bunny's voice above.

Maggie heard Jem's mouth slavering on the girl's slippery slit. A moan of pleasure whispered from the bunny's lips. The sound tore at Maggie's loins. "Fuck me, Jem. Fuck me NOW!" she pleaded.

He entered her with the suddenness and force of a ramrod. Maggie's knees lifted from the marble and for a moment her whole body quivered on the tip of that pounding cock. He lunged inside her, grabbed hold of both breasts, his fingers squeezing the tender nipples, pinching them until they perched like throbbing pinnacles. Her tits were two glowing moons. His cock slid and plunged. His whole body engulfed her.

Concentrating on her own pleasure, Maggie could still hear his tongue, busy licking and sucking at the bunny's cunt. Groans and grunts of enjoyment drooled from the girl's lips, and drops of juice fell onto Maggie's collared neck.

The prick was moving fast. His balls pounded her thighs. Her clit pulsated. Beads of perspiration ran between her breasts. Waves of pleasure filled her belly. The non-stop pumping of Jem's prick swamped her with such desire that, had she been in control of her thoughts, she would have been shocked at herself.

But she was beyond control. A liquid heat glowed in her loins, her breath came in gasps, her eyes stared glassily at the white of the cold marble. She was unseeing, unhearing, Maggie's whole being was concentrated in her pussy. Pulses of pleasure pricked and gushed. Her cunt vibrated with undiluted pleasure. Wave after wave of rapture surged through her. The bunny was crying out in ecstasy. Jem, his head buried in her soggy crotch, grunted his fulfilment in a muffled throbbing choke.

The three agitated bodies relaxed and Maggie could feel the warm wet trickle of Jem's load oozing from the passion of her soft lips.

She slumped onto the marble slab. The bunny, suspended by ropes, subsided onto their support. Exhausted, weak with pleasure, the two girls were unable to move.

The sudden bite of the crop on Maggie's sodden slit made her cry out. Jem's voice was harsh and abrupt. "Get up you lazy bitch," he yelled. "Now the fucking's over, now we can get on with some serious training." At the same time, the crop lashed at the bunny's legs.

Once again unheard, the door to the temple creaked on its hinges, and Damien, pleased with what he'd seen, slipped away into the darkness under the trees.

16: Davy Goes looking For Damien And Finds Daisy

The stable felt cool after the hot sun in the yard and Daisy pressed her body, warm and sweaty from the constant activity of the day, against the cold stone wall to which her lead was fastened. Gradually, she took in her surroundings. There was not much to see. She was in a stall. It was the first one next to the main entrance. Two of the walls were outer and made of stone, the door, was wooden with slats, and a high partition separated her from whatever lay on the other side.

Even Daisy understood that in this place, it was likely that every stall in the stable contained a tethered girl like herself. She had noticed bridled heads peering through the slats in the doors when Nico thrust her in here. She could hear feet shuffling and some light humming. But there was no conversation.

"Is there anybody there?" Daisy called softly, very softly. There was no reply. The small noises she had noticed earlier, ceased. The only sound was the twittering of birds perched high in the rafters.

Despondent, Daisy's attention turned back to her own stall. A bench was fixed along one wall. A manger stood at the far end. A bridle hung above it. Daisy regarded this with interest. She had enjoyed her morning's training in pony discipline. With Jem in charge, she would enjoy anything. He was so clever, so masterful, so manly. The thought of him, the memory of his touch on her flesh, the sound of his voice, all these things sent quivers of pleasure through Daisy. Her full breasts, the paint glimmering in the dim light of the stable, her nipples, the scarlet paint glowing, swelled and plumped. With arms tightly sheathed she squeezed and rubbed her thighs together, and tingles of pleasure rippled through her aching loins.

Surrounded by girls, Daisy still felt lonely. CJ had been taken away at dawn, now Jo had disappeared. Daisy sniffed. The big bloke, the one who never said anything - Damien - had brought them here and then even he had gone away again. Daisy felt abandoned and frustrated. She needed a fuck. She'd have liked it to be Jem. But, at this moment, anybody would do.

In the distance she heard a loud bang.

She strained her ears. Feet thudded on the cobbles. A voice rang out, sharp and annoyed. "Damien! Damien! Where the hell are you, Damien? I told you to come straight back to the camp." The lock on the outer door of the stables slid back. Somebody had entered the building. The door to

Daisy's stall, the first one in the long line, swung open.

"Well, hello, sweetheart. You're one of the ponies Damien brought up here aren't you?"

Daisy nodded.

"So where is he? My instructions to him were quite clear. I said not to hang around here gawping. I told him to come straight back. Where is the little ray of sunshine? And come to that, where's Nico?"

Daisy gazed at Davy. He was standing in the doorway to her stall. He looked her up and down, then shaded his eyes and stared into the dimness of the stable.

"Can you tell me where everybody's got to, darling?" He ambled into Daisy's stall, his hand reaching out to touch the scarlet-painted nipples. Daisy shuddered.

"Damien's not here," she mumbled, thrusting her nipples into Davy's palm. He cupped the ample breasts, squeezing the flesh with sharp fingers. "He brought us here, me and Jo, and then he left, I don't know where." She squirmed as Davy pinched the rigid thimbles perched erect on the silver moons of her breasts.

"And Nico, do you know where Nico is?" Davy was standing close now. His slight but muscular body pressed against the plump warm curve of Daisy's belly.

"He - he - took Jo," Daisy gasped as his fingers kneaded the responsive flesh. "He took Jo into the house, I think." She moaned as his expert fingers glided from her breasts, then his strong arms were pulling her close, his hands grasping the peachy mounds of her bum. She could feel the solid rod of Davy's cock nudging her thigh. Daisy spread her legs in happy expectation.

"Ah-ha! You're all excited as a pony girl are you? If it's pony gear you like, you're in the right place." Davy shoved her away and Daisy staggered, disappointment crushing her.

Davy retreated a couple of paces and scrutinised her closely. Sunlight glanced through high, dust-smeared windows and Daisy shone. Her body paint gleamed, the pony strapping clung to every curve. Her hair, the scarlet ribbons unwinding from the ringlets, drooped about her shoulders in golden waves. She stared back at Davy from soft grey eyes, eyes that sparkled with flashes of brilliant blue.

Her lips pouted their disappointment. She wriggled on her lead, thrusting her pussy towards Davy. He glanced at the girl-harness hanging on the wall, rattled it so that it jangled enticingly.

The excited girl was staring already, her eyes big with desire. Davy unfastened her leash and led her, trembling, from the stall. She followed, demure but perky, and they proceeded along the passageway between the other stalls.

The stable was long. At the far end a window, set high up in the old stone wall, allowed dusty light to filter into the murky depths. Beneath this window was a mounting block. It was wide, wooden and padded with leather. Shallow steps led up one side, rings to tether a horse were embedded in one end. It was fixed firmly to the floor and was about three foot high.

Davy stopped and drew Daisy close to the block. Untangling the bridle, he raised it above her head and it slid over the buttery-gold curls. He fastened it in place. The straps crossed the bridge of her nose, hugged her plump cheeks, cut over her ears, and he buckled them securely at the back of her head.

Tongue protruding in concentration, he gave a final adjustment to the straps. Shoving his fingers between her lips Davy inserted the curb-bit, tugging it into place until Daisy's mouth yawned wide. She shook her pretty head and the bridle tinkled. Davy straightened the straps and buckles until the girl-harness fitted snug and tight.

Daisy was becoming impatient. Her arms were sheathed, her face was smothered by bridle. What did Davy plan next? All she wanted was a fuck. He tied the reins to one of the rings set into the block and leapt onto the padded surface, his legs dangled on either side as if seated on a pony as he tugged on the rein, pulling her closer.

"Climb the steps girl, climb the steps."

Daisy was aghast. She'd fall. She had nothing to catch hold of. Her arms were sheathed. But, terrified, she did as she was told. Precariously she mounted, one step at a time. One foot, then both planted on each step. She climbed with infinite care. Davy was grinning. Did he want her to fall? Daisy became all the more determined to perform well. Her breasts and bottom wobbled with the effort. Her feet were bare, which was a good thing, it allowed her to use her toes to grip. The mounting block was solid and wide and for this she was grateful. She reached the top. She stood over the seated Davy and he smiled up at her.

"Sit down, girlie. Sit down. I may have a long prick, but not that long. If you and I are going to make ends meet, you'll have to sit down here, on top of me." Davy pointed at the cock protruding from his unzipped jeans.

Daisy stared in disbelief. Was he serious?

He was. He sat there, legs dangling on either side of the block, his cock thrusting towards her, long, curved and very inviting. Daisy moaned behind her bit. She wanted some cock, and soon. She swayed where she stood, her eyes filling with tears. She was a pitiful sight and Davy held out his arms to her. Without thinking, she tipped gratefully into his waiting arms. He caught her by her magnificent breasts. Secure in his grasp she lowered her knees onto the block. The long curved cock waved, glistening and urgent only inches from her pussy. Whimpering, Daisy shuffled forwards. Her tits firmly in Davy's grasp. His thumbs rolled her scarlet nipples, pulling her towards him and she shuffled on her knees.

Her slit was wet and the cock glided into position effortlessly. She sank onto it. She tossed her bridled head, raised her strapped body high and sank once more, exhilarated at sensation of long hard cock sliding deep, deep inside her. Davy was still grinning. His finger tips dug into the soft and pillowing flesh of her breasts.

Daisy squirmed, her plush pussy embedded tightly on the thrusting cock. Her hips rotated, her breasts oscillated, her eyes dilated and darkened. She jiggled her body, she squeezed her cunt, she heaved her ample hips up and down on Davy's rock-hard prick.

The expression on Davy's face changed from impish delight to concentrated pleasure. His mouth fell open, his eyes rolled upwards, his breath came in short sharp gasps. Daisy bounced, she gyrated, she ground her hips hard onto his, her bottom squashed his balls, and the tips of her fingers, protruding from the sheath, tickled his thighs. The muscles in Davy's belly tightened and the spurt of liquid gushed into her. Davy groaned and his shoulders shook. Daisy sighed and bowed her head.

Davy slid out of Daisy and zipped his jeans, pleased with himself. He led Daisy back to her stall and tethered her there, then sauntered out into the sunlight, whistling.

17: Snookered!

Turning the key in the snooker room door, Nico slipped it into the pocket of his jeans, never once taking his eyes off Jo. "Get up." His booted foot pressed hard into her belly, and, smirking, he dragged her to her feet. "Right, now we seem to have got it sorted exactly who is in charge here."

Dishevelled and ashamed, Jo struggled to regain her balance. He had defeated her - not that he could have done it on his own - that giggling bound and be-ringed little slut wriggling her bare bottom on the shiny floorboards, she was the guilty one, the who had tripped her up.

Jo's eyes were huge. "What - what are you going to do?"

"Gag that big mouth of yours for a start." Nico grunted and drew a large round ball of leather from inside his shirt and tossed it from palm to palm. "Until I have a use for it!"

Both bunnies giggled with delight.

"Anyway, I think you quite fancy the being gagged!"

Without thinking, Jo nodded.

Ignoring Jo, Nico released the bunnies from their restraints and hauled them to their feet. Scampering with delight, wriggling their toes and shaking their heads, the two girls charged round the room, whooping and calling. The rings piercing two pairs of nipples and four ear lobes tinkled in the headlong rush. They clapped their hands and spun their small bodies on heels made tough by constant walking in bare feet.

Jo watched them, her gaze transfixed by the sight of these two dusky naked bodies, the gold of their many rings glittering in the filtered sunlight and glancing off the manacles that encircled their necks, wrists, and ankles.

"Enough!" The voice was not angry but was instantly obeyed. The two girls flung themselves at Nico's feet. They were panting, their breasts heaving, their eyes shining with excitement as they awaited orders, impatient to be about their business.

A clinking noise attracted Jo's attention. Her tummy tightened - excitement or fear, she was not sure which. Nico was extracting implements, gags, ropes and straps of leather, from a cupboard concealed within the dark oak panelling of the snooker room wall. Implements appeared from nowhere and joined the chain still nestling in the pockets of the billiard table. He heaped everything onto the smooth green baize, fingering and turning various bits and pieces, examining every item with care. He picked up a strap and sniffed the leather, tested the strength of a rope with strong fists, stroked the lengths of chain between hard fingers.

Jo eyed the chains nervously. For as long as she could remember, her desire had been to chain up others, stand over them, whip in hand, boots stretching to her crotch, gloves clinging to her arms like a second skin, and have some man - or girl, Jo didn't mind which - crawl on all fours to her command. But that was not going to be the case today. She shuffled her feet, nervous and wary, smoothed damp hands over the curve of her generous haunches and wondered how it would feel to be totally restrained.

What Jo found surprising, and was only prepared to admit to herself, was that during the few hours she had spent in the gipsy camp, the touch of leather arm restraints, the clink of chain, the feel of manacles biting her skin, had become enticing. This was unexpected. She was even beginning to relish the idea of Nico taking her, fucking her again, and she in no position to do anything about it. Jo felt her blush deepen. Crimson heat spread from the top of her cheek bones to the tip of tits already heavy with desire.

"You see that, bunnies? She's got herself excited just looking at the gear. She's randy as hell before she's even felt the magic touch." Nico's fingers delved into the pile on the table and a shiver of anticipation ran through the all three girls.

"Let's have a model."

A girl, petite and agile, leapt to her feet, clapped her hands and won the race to stand beside Jo.

"Good. Show her how pleased you are to be my assistant."

The bunny raised her face and stared hard from eyes that were dark and lustrous, and winked, a slow heavy drooping of the eyelid. Her lips parted, her tongue moistened the already damp mouth and a face just on a level with Jo's breasts sank onto skin, aflame with anticipation. The rings dangling from her ears swept over Jo's breasts, breasts that were full and ripe. The tongue made Jo gasp. It shot from between the small white teeth, tickled the puckered skin and trembled on the rosy tip of her right nipple.

It darted and danced. The light and delicate touch of that scarlet tongue was electrifying. Jo's breasts seemed to burst into life, crackle with impulses she had never previously experienced. She felt weak. She leant against the edge of the table, her legs ready to crumple under her.

"Well done!" Nico's fist grabbed the small girl by the hair, dragging her away from Jo's urgent longing. "You've an active tongue there. We'll put it to better use later. First, we're going to get this one nicely trussed up." His voice was slow and throaty. Grabbing Jo's arms, he twisted them behind her back and, with expert efficiency, thrust her face down onto the billiard table.

Jo screamed. She couldn't help it. Her legs kicked, her breasts squashed hard onto the flat surface.

"The gag. You can do that as well."

The small girl, keen to demonstrate her nimbleness, climbed onto the table. The other stayed where she was, awaiting her orders.

"Take the ball and fill her mouth with it." Nico held out his hand to the small girl. She clasped the orb with eager fingers and dropped onto the baize, her knees splayed. Jo's face was twisted, the eyes open, the mouth closed. With a smile of triumph, the bunny first pinched Jo's nose and when her mouth fell open, slipped the hard leather-covered ball between her parted lips.

Shocked, Jo gulped. The ball was harder than she had expected. Her tongue licked the smooth surface. The slightly salty taste of it surprised her.

"Now, girl, how shall we keep that ball in position?"

The bunny sat back on her haunches, head perched to one side, looked first at Jo, then at the pile of equipment. "The face mask, Nico. The black leather one. The one with all the straps and buckles. That'll keep her quiet. And it'll look good next to all this lovely, long, blonde hair." She ran sharp little fingers through Jo's long tresses, draped the glinting hair over her thighs, smoothed it with slow strokes, her eyes alight with envy at the abundance and colour of it.

"What do you think?" he asked the other bunny. "Do you want to give her a hand?"

"Sure!" Taking no notice of the wail of annoyance from her companion, she leapt up and clambered onto the table. She ran on light feet over the baize and selected the face mask. She simpered at Nico, shook her tits at him, the nipple rings jangling, and trotted over to join her friend.

Nico changed his position slightly, stood closer to where Jo's feet hung over the edge of the table. His one hand still gripped her wrists, twisting them in the small of her back, the other hand rested on the back of her calf. His fingers stroked the rounded smoothness of the supple skin. He pinched it lightly and Jo shivered at his touch.

The larger bunny, face mask dangling from her fingers, knelt opposite her companion. The two girls giggled at each other. The hand of the first, the one that had so lovingly stroked Jo's long and silky locks only moments earlier, now twisted them in her fist, bringing tears to Jo's eyes.

Jo couldn't see the mask but she could smell its pungent odour, hear the jingle of the buckles, feel the tension in her two tormentors as they held it over her head. The first pulled Jo's hair high, long and taut, in a tail, scraping it tightly back from her skull. The second dropped the mask, delicately, carefully, over her head while the first fed the blonde hair through a hole and allowed it to cascade in a shower of fine golden strands over the inky blackness of the leather. The contrast was eye-catching.

With Jo's face now hidden, the two bunnies tugged on the straps, snapped buckles into position, plucked supple leather into place over forehead, cheeks and chin. A strap pulled across her mouth. It fitted snugly over the ball and jammed it inside her already gaping jaws. She gasped for breath, breathing heavily through nostrils restricted by the pressure of a nose shield. The tightness of the mask pressed on every part of her skull.

Jo's ears were covered, her eyes shielded. The mask cut into the tender flesh below her brows and on the edge of her lower lids. She could see, dimly, she could breathe with difficulty, she could talk not at all. Her hearing was deadened, all sounds muffled.

But, she realised with amazement, the restrictions placed on these senses had enhanced the remaining one, the sense of touch. The surface of her skin tingled. The nerve-endings quivered and the lightest stroke from a bunny's finger tip sent waves of sensuous pleasure rippling through her.

"Turn her over. Let's take a look at that face - what's left to see of it." Nico let her wrists drop from his clutch.

The bunnies, small but strong, grabbed a wrist and ankle each. They turned her onto her back. They stretched her limbs until her back arched and her mound, shaven and moist, jutted directly at Nico's staring eyes.

He leant towards her and caressed the skin of her inner thigh. Jo shivered and shook. Her whole body throbbed with longing. Without waiting for any order, she thrust her pussy towards Nico. The crimson slit, exposed and quivering, urged his fingers on. His hand, one moment gently caressing, now slapped, a stinging painful thwack on her trembling flesh. Jo moaned behind her mask. The bunnies wriggled their bottoms with pleasure. Nico grinned, then laughed out loud at her disappointment.

"Go get some ropes, girls."

The bunnies clapped their hands and chanted in sing-song voices:

"Ropes, bunnies, ropes.
Thighs, bunnies, thighs.
Thighs, ropes, ropes, thighs,
Stretch them wide, wide, WIDE."

The first hopped skipped and somersaulted across the expanse of table. The second spun on her heel, clapped her hands above her head, whooped and dropped to the surface in a graceful spread-legged split. Together, they scampered across the table, selected long ropes of black silk, the thickness of a man's little finger, and hurried back to their captive.

Startled, and weak with longing, Jo lay where they left her. Through the slits in her mask, she watched their antics, watched as they roped her wrists and pulled her arms wide and bound the ropes to the thick wooden surrounds of the corner pockets. The pressure of the mask, the ache of the ball-gag filling her mouth, she noticed none of that. Her whole mind was concentrated on her pussy. A pussy swollen with lust, dripping with desire, foaming with a sexual frenzy she had never previously known existed.

Then she felt the hands of the two girls dragging on her ankles. With difficulty, she forced her head from the table, held it at an angle, and watched their every move.

Black ropes grasped between their nimble fingers, they knelt at Jo's ankles, clasping them between hands that pinched and pressed and pummelled. Her legs were stretched towards the corners of the table, but even Jo's legs, long and elegant as they were, could not reach. It wasn't physically possible, but this did not stop the bunnies. They looped a rope round each ankle, knotted it with skill, heaved on the ends, pulled the knots tight, bruising the flesh and reddening the golden skin.

In unison they jumped to the ground, the ends of the ropes draped over their shoulders. Like two mariners, they pulled on those ropes, jerking Jo's legs into position, heaving until they were satisfied they could heave no more.

Jo's eyes flickered from side to side. Beneath her mask she could just make out the shapes of both girls busy looping and knotting the ropes around the wooden rims of the corner pockets. Each one wove her own rope through the basket, tugged on the knots, winked at each other, bowed to Nico and climbed back onto the table.

"She's ready, Nico, bound, gagged and primed."

"You're ready, Nico. Well pricked up and ready to go."

"And we're ready, Nico," they sang in unison. "Let's get fucking, Nico!"

Jo could not see Nico, but from where she lay, roped, gagged and almost blinded by the mask, she could hear him moving about the room. There was a muffled thud and then another. The table, solid as it was, creaked. She could feel the vibration of a heavy person moving across the smooth, baize-covered slate. Jo's heart thundered in her breast. Her face was hot. The muscles in her legs and arms, tense. He was standing over her. His feet were bare, his breeches loosened. And protruding from the silky blackness, thick and long, the tip glowing with urgent fullness, his cock waved directly above her head.

He swung the whip from his right hand, hung it lightly over Jo's breasts. She shuddered when it touched the tip of her nipple, a nipple so sensitive that at that touch her bottom jerked, an involuntary movement that pulled hopelessly against the ropes binding her ankles. The bunnies squealed with pleasure. She heard the swoosh of the whip as Nico swung it above his head, heard the sharp intake of breath when the lash landed on first one bunny rump and then the other.

"On your knees, you two." His voice rasped in his throat. "You, get down between her thighs."

Jo heard the thump of a bunny sinking to her knees, felt the soft warmth of female flesh brushing against her inner thigh.

"And, you," the whip sang through the air, cutting the bunny across her breasts. "You get down on her tits. Get nibbling on those swollen buds. Do you think they'll be tasty enough for bunny food?"

"Oh, yes, yes!"

Jo lay completely still. The soft lips and tongue of a bunny applied strokes that were long and languorous to the full, melon-heavy roundness of Jo's breasts. The actions were skilful, her touch sensuous. She purred and murmured her delight as she went about her business. She buried her face between the ample curves. The lickings became more ardent as she lapped at the gold-painted flesh. Her small white teeth nipped at the succulent mounds. She drew into her eager mouth nipples that were erect and sensitive. She gently bit the crimson orbs and her sharp pointed talons scratched at the ripe and resilient flesh. A groan of pleasure rose in Jo's throat. The mask aborted all sound. She could only roll her eyes in gratification.

"Me, me, me!" The other bunny jiggled impatiently between Jo's parted legs.

"Okay, get sucking. She looks like she could do with a good suck."

The bunny lowered her head and Jo felt the tickle of her fringe as she nestled between her thighs, and began to nuzzle. The sensations were exquisite. The warm wet tongue lapped at parted lips, prodded and darted between musky folds. It searched and found. It circled and sucked and Jo's clit quivered with desire. Never before had she experienced two girls licking her most sensitive and delicious flesh. Her whole body prickled and tingled. She longed to open her mouth and shout with joy, but her mouth was filled by the hard round ball-gag.

"Good, girls. Keep at it. I think I'll join you."

Jo felt rather than saw the large body lower over her face. She felt his fingers fiddling with the buckle of the mask. It began to loosen slightly. The ball slipped from between her lips. She took a deep and satisfying breath. At last she would be able to voice her pleasure. She opened her mouth to cry out and Nico's cock slid effortlessly between those parted lips, filling her mouth completely. It slithered towards her throat. She could feel the hot tip thrusting into her. The weight of him pressed onto her shoulders and he rotated his hips, filling every inch of her aching mouth.

Jo glanced up at him. He gazed arrogantly back, lifting his body away and jerking it back, forcing the rigid rod even further into her.

The long slow glide of Nico's cock in her mouth swept Jo further onto the roller-coaster of desire. The bunny lickings of tit and clit brought rapture to her ravished body. She felt ready to carry on with this orgy of excitement for ever. She didn't want any of it to stop. Sensations of pure joy shot through her from head to heels. The prick in her mouth was swelling. She could feel it growing as her tongue, mobile and fluid, swept over the silky surface. She sucked and licked, her whole body shook, and the bunnies never paused in their attentions. She jerked uncontrollably as spasm after spasm of delirious energy flowed through her. All she wanted now was to feel the hot gush of Nico's cum jetting down her throat.

Her ankles and wrist burned with the tightness of the ropes. Her scalp hurt. Her hair, pulled through the hole in the top of the mask, was spread over the green baize like a sheet of golden gossamer.

Nico withdrew from her mouth leaving it bruised and aching. The mask shielding her eyes had loosened and she saw his bare feet kick the bunnies away. They tumbled into heap, clasping each other close. The tongues that had so ardently licked her own longings now licked each other's. Their bodies, side by side, nose to tail, cleaved together. Two dark heads buried between thighs that were plump and wet.

"Me!" she shouted. "More!" She was pleading and desperate.

But Nico had his own longings. "Shut up bitch." His hands were under her bottom. Where a bunny had knelt, licking and sucking, encouraging her clit to levels of ecstasy she had never known, Nico now crouched. His prick swung heavily in front of him. The taut dark skin still glistened with the suckings of her own mouth.

He settled between her thighs. His fingers squeezed her sodden lips. He pulled them apart, stared at her cunt, swollen, still shaking with the exquisite pleasure the bunny had imparted. His thrust was quick and deep and he sank into her. She cried out. The hardness of him filled her totally. He thrust, jerking her body in its restraints. He was ready to take her and she was willing to be taken. Sweat ran from his face, his shirt clung to his heaving chest, the muscles of his belly flexed, firm and strong. He ran his prick deep inside her. Jo groaned. The peak of her enjoyment tumbled and her body accepted his load with a sigh of exhausted relief.

Mewing cries of pleasure told of the bunnies own fulfilment. The table creaked and sunlight played over four intensely satiated people.

THE BIG DAY

18: CJ Receives A Proposition

For the first time since Tuesday the camp was quiet. Everyone was exhausted. The effort, put in by men and girls alike, had drained them of energy. Everybody was taking this opportunity to rest before the final preparations for the Big Man's arrival at six.

The camp fire glowed, dull beneath its coating of ash. The mid-day meal had been cooked, eaten and cleared away. Men stretched on bunks, belts loosened, shirts open. Some had girls, recently used, lying on the floor at their feet. Others, preferring the outdoor life, slept under hedges or luxuriated in the lush grass bordering the stream, their aching muscles relaxing in the cool surroundings.

The bunnies had been busy since dawn preparing the chosen ones for this evening. After this break there was yet more work for them to do. But now, even the bunnies snoozed, grateful for the opportunity to rest their aching bodies.

Only one girl remained alert, eyes watchful, body tingling with anticipation. CJ had never felt so alive. The week, as far as she was concerned, had been the most wonderful experience of her young life. She relished every moment, the binding, the whipping, the frenzied training - the fucking - it was exhilarating, and she longed for it to continue.

Troy, like all the other men, was dozing. As Chief Trainer, this week had been more of a strain for him. It was to him they turned to sort out problems, work out routines, appease short-tempered men and allot girls to their appointed tasks. CJ had watched his expertise grow with pride, delighted to be involved.

She hoped she had been of some help. She had washed and scrubbed, laundered his clothes, cooked his food. She had also learnt the necessary skills for pleasing him in other ways. The rack outside Troy's van had seen her stretched every evening. At first the ache in her limbs had been almost unbearable, but now, now she was well practised in the art of bondage, CJ looked forward to it, regretted when she was not chained and gagged, legs spread, everything exposed, ready for Troy to take her whenever he felt so inclined.

She shifted lightly in her chains. The van felt stuffy. The sun was hot and she would have preferred to be outside, on the rack. But, when she had finished tidying the van after his meal, Troy had chained her in here and fallen instantly asleep. CJ was disappointed. She always looked forward to her mid-day fuck, but she was sure their would be some kind of activity later.

Troy needed to rest, of course, needed to regain his strength. Today, CJ shivered at the thought, today was the day, the big day, the day they had all been working towards so industriously. This evening the 'Big Man' and his entourage arrived. What would he be like? Why was everyone so nervous? She had watched the dozen or so girls Troy had been putting through their paces himself, intrigued. Just what would be the culmination of all this frenzied activity? For all her probing and subtle questioning, this still remained a mystery.

A whisper from the van steps caught her attention.

"Is he awake yet?" A dark head popped through the open doorway, eyes sooty, the corners crinkled by a questioning smile.

CJ shook her head and Davy perched his backside on the top step, just outside the van. "You've come a long way since we met on the lane."

"Six days!" whispered CJ. "And I want to thank you. I was looking for the holiday of a lifetime when I met you and Damien and what I actually found was a whole new way of living." She glanced at Troy's sleeping form with affection and desire.

Davy stared at her, his eyes quizzical, his expression thoughtful "If Troy's really asleep I'll just slip inside and sit a little closer. You stay where you are, Damien." She might have known Damien would be there too. "There's something I want to discuss with CJ."

"I'm listening, aren't I?" But CJ frowned, uneasy at keeping anything secret from Troy, Troy who knew every inch of her, to whom she bared her soul as well as her entire body.

Davy slid silently over the Turkish rug, his gaze never leaving the face of the sleeping Troy. His whole body spoke of subterfuge and secrets.

"It's not something he won't know about, eventually, sweetheart. But - I thought - maybe if I explained things to you a little first, between us, we could work something out to the advantage of us both."

"I don't know what you're talking about, Davy. I'm okay as I am. Things couldn't be better. I'm happy to stay like this for ever and ever."

"Ah, CJ, that's my point, my point exactly." His small pixie face was close to hers. She could see his eyes glittering in the subdued light, his teeth gleaming as he smiled a wide and not completely trustworthy smile. "You see, CJ, today is a big day for Troy. The Big Man is - well, he's a very important person. He holds Troy's future prospects in his hands. Everything has to be just right."

"For goodness sake Davy," CJ's voice spluttered her exasperation.

"Ssh, ssh, girl, we don't want to wake his lordship now, do we?"

CJ licked her lips and shook her head. "Are you suggesting it's in my power to make things even better for Troy?"

Davy stroked his chin, crossed his legs and sat comfortably close to the chained girl. His hand reached out and stroked her hair. It glowed like the flames of a fire in the darkened interior. The auburn curls tumbled about her shoulders, loose tendrils brushing the curve of her freckled breast. He stared at the nipples, shell-pink, delicate, perched like the petals of an opening rosebud on the soft white mounds of her naked breasts. Rings of gold, in links of three, pierced the tender flesh, they swayed with every movement of her chained body. She was young fresh, glowing with health and energy. She was everything Davy needed if he was to succeed in his plans for the future.

"You're a real beauty, CJ." His hand touched her cheek, her lips. His fingers traced a pattern over the white skin and flicked the dangling nipple rings. They tinkled, knocking one against the other.

CJ smiled, an amused and cynical smile. "What are you after, Davy. What have I got that you want - besides the obvious?"

"CJ, CJ, don't talk like that. It's what both of us have got that's important. It's you and me together, that's what's important. A girl like you and a boy like me, together, we could go anywhere, anywhere."

"Davy," exasperation edged CJ's voice, "Davy, I've already told you, I like it here. I don't want to go anywhere else."

"Girlie, believe me, if you like it here, you'll love it where I'm planning to take you."

CJ's jaw dropped. The cheek of him. She was Troy's woman. She had ousted that no-good bitch, Maggie. She was the most important female in the gipsy camp. Why should she up and off somewhere else unknown, with Davy?

"I suppose you want us both to run away and join a circus or something," she mocked, biting her lip to stop the giggle turning into laughter that might awaken Troy.

Davy stared at her in awe. "You must have a touch of the second sight, CJ. That's it exactly. It's a circus I'm talking about. No, no, not *a* circus, *the* circus. Mr Columbus's Speciality Circus to be precise."

CJ rocked on her heels. "And just who, when he's at home, is Mr Columbus?"

"He's the Big Man, CJ, the Big Man. And this evening he'll be here. And I want to go away with him when he leaves."

"Why? What's so special about his circus?"

Davy looked round nervously. Troy still slept. Heavy slumbering sounds came from his mouth. His eyes were firmly shut, his body relaxed in sleep. Early afternoon sunlight poured in through the open door and Damien, head bent, hands busy whittling a piece of wood, was their only audience.

"Believe me CJ, it is a very special circus and Mr Columbus is a very important man. I know, I've a cousin who works there. His name's Bernardo. I've heard about it from him. And from what he's told me, you and I would have the time of our lives if only we could get to join."

"No! I'm Troy's girl!"

"There's cages, CJ. There's racks and chains, There's costumes and glamour. There's whips and there's punishment. And you get to perform in front of an audience. An audience, CJ!! It's the most wonderful circus in the world."

"Anyway, if it's that wonderful, why would he choose me? I don't know any performing tricks. I'm not glamorous. Jo's glamorous, and Daisy's striking. He might well choose them for their looks, but not me."

"But he might, CJ, he might. And if he does, you've to tell him that I'm the one who discovered you. That's important. Then he'll see I have an eye for his kind of girl."

"What do you mean - his kind of girl?"

"Nothing, CJ, nothing for you to worry about. It's just that this cousin of mine, Bernardo, he's told me that Columbus is looking for red-heads who are tiny and tight cunted. He likes them small, petite - like you."

"Troy would never allow it!"

"That's my problem CJ - Troy." He glanced at the slumbering body. "Somehow, I've got to organise things in such a way that Columbus gets to see you in all your naked glory, and Troy won't be in a position to stop him." His hand slid up her thigh. His fingers pressed into the warm soft slit, pressing and pinching with expert awareness. "Then it'll be the circus life for you and me, my girl. A life of wonder and excitement, spectacle and fun."

"Do you have a plan to achieve all this, Davy?" CJ was astounded at his audacity but could not stop her hips wriggling as his fingers delved deeper. Of course, she would have to see this Columbus before she finally made up her mind. But if he was as powerful as Davy implied - it might be worth thinking about. There was something about a powerful man, a man in charge of his own destiny. The thought of it turned CJ's belly to honey.

A clatter on the van steps made them both jump. Guilt at their actions and their secret planning made them both gasp in surprise. It was Damien - he had got up and was standing, both arms at his sides, hands loose, the penknife and piece of wood he had been working on, discarded, thrown down the steps in a fit of - despair?

A snort and a rustle of limbs and clothing, a stirring from the bunk, made three heads spin round in consternation.

"Just think about it!"

Nodding vigorously, her green eyes wide with alarm, CJ mouthed at Davy to get out NOW! His eel-like body slithered across the floor. Keeping his head down, he moved soundlessly. With a quick, and she thought, suspicious glance in CJ's direction, Damien leapt down the steps out of his way. Davy rolled, agile and silent, after him. He turned to wave at his co-conspirator, then the two brothers loped off across the field, into the sunlight and out of CJ's sight.

19: Visitors approach

The large car, silver paint gleaming, the chrome polished until it hurt the eyes, nosed its way down the narrow country lanes.

The tinted windows reflected trees and hedgerows. The bulky vehicle filled the road, its radiator grill leering, its fins sharp and threatening. It dared any other car to impede its progress. This stretch limo, the best nineteen-fifties America ever produced, purred. The driver, humming with contentment, steered with aplomb. One hand swivelled the wheel, the other caressed the gear stick with supple fingers tipped by talons of shining bronze. Hair of burnished gold was tucked beneath a black cap, the glossy peak pulled low. Rebecca was pleased to be on the road, enjoying driving her master on a very important mission.

Every other driver, and any pedestrian foolish enough to get in her way, she treated with contempt. If they had glimpsed her behind the tinted windows, the road would have been littered with casualties.

Below the shiny peak, eyes, tawny, flecked with gold, glinted. A nose, pert, upturned, sniffed the air, and her full-lipped mouth pouted. Around her neck a leather collar, black studded with gold, was tightly circled. Gilded chain, fine-linked but strong, descended from this collar and cut between, under, and around her breasts, thrusting the bronze-nippled mounds into golden balls. A wide belt circled her waist, and more chain slashed over a trimly contoured belly, disappearing into the depths of tawny-haired pussy, before re-appearing, snug and secure, clenched between firm bottom cheeks.

Her long legs, tanned and smooth, the skin softened and fed by creams and oils, operated the foot controls with skill and dexterity. Sandals of shiny black clung to her small feet. Thin straps of leather cut between her toes, crossed over her instep, wrapped round her narrow ankles and a buckle, a glittering tiger's head, held the ankle strap firmly in place. The four inch heels dug into the floor mat, and her toenails glowed with the bronze lacquer applied that morning.

Slouched on the other half of the banquette seat was a young man, his hand grasping the lead attached to Rebecca's collar. He was small and wiry, his dark hair shaved close to the skull. A long lock had been left uncut, and hung, thick and greasy, scraped into a tail that swung from the crown of his head. Muscles bulged on his small frame. His mouth was thin, his jaws silently working, his deep-set eyes assessed the scenery. He looked at his watch and turned to the figure spread on the well-padded seat in the rear of the Cadillac.

"There's about forty miles driving left boss. We'll be early at this rate. Want to stop to fuck this one?" He indicated Rebecca.

Behind him, huge bulk spreading over the spacious rear seat, cigar smoke swirling above his head, sat Mr Columbus, the Big Man. Fleshy face, half-hidden behind mutton-chop whiskers and bristling eyebrows, he chewed on the cigar stub clenched between moist lips. His white silk shirt glimmered in the shadowy light, a scarf of brilliant blue was knotted round his neck, and his breeches stretched tightly over massive thighs. The well-worn leather of the seat squeaked and groaned as he eased his bulk.

"No, Bernardo, we won't stop." The voice boomed within the narrow confines of the car. "Keep going, keep going. There'll be plenty of fucking later. I think it might be a good idea to arrive earlier than arranged. Surprise them. See what's going on behind the scenes."

Bernardo nodded. "Okay boss." He glanced at the map on his lap. "We take the next turning left. Then the going gets more difficult. There's this town here," he jabbed with his finger. "We should reach that in about an hour, then Dropwell's only a couple of miles on the other side."

"And what time will that be, Bernardo?"

"About five-fifteen, boss. So long as nothing holds us up."

Rebecca snorted.

"Fine, very good. That's what we'll do. We'll arrive early. Have a bit of a snoop round. See if Troy's up to the mark." The large man sank back into the soft enveloping luxury and stubbed the butt of his cigar into the already over-full ashtray. He picked up a tumbler of scotch and downed the remains. "Are you looking forward to this visit, Bernardo?"

Bernardo turned, the arm that held Rebecca's lead stretched along the back of the seat. "Sure boss, sure. It's always good to see new recruits. Fresh young female flesh, barely trained." He licked his lips, chewed on his gum, and ran a hand over the close bristle on his head.

"Not *barely* trained, surely? I'm looking for girls who are *well* trained, ready to join my new troupe. I need these girls to be up to scratch and raring to go. A team of girls, all blondes and red-heads, wonderful costumes, new equipment designed by myself, spectacular, very spectacular. And new! Spectacular, Bernardo, new and spectacular!"

He set the empty glass down on the cocktail cabinet, sank back and spread brawny arms wide. His mouth beamed behind curly whiskers. His eyes glinted darkly from beneath bushy brows. He gazed at Bernardo. His assistant was nervous. Why? Was there something going on behind his back? Something he, Mr Columbus, the owner of the only Speciality

Circus in the world, should know about? He leant forward. His hands, large, hairy, the nails manicured to perfection, rested on bulging knees. "Did you say, Bernardo, you had heard from your cousin, the one who works for Dapper Troy? What's his name? It's slipped my memory."

"Davy, boss. He's got a twin brother, Damien, but he's a bit - well, Davy looks after him. Davy's the brains and Damien's the brawn."

Mr Columbus nodded, closed his eyes and settled himself comfortably. These new girls were important and he was looking forward to seeing how Troy had got on. He did not hold Dapper Troy Dempsey in very high esteem, but it had been his turn to take over the training. This consignment of girls were an intrinsic part of Mr Columbus's plan. He needed new acts, something to take on tour overseas. It was essential this troupe was impressive. He needed them to turn the heads of those Yanks.

Mr Columbus had not decided exactly where he was going yet, but going he was, for at least twelve months. Men, girls, big top and cages, the whole shebang was off on foreign travels.

Behind closed lids images of girls, some tall, some short, well-built or slender, danced before his eyes. Female flesh in all shapes and sizes never ceased to please him, but this time, they were all to be blonde or auburn, and, he hoped, at least one or two would prove to be tiny, petite, tight-cunted.

His massive organ swelled at the thought of all those new and willing girls just waiting for him to arrive, waiting for the touch of his whip.

Pleased with himself, he felt inside the jacket lying on the seat beside him, and pulled out another cigar. He cut the end with a silver penknife, sharp and shiny with use, and fumbled for his lighter. Bernardo leant over the back of the front seat, lighted match in hand, black eyes glittering, the reflection of the flame dancing in his narrow pupils.

"Thank you, Bernardo, most kind." From beneath half-closed lids, Mr Columbus regarded his eager assistant with interest.

20: A Missed Opportunity For CJ

Troy Dempsey's woman had to be adaptable and CJ had experienced many different positions and methods of bondage since arriving in the gipsy camp. And now, with Troy towering over her, ready and randy after his after-lunch snooze, she wondered what to expect. At his command she rose to her feet, and her chained hands stroked the bulge in his breeches. She shivered at the hardness of it and the touch concentrated her attention. He was certainly ready for her.

He unlocked her wrist and ankle chains and they slid to the ground. CJ stood, naked, quivering with excitement, but perplexed. It was a rare occasion when Troy did not want her bound for fucking.

Tinglingly aware of Troy and his insistent presence, CJ could not forget the words Davy had whispered in her ear whilst her master slept. This gipsy encampment had been a wonderful experience, opened her eyes, taught her things she had never dreamt of but - perhaps - could there really be somewhere even more fulfilling? This circus Davy spoke of, and its owner, Mr Columbus was it, could they possibly be the keys to her future? Silent, her mind racing, CJ watched Troy moving about the van. He was opening cupboards, tugging at drawers, riffling through clothes hanging in the wardrobe. He was looking for something.

"Ah ha. Here it is. You and Maggie are about the same size - inside and out - it should fit you okay." He held up what appeared to be an elaborate corset. Scarlet leather gleamed in the afternoon light, and buckles jangled as Troy shook the garment, examining it carefully then tossing onto his bunk.

CJ stared at it resting gaudily on the white sheet. She could see it was made for a slender waist and took a deep breath, but there was an extra piece, solid but curved, dangling from the bottom edge. Not sure where all the bits and pieces were meant to fit, she prepared herself for shocks.

Troy followed her gaze. "Interested? You'll have to wait a while. First," he glanced up towards the ceiling, "first I shall have to check the ceiling rings."

CJ looked up in surprise. Ceiling rings? She screwed up her eyes, and in the dark recesses, where light hardly penetrated, she saw them for the first time, two iron rings. They lay flat against the surface about three feet apart. Troy's fingers fiddled with a clasp, there was a sharp click, and first one and then the other swung down. They hung quite still, fixed to the roof of the van by bars and rivets. These rings looked serious, their purpose was not frivolous. These rings were intended to carry a considerable amount of weight.

"Stand here, girl." Troy indicated a spot on the floor immediately under the left-hand ring. "Put your hands above your head. Stand still!" The flat of his hand stung onto her clenched backside.

CJ did as she was told. She placed both hands together and stretched them up towards the ceiling. Her body quivered and she spread her legs to retain her balance. She wondered what punishment Troy was planning this time.

He was standing behind her and she wanted to look, but her training had taught her to control any inquisitiveness. There was a rustle of movement, a hand tugged at her jaw, and a gag, stiff strips of cloth, slipped between her teeth. It parted her lips and cut into the tender flesh of her cheeks.

Troy pulled the ends tight behind her head and fastened them. His fingers tangled in the tumble of russet curls and CJ winced as he tugged a wilful tendril, pulling at the roots on her scalp. She braced herself for his next move. Her arms were aching, but still she held them upright, straining towards the ceiling. It was her arms he dealt with next. A manacle snapped round her wrists. The manacle was heavy and her arms sagged under the weight. Troy's hand slapped her breasts, sharply, quickly, one precise slap on each breast.

"Keep those arms up. Keep them exactly where they are." He moved away, moved back to one of the cupboards he had searched earlier. She watched his strong broad bare back. The muscles bulged over sharp shoulder blades, shimmied down his back, formed a trim waistline then curved beneath the tough cloth of his jeans.

CJ's tummy flipped as she saw the muscles ripple and glide and hoped that, whatever Troy had in mind, she would soon be feeling those muscles pressing the soft warmth of her own flesh.

He had found what he was looking for and was walking back towards her, staring at the ceiling, staring at the rings that dangled there. Draped over his arm was a chain. It was long and heavy, the links large and strong.

The roof, several feet above CJ's head, was easily reached by Troy's out-stretched arms. And, like a ship dropping anchor, he fed the chain through first one ring, then the other. The ends dangled and between the rings it bellied slightly. The loose end hanging over CJ's head brushed her shoulder and she shivered at its touch.

Stepping back, Troy surveyed his handiwork. He pulled the end of chain and it rattled noisily through the rings. He positioned it carefully. A snap of metal on metal and a sudden wrench on her shoulders told CJ she and the chain were now attached to her wrist manacles. Troy walked away, tugged on the other end and her feet lifted from the floor.

After six days in the camp CJ understood a lot about bondage, it had become familiar and welcome. She had seen and learnt a lot, but all this equipment was new to her. With the gag cutting into her mouth, her arms taut above her head, she pondered. She eyed the chain with interest and wondered what it was Troy planned to do with the opposite end, the one still hanging loose from the second ring. She stretched her lips over the gag and swallowed hard. Her fingers wriggled in the handcuff and the tips brushed the links chaining her to the ceiling. She waited, patient and demure, her naked body, stretched and drawn, jiggling lightly backwards and forwards.

As Troy moved about the van she followed him with her eyes. He walked towards the bunk. The corset lay where he had tossed it. He picked it up, shook it out and smiled.

It really was a most peculiar looking item. Scarlet leather gleamed, the buckles of shining chrome jangled. The garment looked very small and she knew would be a tight fit, but that did not worry her. What intrigued her was the long object hanging from the lower edge. It also was scarlet leather, but there were no buckles or loops. It swayed, its curved solidity pendulous.

Three easy strides and he was standing at her side. His arm, thick with muscle and corded by sinew, stretched across her and he slipped the corset over her stomach. His hard body pressed close and he fastened the buckles, pulling them hard, pinching her flesh, squeezing the breath from her lungs. CJ was fascinated. Troy continued to pull on the buckles. This corset would not slip out of place, he was making sure of that. He twirled her round in her chains, tugged vigorously on the remaining straps, and seemed satisfied at last that everything was as it should be.

CJ lowered her eyes. She was keen to see the effect this garment was having on her body. She stared, gratified by what she saw. Her breasts bulged. The nipples, usually small and delicate, stood rigid, like two pink thimbles. The corset cut a scarlet swathe across her middle and her belly. The skin, shockingly white against the vivid red, swelled softly beneath its lower edge. Her bush of red-gold hair shone, and the solid object attached to the hem nodded backwards and forwards between her legs.

Light began to dawn. A furious blush burnt her face. That thing, the long solid curved object - now she understood exactly where that was designed to fit. The corset pressed on her belly and CJ tightened her muscles.

A dildo hung between her legs.

When Troy had lifted the chain from the cupboard, another implement had also nestled in his arms. Now he dropped to his knees and CJ glanced down when she felt the touch of cold metal encircling her ankle. It was a shackle, but very different from the one binding her wrists. This one was a solid bar, about twelve inches long, a small ring welded to the middle, iron ankle cuffs attached to either end.

"This should keep those thighs well parted." Troy was talking to himself. He had to. CJ could only mumble incoherently behind her gag. He thrust her legs into position and snapped the second fetter into place. He stood up and stared. CJ stared back, her emerald eyes large and questioning. The heavy chain pulled on her arms, more than a match for her slight body, but she did not dare to tug or wriggle.

"You're behaving very well, but somehow those eyes look just a little bit concerned." Troy brushed his fingers over her cheeks and laughed, squeezing her gag-distorted face with steely hands. "You've nothing to worry about, CJ. The next bit is the fun bit."

He stepped away from her, and grabbed the free end of the chain. He wrapped it round his forearm and pulled hard, bending his knees to gain greater purchase. CJ's arms dragged in their sockets. Her feet left the floor, and she hung, suspended by the wrist cuffs. Troy continued pulling and the tendons in his neck stood out with the strain. Blood suffused his cheeks. He heaved on the chain and with a massive effort she rose higher, until her curls brushed the ceiling and her feet were on a level with his hands. With the chain wrapped tight to his elbow, Troy grabbed the bar between her ankles, flicked open the ring with his thumb, and counted links on the chain. "One, two, three, four, one more should do it." He was breathing hard. With a sigh he threaded the centre ring through the chosen link.

The chain rattled through the rings, and CJ hung suspended from the ceiling by wrists and ankles, as if swinging in an invisible hammock. Her body rocked, her back bowed, her head dropped back. Troy's hands eased away and she shivered and shook. She swung in mid-air, her hair flowed towards the ground, her neck stretched and, through the open door, she could see that the sky was her carpet and the swaying branches of the trees, hazy with new leaf, her cushions.

She strained to look at Troy. He was nodding, a satisfied smile on his face. He disappeared from view and she felt his finger slide into her hot slit. He spread her lips, stretching and stroking the moist flesh. CJ moaned behind her gag. Her juices flowed. She was ready for him. She longed for him to enter her, take her, thrust deep inside her quivering body. She arched her mound towards him and suddenly she was full. Fuller than she had ever been. The prick delved deep, deep and hard inside her. She thrust her hips, the chain overhead rattled and clattered.

It was noisy and shook to her every undulation. The more she wriggled the deeper the prick delved. CJ gasped at its ferocity. Her mouth ached and she longed to shout out, but the gag, tight and cutting, prevented her.

She opened her eyes and saw Troy standing over her. He tore the gag from her mouth. She cried out in surprise. His cock, long and thick, lay in the palm of his hand. He thrust it into her open mouth. CJ gulped. Her mind was in a turmoil. Troy was fucking her mouth, fast and furious. So who was fucking her pussy?

Then she remembered the dildo. Long, scarlet, hard and curved. She was fucking herself. With every sway of her body, every wriggle of her hips, the dildo, attached to the leather corset bound round her waist, dug ever deeper inside her accommodating cunt. CJ wanted to giggle. But her mouth was full to bursting. Troy was thrusting deep, long and hard, down her throat. His body was shaking and she knew that soon the hot spurt of spunk would jet into her.

Excitement filled her belly. The dildo was nicely placed. It rubbed and stroked her clit and her body was vibrating. Shafts of pure joy shot through her. She shook and trembled. The van creaked and swayed. The chain rattled and clanked. Her body jerked, and Troy groaned as hot sweet liquid jetted down her gulping throat. He clutched her breasts, squeezing and manipulating the bulging flesh. A look of fierce fulfilment flitted across his face.

"You're good, CJ. I'm not going to let you go. I've plenty of other girls to show the Big Man. He won't miss one, especially one he doesn't even know exists." Troy withdrew from her aching mouth and strapped the gag back in place. "We don't want you enjoying yourself while I'm not here, do we?" He unbuckled the scarlet leather and, with regret, CJ felt the dildo slide, wet and glistening, from her pussy. Troy tossed the garment back onto the bunk, slipped his cock inside his jeans, pulled a clean shirt over his head, and went out, slamming the van door behind him.

21: Success For Maggie: Abduction For CJ

"All you bunnies, up here, NOW." Troy's tone was excited, elated even. It was still not five-thirty, and everything was ready. When the boss, The Big Man, arrived in about half-an-hour, Troy would be prepared.

Panting and giggling, the bunnies formed themselves into a group, make-up boxes clutched in hot sticky hands. They had worked hard and were ready for their efforts to be recognised, to receive an appropriate reward from Dapper Troy.

"All kneel."

Willingly they obeyed.

"Heads bowed. Good. Right men, fix the leads. Take them back to the cages. Bind them tightly. I don't want any trouble tonight."

A groan of dismay reverberated round the clearing.

"Troy! That's not fair! We've worked our butts off for you today."

"Shut up! I won't take any lip from any of you. Gag them all, boys, gag them well."

The men moved swiftly, moving among the kneeling girls, snapping leads into position, thrusting ball-gags into protesting mouths.

Only one bunny, unable to believe what she had just heard, rose to her feet. Maggie stared at Troy, her dark eyes luminous with dismay. "Me, Troy, me. You can't mean to include me in these orders, surely?" Maggie had been living and working as a bunny all week. She had obeyed orders, caused no trouble. But now her punishment must come to end. Troy must be missing her by now.

"Who said that? Who spoke? I'll take the whip to her personally." Veins stood out on Troy's forehead. His patience was short. He was not going to take any cheek from these girls.

Boldly, Maggie stepped out of line. The others stared, those not yet gagged, giggled, jeered at the nerve of the girl. To them Maggie was a hutch bunny now. "It's me Troy, Maggie." She stood in front of the others, naked and shaking.

"Well, well, well. So it's Maggie is it? I almost didn't recognise you. You're thinner. Finding life hard? Longing to get back to a life of ease and luxury in the van, are you?"

Maggie hung her head and did not reply.

"I've been managing very well without you all week. I think I might just leave you where you are."

Silence hung over the gipsies. They all stared at Maggie. Troy was heaping humiliation on her already bowed back. She had not been born to be a bunny. She was a helper, a performer, to be used, yes, but not to be treated like this. Feet shuffled, someone cleared their throat, the fire crackled in the middle of the clearing.

"You can't do that, Troy." A voice rang out, sharp and clear from a group of girls to Troy's left.

He span on his heel, glared at the group. "Who thinks they can tell me what to do?"

Shorsa stepped forward. "I'm thinking no such thing, Troy," she smiled sweetly at him. "But have you forgotten tonight, the Big Man, the entertainment? Our dance, me and Maggie together, we're a spectacular team. You don't want to deprive the man of that, do you Troy?"

Troy glared at Shorsa. She stood, her long purple skirt swirling about her ankles, her breasts pert, dark-nippled, the nipple rings glittering and tinkling as she shook her tits in his direction.

"We're a good team, Troy. I can't dance alone. It just wouldn't be the same."

Troy glowered at her, swung his whip against his boot, tapped his foot. What she said made sense, Troy understood that, but no chit of a girl was going to tell him what was what. He raised his whip and pointed the handle in Maggie's direction. "Okay," he growled, "Okay, tonight she dances, but tomorrow, it's back with the bunnies."

With heart thudding painfully beneath her ribs, Maggie fell to one knee, bowed her head, and moved her lips in silent thanks. One evening of dancing, one night of bondage and punishment, that was all it would take to get back into Troy's bed. That red-haired bitch would be gone by the morning, Maggie felt sure of that.

A twittering and rustling of disapproval ran through the bunnies' ranks. Troy must be going soft. That girl was a liability. He'd regret giving in to her so easily, you see if he didn't.

Maggie stayed where she was. Men strode past her, leather leads and chains clutched in their fists. The bunnies were dragged away, their protests silent now. A smirk flitted across Maggie's face.

"Wait, Seth." Troy barked out an order. "That bunny, number three, you can leave her where she is. She could be useful tonight."

Maggie's face darkened, her thoughts mutinous.

CJ was becoming restive. She hung as Troy had left her and her arms and legs smarted with pins and needles. The gag split her face and her jaw ached. Every move she made was accompanied by the jangle and rattle of the chain sliding through the ceiling rings.

She could hear shouting and pounding of feet in the distance: men and girls, all desperately busy, too busy to remember her. CJ wanted to take part in all this activity, to play an essential role, to get a good look at the Big Man. Instead she was trussed, unable to move, and alone.

She wiggled her fingers. She shook her toes. It was useless. She was trapped. She wondered what the time was. How long before the Big Man arrived? Tears of frustration welled in her eyes. She hated not getting her own way, and was beginning to despise Troy, to see him differently: a puffed up braggart.

The door of the van was closed, She couldn't even see any of the hustle and bustle taking place outside. The meadow might as well have been a foreign country. She was stuck here, alone, silent, separated from her friends, and prevented from discovering about Mr Columbus's Speciality Circus. CJ shook her bottom in frustration.

A shuffling noise, close, just outside the van, caught her attention. Somebody was on the steps. They were moving cautiously. It wasn't Troy. Troy would have burst in through the door, full of confidence and vigour. Whoever it was out there, sounded unsure, not convinced of their right to be lurking on the steps of the master's caravan.

CJ's hearing was acute, and slowly, very slowly, the door handle turned. It was not locked, no one in Troy's camp would have the nerve to invade his privacy. But someone had the nerve. Someone felt strongly enough about something to gather up all their courage - approach the van - climb the steps - turn the handle - open the door -

It was Damien.

He stood there, on the threshold, staring at the chained and gagged CJ. She stared back. Her heart was racing. Had Troy sent him - or Davy? Damien glanced over his shoulder and slid silently into the van. He strode towards her, looked at the chains, ran stubby fingers over the heavy links. He grunted, glanced up at the ceiling, stared at CJ, reached up, and with one arm supporting her knees, unclasped the chain from the far ring. Her legs slumped into his arms. He soon released the second clasp, and her body, stiff and sore, slipped into his waiting grasp.

The gag stifled all questions. She was dumb. And so was Damien. She had never known him speak to anyone but Davy. CJ was alone with him, glad to be released from the chains, but alone and frightened.

With Damien clasping her trembling body to his chest, they were out the van. It was late afternoon. He looked round anxiously, but there was no-one in sight. Carefully, Damien descended the steps and with long leisurely strides, loped over the field towards the wood. His body was hot beneath his shirt.

Naked, CJ shivered and cuddled closer for warmth. She buried her face in the taut muscles of his stomach and together they lurched towards to the cover of the trees, Damien intent, his mind concentrating on his self-appointed task.

Neither of them noticed the silver Cadillac gliding silently down the track from Dropwell Park. With engine disengaged, the stately vehicle free-wheeled, swiftly, soundlessly, stopping with a whisper of rubber on grass just out of sight of the camp.

Neither of them saw three pairs of eyes behind the smoky glass observing the abduction. Neither was aware that their disappearance into the wood was watched with interest. They were both ignorant of the fact that one particular pair of eyes observed the flaming red of CJ's hair flowing over Damien's arms, or saw with what ease she was carried. Observed all this with the skill and knowledge of someone well versed in the weight and size of girls in relation to transport. Someone who knew such details intimately because that was his job, his profession, his innate and well-honed skill.

22: Is This Folly?

"We'll leave the car here, Rebecca, parked under these trees. I don't think anyone saw us arrive. But our short time here has already proved very interesting."

"Yes master." Rebecca slid the car to a halt on the edge of the wood, the same wood the large man had scurried into, girl clutched firmly in his arms. Easing the handbrake on, she stroked her breasts and peered at her surroundings from beneath the peak of the black cap pulled low over her eyes. "It's a nice place, boss."

She glanced at her master, his massive body spread over the rear seat. "It's well out of sight of the encampment. But it's quite a long walk up the field to the vans." She grinned cheekily. "Are you sure you can manage?" Mr Columbus roared, a guffaw that rocked the limousine. Bernardo slapped Rebecca's face for her insolence, and dragged her, giggling, from the driving seat.

Still chuckling at her impertinence, Mr Columbus eased his bulk from the car, brushed ash from the front of his shirt and slipped his arms into his jacket. It was a snug fit. The material was blue velvet, the colour clear, dazzling, aquamarine. It shimmered in the light of late afternoon. His breeches, black and straining over ample haunches, were of silk, his boots, black with silver studs, clung to thick calf muscles. His hair, gipsy dark, flowed back from his forehead and curled greasily over his collar. The two men wore ear rings.

"This spot is perfect, Rebecca. Now come here. Let me take your lead. You might as well come with us. You have an experienced eye where female flesh is concerned."

"Oh, thank you sir," Rebecca simpered, bowing her head low. A tawny curl escaped from under her cap and corkscrewed over her left ear. She kicked one leg high into the air. The taut muscles rippled, smooth beneath the supple skin, her cunt ring flashed, her bronze-tipped breasts bounced, and she twirled and twisted on the end of her leash, happily performing a series of loosening-up exercises. "I've been cooped up in the car for three hours, and I'm not used to it. I lead an active outdoor life, as you know."

Mr Columbus snorted, slapped the apple-round cheeks of her bottom and wound the lead round his hand. Together, they started the long climb up the hill to the encampment. He glanced over his shoulder at his assistant. "Make sure the car is secure, Bernardo, then follow me."

Car keys safe in the pocket of his jeans, Bernardo followed. This was a good spot. He had known the minute he saw it for the first time that the boss would be impressed. But he was worried. That had been Damien they had seen sliding out of the big caravan, gagged red-head clutched in his brawny arms. What on earth had been up to? Just what had been going on here? If Davy wanted to join the circus, and until now Bernardo had seen no reason why he shouldn't, there must be nothing in his past that would make the boss mistrust him in any way.

"Come along, Bernardo, come along." The big voice boomed along the valley. "We don't want to keep our hosts waiting, do we?"

"I'm with you, boss." Bernardo sprinted up the slope, his gaze fixed on the hypnotic sway of Rebecca's gleaming hips.

CJ felt battered and bruised. Her head was swimming, the gag cut tightly across her mouth, her arms and legs were numb and she was sure there was hardly a breath left in her body. Once Damien had released her from the sling of chains he had gathered her close, and hurried away from the van and the camp.

They had trotted through the countryside for what felt like hours but was probably less than twenty minutes in reality. From the start he had seemed to know where he was going and they had hastened down the steep slope towards the stream and into the trees. She would have liked to ask him where they were going, but she was gagged and Damien was no conversationalist.

Since entering the camp less than a week ago, CJ had seen very little of her surroundings. The corral, the meadow, Troy's van, these had been her horizons. Being with Troy, looking after him, learning the art of bondage, had satisfied her completely. She had thrilled to the new experiences, and was ashamed to admit that she had not even thought about her new friends Daisy and Jo.

They were out of the trees now and the sound of rushing water attracted her attention - a weir, a waterfall? Turning her face away from Damien's chest, she peeped over his forearm. They were approaching a lake. It was wide, calm, wild fowl glided on its tranquil waters. So where was the noise coming from? Damien veered to the left. The noise grew louder. She craned her neck. Ahead she could see a bridge. The lake narrowed at this point, its volume compressed by rocks. The bridge arched over that slender neck and the water tumbled and roared in a foaming, spitting, wildly natural waterfall beneath the elegant span.

Looking to left and right, but there was no one to see, Damien trotted over the bridge, turned, and followed a rocky path, twisting beneath the trees. He clutched CJ tighter and she felt his body stiffen. Whatever goal he had, Damien must have nearly reached it.

He came to a halt, took a deep breath, and slowly, laboriously, for even CJ's light weight was straining his arms, climbed a flight of steps. At the top of those steps she glimpsed a large wooden door. With one booted foot Damien pushed it open.

He strode into the building and she caught her breath. A central dome, glass covered, sent shafts of late afternoon light glancing through the interior. Motes of dust danced within the shafts and ropes, suspended from the rim of the dome, rustled in the draft from the open door.

With easy strides, his step lighter now, Damien walked towards the centre of the building, and lowered her gently onto a flat surface. It was cold and hard. CJ shivered, with nipples prickling, and lay completely still, mind racing.

This was a strange place. It looked like some kind of temple. She could see niches in the walls, some with tiny figures perched. Candle sconces were fixed at intervals, and the slab, the one on which she lay, was this the altar? It didn't seem quite right. An arch sprang from it and the arch was made up of carved and writhing figures, men and women, clambering and kissing, feeling and fornicating. Anxiety engulfed her. Damien was a strange lad, she did not understand him at all. Was this temple of significance to him? And if so, was she to be his sacrifice?

With the sun moving towards evening, Damien grinned at his captive.

23: An Unforgettable Evening

It was getting late and Rebecca moped, sulky and annoyed. Tied by a chain that led from her neck-bond, she was fixed to an iron ring sunk into a hefty post of well-seasoned oak. That, she didn't mind. It was where the boss had left her, away from the camp fire that Rebecca did not take kindly to. The crowd grouped round it were ignoring her. She scuffed her feet, the thin tapering heels of her sandals digging into the soft earth, the fetters round her ankles reflecting the light from the flames as they leapt skywards.

She considered creating a diversion; tried jiggling around, shaking her chains, thrusting her pussy forward. She would have made ribald comments but her mouth was stopped by a gag. She was bored. Then she remembered the look on Dapper Troy's face when the boss, with herself and Bernardo in tow, had turned up earlier than expected. He had looked stunned. She sniggered through her gag.

Today was not the first time she had come across Dapper Troy. Rebecca had met him before. He had visited the circus where she lived. He had fucked her. He was okay. But his abilities, in Rebecca's eyes, were nothing compared to those of the boss. He lacked the presence, the stature, the overwhelming unforgettabilty of a Mr Columbus. Dapper Troy thought a lot of himself, that was true, and the girls round here seemed to moon over him, but it didn't impress her at all.

She glanced round the clearing. Rebecca's eyes, a clear translucent amber in daylight, darkened at night. The pupils widened, became huge and velvety black, and it was these all-seeing eyes that gazed with contempt at the gipsy girls. There was hardly a one here fit to join Mr Columbus's Speciality Circus, and the boss was getting restive, Rebecca could see that.

"Is there any more of that delicious claret left, Troy?" Mr Columbus waved an empty goblet. He had eaten and drunk well. The satisfying of his stomach was of great importance to him and only rivalled in enormity his appetite for sex.

"Yes, sir. At once." Troy looked harassed. "Here, you, girl, bring the wine, fill the glass."

Bunny three did as she was ordered. She smiled at the Big Man. The rings in her nipples jangled.

Rebecca eyed her critically. She wasn't bad. Small, sloe-eyed, tip-tilted nose. Lots of black hair scraped into a shining tail. But the boss wanted blondes and red-heads. She shook her own tawny curls with pride. Nearly all the girls Rebecca had seen since arriving here had been dark-haired gipsy types, and they weren't what the boss was after.

There had been those two dancing girls, they hadn't been too bad. The dance had been energetic and the boss had applauded enthusiastically. But then he always enjoyed the sight of shaven and perforated cunts. And these two had been particularly attractive. The rings sliding through the plump lips had been decorated with ribbons. They had flashed and flown, waving vigorously with each sinuous pelvic thrust. It had looked impressive. But both Rebecca and Mr Columbus were waiting, impatient to see the girls gathered and trained specially, at his request.

She glanced round the gipsy camp. In the distance she could see old animal cages, and the small, dark-haired bunnies crouching in the narrow confines. She smiled. It reminded her of home. Not that her cage, the one she shared with her best friend, Tracy, was small like these hutches. Her cage was spacious, even plush compared with these humble boxes. But she could see the attraction of such limited living quarters. She ran bronze-tipped nails over golden breasts and longed for some action.

Tossing back his great head, Mr Columbus gulped the remains of his wine, threw the glass to the ground and declared, "Well, Troy, its time, don't you think? We, Bernardo and myself, have not come all this way merely to sample your generous hospitality." He smiled a wolfish smile at Troy, who grinned nervously back. "As you know, we are here on business. We have come to view your new recruits. You followed my instructions?" Troy nodded and brushed back a lock of hair that had fallen into his eyes. Mr Columbus beamed. "And they are all - what shall I say - they are all of the paler hue?"

Troy stood up, planted his feet firmly apart, swallowed the dregs of his own glass, cleared his throat, and pulled the carefully prepared speech from his back pocket. He had composed it for just this moment.

"Mr Columbus, sir, we, the gipsy training camp, we are delighted to receive you into our midst. Preparations have been a little - hurried. We did not expect you so soon -"

"Quiet," snapped the Big Man. "There's no need for speechifying. Either the girls are ready or they aren't. Bring forth the goods."

Rebecca sneered as she saw a blush of embarrassment colour Troy's cheeks. He wasn't used to being ordered about, and especially not in front of his own minions. The boss had got the upper hand and Dapper Troy would have to work hard to regain it.

The day was drawing to a close. The sun was low on the horizon. Streaks of cloud, cerise and scarlet, slashed across the azure backcloth.

The wood in the valley below the clearing, each freshly opened leaf rustling and whispering on the evening breeze, turned black and ominous. The stream that rushed along the wood's edge before disappearing into the inky depths, echoed through the valley. The sound of water gurgling and leaping over rocks was clearly heard on the evening air. A shiver ran through the assembled company and fresh logs were thrown onto the fading fire. Crimson and gold flames shone on the faces of the men gathered in the darkness. Sparks shot into the night sky. The sun withdrew beyond the horizon and soft night fell on the darkling camp.

"You do have girls to show me, don't you Troy?"

Rebecca heard the edge in her master's voice. He was becoming impatient. If Troy didn't pull his finger out, trouble was brewing. She noticed Bernardo shift uncomfortably. He sat cross-legged on the grass with the other gipsies. Only Troy and Mr Columbus sat on stools, and the ample haunches of the boss oozed over the narrow edges of his.

"Of course, sir. Of course I've got girls. Beautiful girls. Well-trained girls. Dozens of them." Troy licked his lips and rubbed the palms of his hands down his immaculate thighs. "Davy, Jem, Nico, Seth - where *is* Damien? - jump to it and bring the girls up here. Mr Columbus is ready to see the results of our hard work. Bring them up here - fast!"

Davy sprang to his feet, looked round anxiously for Damien, winked at Bernardo, and scurried away into the darkness. Troy's other trainers strode ahead of him. They hurried down the slope, out of Rebecca's sight.

Those left behind held their own counsel. Silence hung in the air. Troy stared into the distance, uneasiness creasing his handsome face. Mr Columbus indicated his glass lying on the ground and bunny three refilled it speedily. She bowed low, her dark-nippled breasts swaying, her bottom angled in Troy's direction. Rebecca smirked. She recognised all the little tricks and admired the bunny's expertise. She must have worked hard on this performance. The girl was enjoying herself and seemed determined to make the smaller dancing girl jealous. The fire crackled, the boss gulped his wine, Troy paced, anxiety seeping from every pore.

A thudding of feet, a tinkling of chains and the murmur of girlish voices, announced the imminent arrival of girls. Rebecca's eyes glowed, lively and animated. Bernardo, lounging on the grass, looked up expectantly. The boss sat up straight, whiskers bristling. Troy stared into the darkness. A sudden burst of nervous energy electrified them all, from the gipsy dancing girls to the bosses themselves, they all waited, anxious to see the presentation of this glittering troupe.

Gradually they appeared through the gloom. Davy came first, Nico to one side, Seth to the other, Jem brought up the rear. Each man clutched a crop or whip and swung it with vigour.

The girls, hair gleaming in the velvety night, trotted, demure and obedient, towards the party waiting in the clearing. Rebecca counted. There were twenty all told - not as many as Troy had insinuated. She noted their outfits with a professional eye.

The bunnies had done their job well, she could see that. Each mane of hair was dressed to perfection, the plumage varying from the brightest of silver blondes to deeply burnished russet. Some was pulled tight into tails that bounced from the domes of smooth round heads. Some hung loose, the flowing locks brushed and arranged into curtains of shining silk. A few, not many, had hair cropped so short it stood proud in haloes of red or gold, framing faces that were heart-shaped and elfin.

Rebecca frowned, shook her chains, glanced at the boss, whose expression was impassive. As the girls trotted closer the flickering flames shone on their lustrous skin, shadows played over, under and between each mound, each curve, each furrow. They were all naked but for fetters and chains. A chain hanging from the neck band of the leading girl joined all twenty in a long and perfumed line. Every girl was harnessed in golden leather. Their arms were tightly bound behind backs that arched, thrusting breasts proudly forward. From every nipple a chain dangled, and below the flawless curves of their breasts, these two chains joined into one. This single chain cleaved to each rounded belly, before nestling into and parting plump pussy lips. When it reappeared from between bottom cheeks, all pillowy and peerless, the chain linked to the nipple rings of the following girl.

The slightest misjudgement of step, a falter, a pause, and it threatened to cut deep into tender flesh and drag on pierced nipple flesh. Any miscreant, wherever her place in the line, hastened to rectify her error. But a quick swish of Jem's whip said her mistake had been noted and would not be forgiven easily.

Rebecca longed to thrust herself forward, to join in the parade, to be admired by an audience.

Number three bunny was poised behind Troy's chair, and watching the performance with interest. The two dancing girls had melted into the background.

The coffle circled a carefully choreographed display. Perched on teetering heels, the girls paraded past the important visitor. They inclined silken tresses towards Troy and Mr Columbus. They followed their instructions assiduously. They wobbled their breasts, displayed their sex, and with every step they took the linking chains massaged and stroked moistened and engorged pussy lips, lips already throbbing with excitement.

Some girls wore ear-rings, long and jangling, rings that pulled on lobes dragging them down by their weight. Others had studs, three in a row, piercing each nostril. Every neck, slender and pale, was tightly circled by a collar of burnished metal and shafts of firelight flashed from the shining surfaces. Finger and toe nails gleamed with lacquer the colour of freshly spilled blood and chains of finest silver, wound from ankle to knee, glistening in the firelight.

Elegant and supreme, the girls circled the clearing, until, at Davy's shouted command, they came to a halt, bound hands resting on plump bottoms, breasts bulging, nipples erect and ready.

Troy, nervous and unsure, fumbled with his whip. Bernardo, kneeling at the feet of his boss, winked at Davy, who raised his eyebrows in mute query. Enigmatic and silent, Mr Columbus stared from beneath bushy brows. His face, crimson with the effects of wine and the heat from the fire, perspired freely. He removed the scarf from his neck and wiped cheeks that were full and ruddy. His ample weight shifted and his stool creaked in complaint. With eyes narrowed, lips pursed, belly bursting over the belt straining to hold his breeches, he stood up. The line of girls trembled exquisitely before him. Slowly, he approached.

Silently he strolled from one girl to the next. He stroked soft hair, examined skin texture, opened mouths, squeezed soft and pliant breasts, jabbed at wet slits with thick fingers. Anxiously, Troy followed him. When they reached the end of the line Mr Columbus made no comment, merely moved to the rear and making his inquisitive way back again. He clutched at tightly bound arms, patted globed bottoms, and thrust inquisitive fingers into secret entrances. Sometimes he stopped, assessed the girl from head to toe, dug deeper inside and growled, a meaningless growl, full of import.

Some squirmed at his silent probing. Others chewed on quivering lips, some gasped as his expert finger tip stroked, delicate and knowing, over sensitive and responsive places.

Two blonde girls in the middle of the row, standing side by side, waited excited and expectant. Daisy and Jo looked perfect. Daisy's hair was piled high, Jo's swung in silver sheets over her straining shoulders. Mr Columbus examined both girls with infinite care. He prodded, he stroked, he squeezed with relish, and eventually came out with 'Humph,' but that was all he said. He fumbled in the inside pocket of his velvet jacket, withdrew a cigar and lit up. Fumes of claret and cigar smoke swirled into the faces of both girls.

Rebecca and Bernardo relished this performance, but both looked uneasy. The boss was not satisfied. Troy was in for a dressing down. To Rebecca's eyes none of these girls looked too bad. There were several she might have chosen herself, but something was upsetting the boss. She glanced at Bernardo, who, gaze hardly shifting from his boss's face, shrugged his shoulders in her direction.

For the past ten minutes no words, except for that one *Humph*, had passed the lips of Mr Columbus. But now the tempo changed and his orders were sharp and incisive. "That one, that one, the one next her and both girls at either end of the line. Detach them. They'll do. I'll take those five."

Startled, Troy nodded, pointed at Jem who extracted a key from his jeans and released the girls from the coffle. Troy coughed. "Only five, sir?" His voice was low, shocked by the Big Man's response. "There are twenty girls on display, all selected and trained to your specifications. Are you sure five is enough? Wouldn't you like a few more?" There was a note of desperation in Troy's voice.

Mr Columbus glared at him. His eyes, always small, had all but disappeared into the glowering countenance. To those who knew him well, the light glimmering from beneath those bushy brows was dangerous. Rebecca shivered with pleasure. She could see the flash of anger in those glittering orbs, the flush of rage colouring his florid face. His body, heavy and bulky, darted with a lightness and swiftness that made Troy step back in alarm.

"No Troy, no, five is not enough. Yes Troy, yes, I would like more - or to be exact *one* more. One more in particular. One more girl of a very specific type."

Troy gazed round in bewilderment. "But this, sir, this is all of them. There aren't any more girls. Not of the type you wanted. I've plenty of gipsy girls available." His voice rose, squeaking in alarm. "Maggie, Shorsa, number three." Number three was instantly at his side. Maggie and Shorsa sidled towards the firelight from the darker reaches of the camp. He grabbed hold of the three dark-haired girls, dragging them into view.

Mr Columbus snorted, threw his cigar to the ground, crushed it beneath his mighty boot, and waved a vigorous finger under Troy's nose. "These girls," he clutched at the gipsy group, "nice girls, juicy girls, no doubt very skilled - I might have room for girls like these at a later date." His arm, always hefty, heavy with anger now, shoved them to one side. "But today, Troy, today I want blondes and red-heads!"

Troy indicated the line chained on the other side of the fire, his mouth opening and closing wordlessly.

"Yes, yes, Troy, I know, I'm not blind." He dismissed the twittering coffle with a sweep of his hand. "I can see *those* girls *there*. But it's not them I am interested in Troy. You are deceiving me, aren't you Troy? You are hiding a girl from me, aren't you Troy? A particularly tasty girl. Small, petite, masses of auburn curls!" His voice roared into the dark night.

Troy opened his mouth, shook his head violently.

"Don't bother to deny it Troy. I've seen her. I caught a glimpse of her when I arrived on the site. You arranged for her to be hidden. You wanted to keep that little piece to yourself, didn't you Troy?" His face crimson, his voice trembling with rage, he grabbed Troy by his immaculate shirt collar.

Looking round wildly, Troy tried to pull away from the iron grip. He gazed at the closed door of his own van. The Big Man, he'd seen CJ? How? Troy was confused. "I - I'm not hiding her sir. Not hiding her, not what you'd call hiding. I'll go and get her, if you insist." He was desperate to appease the fury of the Big Man, a fury that buffeted his body, shaking him as if he was no more than a young bunny on the end of a rope.

"I honestly didn't think she'd be quite right for you. I was sure she wasn't what you had in mind. She really is a bit on the short side. I had no intention, no intention at all of deceiving you, sir."

Mr Columbus let go his grip. Quaking, Troy turned towards his van.

"Just stop right there, Troy, and don't try to act the innocent with me. She's not in the van, is she? As I said, I've seen her. Your assistant was in the process of bundling the delightful little gem out of sight when I arrived - earlier than expected. I saw, we all saw, everything.

If Troy had looked bewildered before, he was totally mystified now. His head swung from the van to Mr Columbus, from Mr Columbus back to his van.

"But - but -" His hands flapped towards the van in confusion."

"Enough!" Mr Columbus towered in front of Troy, who looked crumpled and defeated. "What I want to know is where have you hidden her? What have you done with that delicious little red-head? I want her, and I shan't be leaving this camp till I have her. So the quicker you tell me where she is, the sooner we can complete all our business.

CJ lay on the marble slab, her gaze fixed on Damien. Since reaching this place, he had given no inclination of his intentions. Why had he been in such a hurry to get her away from the gipsy camp? Why had he brought her here? Even Damien must have a reason for his actions. He must have some kind of plan, but what was it? After laying her on the platform on arrival, he had not touched her again. CJ, arms and legs still stiff from her earlier chaining, began to relax. Whatever it was Damien had in mind, from the way he moved, ignored her, surveyed his surroundings, she had the feeling he wasn't intending to do her any harm. He seemed pleased with himself. Almost as if just having her here, hiding her here, was enough.

Grunting and mumbling, Damien shuffled round the temple. CJ's mouth was dry behind the gag. It would have been nice just to talk to him, even if he didn't reply. The cold of the stone made her shiver. Her shoulder blades ached from the pressure, her bottom felt numb. She wriggled slightly but didn't dare move too much, she certainly didn't want to provoke him.

The bright sunlight, which had filtered through the glass of the dome when they arrived, was fading, was turning rosy, the sky deepening into shades of turquoise and aquamarine tinged with crimson. It made a spectacular sight. There was a raw edge to the air. It was only May, and when the sun set, a sharp chill penetrated through the partly open door.

Suddenly, the striking skyscape CJ had been dreamily contemplating was blotted out by the moon of Damien's face. He was leaning over her, staring into her emerald eyes. She stared back, opened her eyes wide and tried to indicate she had a question to ask. But even if he understood her expression, Damien chose to ignore it. He pinched her pale flesh, stroked the auburn curls and tweaked nipples, stiff with cold and anxiety.

Leaving the gag in place, he slid brawny arms beneath her shivering body and lifted her from the slab. His large head, long hair hanging to his shoulders, swung from side to side as he stood, surveying the scene. He looked towards the door, the various niches, stared up at the dome itself. With CJ clutched in his arms he wandered round the temple, seemingly unsure of his next move. She quivered and clung to his warmth. Then, with a satisfied grunt of understanding, he carried her towards the ropes that hung at the head of the marble platform.

She was back where she started, on the block, but this time standing. Her legs were weak, and when he let go, CJ thought they would crumple, and she clung to his reassuring bulk. Damien gazed at her, a look of puzzled wonder on his normally impassive face. He brushed her hand away and CJ clung to a rope for support.

The sun had set, the moon was in its first quarter, a slim sliver of silver hanging in the deep navy blue of the summer evening sky. She could barely see Damien now. The light had almost gone but she noticed, whilst she had been staring at the spectacular sunset, he had placed candles, long, red and straight, in each of the sconces. There must have been twenty candles altogether, all waiting to be lit.

Damien struck a match. The blaze illuminated his face and it seemed to hover in the glare of the dancing flame. Slowly, he lit one candle then another. The light flickered in the draft from the open door. Damien looked from the flames to the door, put down his box of matches, and slammed the door shut. The noise echoed round the stone interior.

He lit the remaining candles. When the last one flickered into life, he put the matches away, rubbed his hands over the seat of his jeans, and strode towards where CJ clung to the flimsy support of a swinging rope.

"I want her Troy, and *you* are going to take me to her." Mr Columbus, arms folded over a looming stomach, did not once take his eyes off the panic-stricken face of the Chief Trainer.

Feeling at his wit's end, Troy looked round wildly at his companions. "Jem, Davy, Nico, Seth, anybody, tell me, if CJ's not in the van, where is she?"

The men shuffled their feet, glanced at one another, shook their heads, shrugged shoulders, unsure how to react.

Troy turned to Mr Columbus, a look of despair clouding his features. "Mr Columbus, sir, if I knew - I'd take you to her willingly. You'd be welcome to the cat. She's obviously trouble as far as I'm concerned. But I've no idea - I don't even know who could have taken her from my van."

"Am I to understand from what you've just admitted Troy, that you are not in control here? Your men can do whatever they choose - and apparently so can the girls?"

"No! That's not true. If I knew who'd taken her I'd flay the skin off his back!"

"It was Damien." Bernardo spoke softly. "He's my cousin. I recognised him."

"Damien!" Davy sprang forward. "If that's true he would only be doing it for the good of the camp, for the reputation of us gipsies. He's loyal and true to the cause, is my brother Damien."

"Well spoken, young man." Mr Columbus gazed at Davy who was rigid with rage.

"He," Davy pointed at Troy, "he was hiding her from you, sir. He wanted to keep the little honey-pot for himself."

Mr Columbus nodded and smiled at Davy. "So - where would your brother have taken this delightful little spitfire? She must be quite something to have aroused so much interest in someone of Troy's insatiable appetite."

"Oh, she's something special all right, Mr Columbus sir. And it was me, me and my brother, Damien, who found her. It was the two of us brought her to this camp less than a week ago. She's young, she's sweet, she's -"

"- disappeared," interjected Mr Columbus. "I want her. Find her." His voice bellowed.

"He might have taken her to the temple." The voice spoke quietly, emerging from the darkness beyond the light of the fire. Maggie stepped forward, her eyes bright with excitement, smiling at Troy.

"That's possible," agreed Jem. "Damien's keen on that place. He showed it to me the other day. I've been using it for training purposes. It was a building he seemed to have taken a fancy to."

"Where, where? Where is this place? Take me there." Mr Columbus's face was puce.

"Really it's a folly." Jem spoke urgently. "It's on the other side of the lake. It's a wonderful place, dedicated to flagellation and bondage."

Mr Columbus, who had been pacing furiously, came to a halt. "Indeed, indeed? Then we shall certainly go there. Bernardo, get Rebecca. You," he pointed at Davy, "you come as he's your brother, and bring along one of these girls."

"I shall have to show you where the place is, sir." Jem looked at Mr Columbus, his hooded eyes calculating.

"Yes, yes, of course you will." He beamed at Jem. "Bring a girl, whichever one takes your fancy. You must come as well, Troy, I want to keep an eye on you. It's obvious you can't be trusted."

Maggie, her dancing skirt tangled round her ankles, clung to Troy's arm. "I'm coming with you, Troy. Please, please let me come with you."

Troy grimaced, then clutched her breasts and slid a lead through the nipple rings.

Jem grabbed Daisy by the wrist. Davy grasped hold of Jo. Rebecca, quivering with excitement, jiggled next to Bernardo. And when nobody was looking, bunny three tagged on behind.

With Mr Columbus in the lead, the group set off into the darkness. Davy snatched a branch from the fire, held it aloft and the evening breeze set it glowing. The light was faint but sufficient.

With Daisy following on her lead, Jem hurried to Mr Columbus's side. "Down the hill. We go down the hill, cut through the woods and the lake is on the other side of the yew hedge. The temple - or folly - is on the other side of the lake."

"Go ahead, lead on. We shall be right behind you."

Excited, Rebecca trotted beside Bernardo. Jo was intrigued, and followed Davy willingly. Daisy was in seventh heaven, and scurried in Jem's wake. She didn't care where they were going, or why, Jem had chosen to take her with him. That was enough for Daisy.

In the temple all the candles glimmered. Shadows played on the walls. The carved figures arching over the marble platform, which had seemed to be writhing in daylight, appeared to be almost living and breathing in the light of the candles.

One figure, suspended above the slab was indeed living and breathing. CJ, ropes wrapped round her arms, her wrists strapped together above her head, dangled from the rim of the dome.

Damien was busy at her feet. Already he had tied one ankle to the upright of the arch. He was busy working on the other leg now. When he finished, her small body stretched at an angle. The upper half suspended by rope extended towards the dome, the lower half, legs spread, pussy gaping, angled towards the door.

Damien seemed pleased with his efforts. He stepped back, tested the tightness of the knots, ran his fingers along the wide open slit of her cunt. His fingers dug inside her and CJ gasped and wriggled in her bonds. Damien grunted, slapped her bottom, and turned away. He walked over to one of the niches. This one was large and contained a figure the height of a full-grown man. In its right hand a whip thrust upwards. CJ followed Damien with her eyes. Was he leaving her here like this? And if so, for how long? She wriggled and swallowed hard behind her gag.

Damien fiddled with the statue and CJ saw the whip it carried was not a carving. This whip was real, its handle polished teak, the thong best cowhide. Damien, who she knew enjoyed producing new equipment, must have made it himself. He flexed it in his huge hands, and the leather, which he always soaked in brine, was tough and stiff. He flicked his wrist. The leather came to life. It curled upwards towards the dome. It sliced through the air and the candles flickered in its down-draught.

CJ watched, her eyes big and round. Was this what Damien had planned all along? Was he jealous? Did he envy Troy his chaining, whipping and fucking of herself. She groaned. She was the boss's girl, the head man's. She was only ever interested in the man at the top. The assistants held little interest for CJ.

Damien walked back towards her. He laid the whip on the slab. His eyes turned towards her naked and vulnerable body, taut and stretched, helpless and gagged. A snort - amusement or desire - rose in his throat. CJ watched with horror. He was slipping off his shirt, unzipping his jeans. He kicked his boots from his feet and the jeans slid to the floor. Underneath he was not naked as CJ had supposed. What she saw made her eyes open even wider.

Damien was dressed in leather. Black and supple, it clung to his torso. The flesh of his back and chest which was not covered by the clinging vest was thick with coarse black hair. The little top bulged, outlining every muscle and sinew, even his nipples prodded the finely clinging fabric. The briefs were skimpy and dug tightly into the chunky flesh of his belly. The bulge between his thighs riveted CJ's attention.

Kneeling, Damien replaced his boots, laced them and stood up. The shadows made by the flickering candlelight deepened the outlines of his well-endowed body. He grasped the whip in his right hand, eyed CJ carefully and raised it slowly and deliberately above his head.

The group of ten pounded over the wooden bridge. The waterfall roared in the night. Their feet clattered and echoed over the lake.

"Not far now," Jem yelled over his shoulder. He was first over the bridge, Daisy, her pretty outfit of chains tinkling as she ran, close behind him. Hurrying, they led the way along the rocky path towards the temple.

Rebecca trotted behind Mr Columbus, her lead still firmly in Bernardo's fist. She was thrilled by the sequence of events that had occurred since supper. She had been bored earlier, but now there was real excitement in the air, and Rebecca was loving every minute of it.

Behind Bernardo ran Davy and Jo. Anxiety creased Davy's features. Damien was his responsibility. If anything went wrong now, there would be no chance of him joining the circus. Jo loped at his heels. She was happy to be here.

Troy followed hard behind Jo. He couldn't believe the way things had turned out. Everything had been planned so carefully. He had put so much work into today. Whose fault was this fiasco? Damien's? That redheaded bitch? It certainly wasn't his. The only mistake he had made was ditching Maggie for CJ. He clutched Maggie's chain in his hand. The nipple rings yanked at her breasts. Breathing hard, Maggie smiled. She was back with Troy. She'd always known she would be. That witch was going to get her comeuppance and it would be good-bye bunny hutch for ever.

Bunny three skipped happily at the rear of the group. She hadn't run so far for a long time. Not since she was quite young. She didn't know where they were going, but she was enjoying herself. She loved being in the wood. She glanced up through the branches of the trees and skidded, amazed by what she saw.

"Look!" she cried, pointing down the path. The group staggered to halt. Girls bumped into men, men felt the soft and yielding naked bodies of girls press close against them. They all stared into the darkness.

"Look!" she yelled again. "Look up, through the branches, about fifty yards ahead."

They all stared. In the darkness a light glimmered. It floated in the tree tops. It was the shape and colour of a full moon. The branches swayed across it, breaking the edges of the soft and golden glow.

"He is in the folly," cried Jem. "That's the dome."

Mr Columbus pushed his way to the front. "So that's where she is," he breathed. "Forward men, forward. We have run our quarry to earth." His breath fully restored, he took over the lead, strode down the path, leapt up the steps and flung wide the door that led into the candle-lit temple.

24: The Future

The door opened with a crash. The huge bulk of the Big Man filled the entrance. The rest of the group, men and girls, huddled behind him, peering over his shoulder or round him.

An astonishing sight confronted and silenced them.

The interior of the temple, built of pale limestone, shone gold. Red candles burnt, wax dripping down the scarlet shafts. Carved figures clambered and writhed in all directions. Stars glittered overhead, an exotic canopy protecting the two people frozen in tableau, in the centre of the glowing building.

The one figure, male, long hair sweeping immense shoulders stood, every muscle and sinew of his torso picked out in finest detail by the tight-fitting costume which clung like a second skin. His arm, raised in salute, the whip grasped in his fist, poised, awaiting the order to spring into life. Huge thighs supported a body, muscular, massive, and toned to perfection. His head did not move at the sound of the intruders. He remained exactly where he was, staring at the vision suspended before his eyes.

Mr Columbus strode into the building. The rest bundled in after him. He gazed at CJ. A sigh of respect and appreciation whistled between his fleshy lips. Her hair, a halo of flaming auburn, seemed almost to be on fire as the flare of the candles danced and shimmered behind the bobbing curls. Her elfin face, framed by this ring of light, stared back at him. Her eyes glittered like two large and perfect emeralds. The skin of her cheeks was pale, almost translucent in this light, and freckles dusted a turned-up nose.

Arms, slender and frail, stretched above her head, the tips of the fingers invisible as they reached towards the dim, star-spangled dome. Her slight body, the breasts tipped by nipples of fragile pink, swung on ropes, and the moist mound of her sex was fully displayed to his devouring eyes. Mr Columbus swelled at the sight of her. Daisy and Jo exclaimed "CJ" in unison.

CJ gazed from one person to another, bewildered by what she saw. Some she recognised, others she didn't. But all the time, her eyes kept returning to the man at the front of the group. Her nipples tingled as she absorbed the aura of vitality surrounding him. She could see Troy, but he seemed to be hanging back. This man, this new man, looked powerful. This man was big. Huge! And, from the way he held everyone at bay, was used to being obeyed. This man was in charge of the situation. This man, strong and virile, was Troy's boss. This was the Big Man himself.

"What a vision of wonder and delight! I am dazzled by what I see." Mr Columbus turned to Troy. "Never, Troy, never, did I believe I could be surprised by anything any more. But what is presented here, thrills me more than I can say."

Troy hurried to the Big Man's side. "You're pleased? You like what you see?"

"Like? Like? What a small and insignificant word for the way I feel at the moment. I am astounded, overwhelmed, tickled pink." He slapped Troy on the shoulder. "This is perfect. Beauty and the Beast - an act - fully presented. The back-lighting is superb. I'll take them, both of them, no quibbling. You have surpassed my expectations."

"Well - well -" Troy blustered, unsure what to say.

"That's good, Troy, isn't it?" Maggie hissed. "Your plan to keep this as a surprise, to finish off the evening on a high note, it was an excellent idea - wasn't it?"

"What, y-yes, of course it was. Yes, thank you, sir. To finish the evening on a high note. I'm delighted you're impressed." He smiled, a look of bemusement evident on his handsome features. Maggie giggled and skipped on the end of her chain. "Keep still, woman. Who gave you permission to move?" Maggie subsided, pleased by the turn of events.

"To be honest, sir," interjected Davy, "if there's anyone who should take the credit for this wonderful scene, it must be me - and Damien - of course."

Damien, who hadn't moved a muscle, since being disturbed by so many people, turned his massive head and blinked at his brother. His mouth opened, his jaw moved stiffly from side to side. His throat gulped and his teeth rattled as a rumbling sound swelled beneath the leather-clad chest. "You," he mumbled - the crowd held their breath - "you - you -" his face coloured, he was breathing hard. Swaying, he pointed the whip at Davy. "You were planning to leave me - you and her." He turned the whip in CJ's direction.

"What!" Damien! I'd never have left you. You thought I was planning to join the cir - I mean, go away and leave you - alone. Never! You'd have come with me."

Puzzled, Damien, looked from his brother to CJ and back to his brother. His perplexed expression eased. He nodded, beamed, and guffawed his sudden understanding of the situation.

The group of men and girls followed this conversation with interest. Most of them had never heard Damien utter a sound before. The bunny, who remembered her double fuck in the field the other day, jumped up and down with delight and waved at the impressive figure in leather.

Mr Columbus gazed at all the faces, white and shadowy in the candle glow. Some looked guilty, some mystified, others were hardly able to stop themselves bursting into shouts of laughter.

"I don't suppose we'll ever know the full story of what has been going on here." Mr Columbus looked at each one of them in turn. "But - I am overjoyed to have discovered something so splendid, so innovative to take on tour."

"He can't go without me!" Davy leapt in front of Damien protectively. "He can't cope on his own, can he Bernardo? You know Damien, tell your boss - tell him, please."

Bernardo stepped into the light, Rebecca close by his side. "He's right, boss. Damien may look impressive, but he couldn't cope, not without Davy's guidance."

"No problem." Mr Columbus placed a massive paw on Davy's shoulder. "There's always room in the circus for likely young men. You will be welcome. Jem as well. I want to instruct Jem myself. So he'll be ready to take over the training camp - when necessary."

Daisy squealed. "We can join the circus together, Jem. Won't that be wonderful!" With arms still tightly sheathed behind her back, she pressed her ample breasts close to his body, squeezing and rubbing in ecstasy.

Davy pulled Jo close, slipping his hand between her thighs.

Mr Columbus eyed the platform, CJ suspended above it. "After all this commotion, I'm sure everyone is ready to finish the evening off in suitable fashion. Bernardo, Troy, Jem, Davy, lift me up. I'm ready and by the look in her eyes so is she."

The four men heaved the bulk of the Big Man onto the marble slab. He towered over them, his breeches strained to near breaking point. Rebecca pouted, disappointed. She'd have to make do with Bernardo by the look of it. The boss only had eyes for the red-head.

CJ, eyes wide with delight, stared at this vision of power and influence standing in front of her. He unfastened his breeches and a prick beyond her wildest dreams leapt forth. "Yes! Yes!" she shouted behind her gag. Nobody understood her words, they didn't need to. The state of her tits and pussy said it all. Mr Columbus slipped the purple-tipped organ between her wet cunt lips and pressed home with a roar. The glass dome shook at the pounding of his bulk on the tiny roped and gagged girl.

Taking their cue from the master, the others set to with a will. This eighteenth century folly, built for just such a purpose, resounded to the groaning of men, the moaning of girls, the slap of flesh on flesh as Davy fucked Jo, Daisy thrust herself onto Jem's responsive prick, Maggie knelt worshipping the cock of her lord with lips and tongue that longed for this bliss to continue for ever.

Damien, whip in hand, watched them all. His tiny leather briefs strained and his cock stood ready for action. Bunny three scampered to his side and bowed down before him. He stared at the smooth round globes, dropped his whip, and clasped them in both hands. Her bottom thrust towards him. She wriggled and screamed with delight when that prick once more slid between her cheeks, split the dark rosebud, nuzzled home, and her hips rotated as he plunged long and deep inside her accommodating bum.

She bounced backwards and forwards on his thrusting prick, her tits swayed, her long tail of hair gyrated. The breath buffeted from her body but she cried out, "Don't forget Damien, this bunny fucks harder than most. This bunny likes double fucks, and double-fucked bunnies taste sweetest."

Grunting, Damien obliged and decided that if he was going to join Mr Columbus's Speciality Circus, so was bunny number three. It was him the Big Man wanted, and at last, Damien realised, he could have some say in his own future. If that future included being a performer in the circus, The Beast as partner to the red-headed Beauty, so be it. But it would also include a non-stop supply of double-fucks with this bunny, and any other girl, if half of what he had heard about the circus was true. And that would suit Damien very well indeed.

The next morning, the silver Cadillac nosed its way back along the narrow country lanes. The circus folk sat comfortably inside, Jem and Davy squashed between Rebecca and Bernardo on the front seat, Damien smiling in the back. His massive thigh pressed against that of Mr Columbus, as he perched on the edge of the seat, a glass of scotch grasped in his large fist, new whip resting on his knee.

Behind the car, a caravan swayed. Inside were Daisy, Jo and CJ plus three other golden-haired girls.

Bunny three was squeezed in at the end. She wriggled and giggled, thrilled and amazed to find herself included in this exotic, and for a bunny, completely unexpected and adventurous future.

WATCH OUT FOR THE CIRCUS ON THE MOVE!!!

IF YOU ENJOY ONE OF OUR BOOKS YOU WILL PROBABLY ENJOY THEM ALL

£4.99 from shops or £5.60 by post
To order from shops quote title and ISBN number. All our ISBNs begin
1-897809- the last three figures only are given below.

The Barbary Series by Allan Aldiss:

01-8 Barbary Slavemaster
03-4 Barbary Slavegirl
08-5 Barbary Pasha
14-X Barbary Enslavement

Books by Rex Saviour

02-6 Erica:Property of Rex
   Balikpan One: Erica Arrives (Mail order only, £10)

Books by Lia Anderssen

04-2 Bikers Girl
07-7 The Training of Samantha
11-5 The Hunted Aristocrat
17-4 Bikers Girl on the Run

Books by Janey Jones

10-7 Circus of Slaves
20-4 Caravan of Slaves

Three in One Special (Gord, Saviour, Darrener)

05-0 Bound for Good

Book by Ray Arneson

16-6 Rorig's Dawn

Silver Mink Books - intended for women, read by men!

09-3 When The Master Speaks
13-1 Amelia
15-8 The Darker Side
19-0 The Training of Annie Corran

SILVER MOON BOOKS PO BOX CR25 LEEDS LS7 3TN